MISHPACHA FAMILY

Rebecca Tomasis

Mishpacha – Family is the story of four women living within the modern state of Israel. Each arrives from a different background—the anti-semitisim of Communist Russia; the exclusive suburbs of Tel Aviv; the poverty of Yemen; the comforts of Middle class America—to live within the confines of one home and one family.

These are the separate stories of these four—the daughter of a Russian immigrant; the daughter of a successful European-Israeli businessman; the daughter of Yemenite Jews; and the daughter of assimilated American liberal Jews. It is also their joint story under one roof with one man, brought together in the name of Judaism and in the name of Family.

DISCLAIMER "The idea for the family which is the subject of "Mishpacha – Family" began in Israel on Independence Day, 2007. We attended a large party to celebrate the day in a park in Tel Aviv. At the park were a group of women with a large number of children. The children all looked vaguely similar but the women not at all—although two of them may have been sisters. Later a man turned up whom the children gathered around as if he was the father of all of them. I assumed this to be the case and the story started from there. I tried to find out what I could about this particular family, while in Israel that time. However the only information I could get was vague. They had been featured in an Israeli newspaper at some point, but no one could really remember their names or any other specific details. Everything about the family in my novel comes completely from my own head. The weekend of 14 February 2010, in Israel this story was ALL over the news, and it seems the family we saw in the park that day was the family in the newspaper. But I knew nothing about the family in the newspaper, apart from what I saw in person that day at the park!" — Rebecca Tomasis

Supported by

Hong Kong Arts Development Council

The Hong Kong Arts Development Council fully supports freedom of artistic expression. The views and opinions expressed in this project do not represent the stand of the Council.

2

MISHPACHA FAMILY

a novel

Rebecca Tomasis

*Winner of the inaugural
Proverse Prize*

Proverse Hong Kong

MISHPACHA – FAMILY
by Rebecca Tomasis
Published in Hong Kong by Proverse Hong Kong, August 2015.
Copyright © Proverse Hong Kong, August 2015.
ISBN: 978-988-8228-13-3
Printed by CreateSpace

1st published in pbk in Hong Kong by Proverse Hong Kong, 23 November 2010.
Copyright © Proverse Hong Kong, 23 November 2010.
ISBN 978-988-19320-1-3

1st edition distribution (Hong Kong and worldwide):
The Chinese University Press of Hong Kong, The Chinese University of Hong Kong,
Shatin, New Territories, Hong Kong SAR.
E-mail: cup-bus@cuhk.edu.hk; Web: chineseupress.com.

Distribution and other enquiries: Proverse Hong Kong, P. O. Box 259, Tung Chung
Post Office, Tung Chung, Lantau, NT, Hong Kong SAR.
E-mail: proverse@netvigator.com Web site: www.proversepublishing.com

The right of Rebecca Tomasis to be identified as the author of this work has been
asserted by her in accordance with the Copyright, Designs and Patents Act 1988.

Cover image "Fillettes et Mamans" © Quost Ernest (1844-1931)/RMN/Imaginechina
Cover design by Proverse Hong Kong and Artist Hong Kong Company.
Page design by Proverse Hong Kong.

Proverse Hong Kong

British Library Cataloguing in Publication Data

Tomasis, Rebecca.
  Mishpacha - family : a novel.
  1. Jewish women--Fiction. 2. Israel--Social life and
  customs--Fiction.
  I. Title
  823.9'2-dc22

  ISBN-13: 9789881932013

Mishpacha — Family
Table of Contents

Characters

The characters in "Mishpacha – Family" are listed below by family and the families themselves are listed in order of appearance.

<u>Dana Finkel</u>
Anton Finkel: brother of Dana. Died aged eighteen in the suicide bombing of a Tel Aviv nightclub.

Anna Finkel: mother of Dana. Brought her children to Israel from Russia after the death of their father. Died of breast cancer five years after the death of her son.

Dimitri Finkel: Russian author and academic, Economics and Sociology expert. Renowned for combining fields of economics and sociology to predict and plan how the economy would grow and develop.

Tamar: eldest daughter of Dana.

Yuval: second daughter of Dana.

Isaac: baby son of Dana.

Mr Peleg: next door neighbour of Dana, Anton and their mother. Immigrant from Russia. One time physician.

Mr Bernstein: next door neighbour of Dana, Anton and their mother. Immigrant from Russia. One time concert pianist.

Elijah: one time boyfriend of Dana.

Hofit: one time girlfriend of Anton's and Elijah's sister.

Mr Cohen: Dana's father's agent in Israel, specialist in publishing and promoting academic works.

Ilan Cohen: son of Mr Cohen, who takes over the business from his father. Dana eventually leaves the family to marry Ilan.

<u>Beruriah</u>
Sara: eldest daughter of Beruriah, the product of Beruriah's rape by her cousin.

Yeshua: Beruriah's second eldest child and first son.

Shoshanna: Beruriah's third child, a daughter.

Yonatan: Beruriah's fourth child, a son. This is the baby Dana sees in the hospital when her own mother is there dying.

Rivka: Beruriah's fifth child, a daughter, born while all the women are living with The Family.

Sara: Beruriah's mother. Migrates from Yemen to Israel.

Avraham: Beruriah's grandfather in Yemen.

David: Beruriah's grandfather's brother, fled to Israel from Yemen with his wife and ten children, and Beruriah's mother, her sister and his own brother-in-law. He is Beruriah's great-uncle.

Soloman: Beruriah's great-uncle's brother-in-law, who married Beruriah's maternal aunt.

Lilach: Beruriah's cousin, born to Beruriah's maternal aunt (sister of her mother) and Solomon.

Abigail: a secular school-friend of Beruriah.

Amelia Lieberman

Tali Lieberman: Amelia's mother, the daughter and granddaughter of famous Zionist partisans, founders of the Israeli state.

Mark Lieberman: Amelia's father, successful businessman.

Lucille Stern: Amelia's sister.

Tal Stern: Amelia's brother-in-law, married to her sister.

Ella Stern: Amelia's niece, daughter of Lucille.

Itai Stern: Amelia's nephew, son of Lucille.

Ifat: Amelia's best friend, they served together in the same army unit during their two-year military service.

Baby boy: born to Amelia. She does not name him, and we never learn his name.

Rachel Friedman

Ben Friedman: Rachel's brother.

Maria Friedman: Rachel's Catholic sister-in-law, married to her brother, Ben.

Jack: Rachel's best friend in the USA.

Leah Schwartz: an acquaintance of Rachel, from the same town in the USA. They grew up together. Leah elopes to Israel with an Orthodox Hasidic Israeli.

Jonathan: Leah Schwartz's husband.

Mishpacha — Family: A dedication

When you walk into a train station, a hotel, a synagogue and open fire on unarmed innocents—men, women and children—
    You are not a freedom fighter you are a terrorist.

When you board a bus, a train, an airplane and blow up innocents—men, women and children—
    You are not a freedom fighter, you are a terrorist.

When you fire a rocket into a kindergarten onto innocents—children at play and teachers at work—
    You are not a freedom fighter, you are a terrorist.

When you enter a bar, a night club, a busy restaurant weighed down with explosives and kill innocents—someone's wife, husband, daughter, son—
    You are not a freedom fighter, you are a terrorist.

When you rob an innocent of their life simply because of the passport they carry, the language they speak, the religion they practise;
    You are not a freedom fighter, you are a terrorist.

When you deny an innocent of their right to live, simply because you feel disenfranchised;
    You are not a freedom fighter, you are a terrorist.

If you are a terrorist, you are not a freedom fighter.
    You are a murderer.

10

Chapter 1—Dana

My Papa had been the star in the system—well-educated, did what he was told, kept his Jewishness nicely hidden. Everything he was supposed to do as a non-practising Jew living in Russia.

And then it happened.

One day he went to bed a Russian who had mistakenly just happened to have been born a Jew who had nicely assimilated within the Soviet system: the next he was a Russian Jew in desperate need of his own identity as a Jew first, and a Russian second.

~~

My Papa was two years old in 1952 on the night of the murdered poets, and only seventeen during the Six Day War of 1967 when Israel triumphed against her Arab neighbours yet again and Russia cut off all contact with the Jewish state.

~~

Throughout all of this my father and his family had been Jewish in name and not in deed and they had sailed through the Stalinist and then Soviet régimes untouched by the anti-Semitism that burdened most Russian Jews. Most practising Russian Jews that is. For there were plenty more, like my Papa's family, who were good Russians first and Jews, well never, and they assimilated within society by virtue of their being as Russian as their neighbours and colleagues.

~~

The Jewish ancestors — the Jewish blood they all contained — well that was just a nasty family secret that no-one outside the family had to know about. All families had secrets, mad uncles, relatives they regretted. Being Jewish for my Papa and his family was no different to that.

Papa used to say, after he had re-embraced his Jewishness, that for years he could never understand why his parents had done it. Why they had denied their own religion and history to blend in. Just for the sake of an easier life. Why they had denied the existence and suffering of their own ancestors.

Even after all the persecution he suffered he never understood why they did it. Not he said until I was born. And he said then as he held me in his arms for the first time, and looked down at my trusting blinking eyes, that refused to open to the bright hospital lights, he realized how he would do anything to protect me. And he realized then that that had been what his parents had been doing all those years. They hadn't been denying their Jewishness, they had been protecting him. But by the time I was born it was too late for him to turn back. Too late for him to assimilate once again. The family secret, so carefully hidden and concealed for all those years, was finally out in the open and no longer deniable. The mad uncle was out from under the bed and on the rampage, running naked down the street for everyone to see and point at.

~~

Anyway we were going to Israel.

~~

In 1972 when he was twenty-two years old — the same year that he told my mother they were going to Israel — the government idelete linentroduced a diploma tax on all Russian Jews educated at universities in the USSR. My father, so proud of his undergraduate and postgraduate degrees, earned at such a young age, suddenly felt the full weight of them crushing against him. The tax was twenty times what my father earned in a year at the university. No-one would lend him the money. The tax was soon repealed but still they refused my Papa a visa.

~~

12

My parents waited nineteen years to go to Israel. Nineteen years in which my father kept his job but never received a promotion, or grant for research. Nineteen years in which they lost most of their friends — some quietly, some not so quietly. Nineteen years in which no-one would play with my brother and me, apart from other Jewish friends. Nineteen years in which my father saw not one article published, not one of his books sold in Russia. What kept us afloat and my father sane were the royalties from the sales of his books outside Russia; for some reason they let him keep on selling them. But my father was an outcast in Russian academia; and my mother an outcast in Russian society.

They, the authorities, made no secret of the fact that my Papa had only himself to blame for his bad luck in life. If he played by the rules, obeyed the system and kept his Jewishness to himself, well then there was no problem in restoring his life to normal. But for as long as he kept playing his little Jewish games, so his life would remain changed. They told him he could sink or swim, but he had to promise to renounce his Jewishness if they were ever to throw him a rope.

He was lucky, in many ways. So many like him found their way to labour camps and jails. And so many lingered and perished there. Papa was too bright, had had too much money and time invested in him by the system in his early academic years for them to throw him away quite so quickly. They wanted him—so they continued to beat him down, rather than shoot him outright, in the hope that one day they would get what they wanted. They wanted his brains, but not his ideals. Nor his religion.

And thus Israel became much more than the biblical land of milk and honey and became for each of us the place where our own individual dreams would come true.

For Papa it was the place where the academic world would once again welcome him with open arms, where once again his star would shine, his articles would be published and his books read.

For my mother it became a land where she would have friends again. Friends to share recipes with, and sewing tips and ideas on how to raise children. Somewhere where she could go to the theatre, the ballet, without people whispering at her behind her back. Somewhere where she could go to the supermarket, to a dress shop and not feel like a leper.

For my brother and me it became a place where our parents would smile again; where our father would remember how to play with us, how to laugh; a place where our mother would be able to relax and rest and somewhere where her frowns would turn to smiles.

Mama had never been religious, never even really knew what it meant to be Jewish—her father as a prominent businessman had decided business was better if he wasn't obviously Jewish and so my mother was raised as a Russian.

My parents fell in love as Russians, not Jews, and my maternal Grandparents were never happy with my father because of his blatant Jewishness. They feared, and not without good reason, for the life of their daughter and their grandchildren.

It must have been a shock for my Mama to have gone from having it all, to having, if not nothing, then very little. At eighteen she had been a debutante and presented to society in a new silk dress. At twenty she was married to my father, a rising star in the academic world whose first book was awaiting publication. She had it all. The friends, the home, the husband and in time she would have the children too.

It's easy to see how she blamed my Papa, and not the system. Her family had always lived very well within the system because they knew what was expected of them—it was just a case of going along with everyone else, and how hard was that? She resented Papa for his attack of conscience, I know she did. And I suppose who could blame her?

My younger brother, Anton, had confused the biblical milk and honey with his own love of ice cream and he had decided that Israel was the land of ice cream—it grew on trees, sat on the top of mountains, ran through rivers and streams. My mother never had the energy or heart to tell him otherwise but at the age of ten I had no such qualms.

"There are no rivers made from ice cream, not anywhere in the world."

"In Israel," Anton's eyes looked so trusting and sure, that something evil in me wanted to destroy that innocence, to let him know that there was nothing you could be so sure about—nothing.

"No. Not in Israel, not in Russia—nowhere!"

"No. Not in Russia, but in Israel!"—Again so sure.

"Ahhhhh!" And I gave up—let the baby find out the hard way that his dream was nothing but that—a dream.

"You will see—in Israel,"

He kept the same dream alive for many years, and two years later we were still having the same argument on a daily basis. Two years later we were still waiting for our visas.

But now I was older—almost twelve—by which point we had been leaving for Russia for my whole life— and I had realized that Israel was just that—a dream. Something we all wanted to happen, somewhere we all wanted to be but a dream all the same. A dream Jewish people had had for over two thousand years and one we would continue to have for another two thousand more. I had, in the back of my mind, begun even to doubt its very

existence. Anton was only eight, a kid, what did he know?
He thought ice cream could grow on trees for G-d's sake.

And when Anton came home from school, black rings
developing around his eyes, his nose a bloody mess, I told
him if he was stupid enough to wear his *kippa* to school
then he deserved everything he got. I told him this as we
sat on the bathroom floor—mopping up the blood with
tissue.

"Stupid, Anton, just stupid. What did you expect
them to do?"

"In Israel I can wear it. In Israel everyone wears one,"
he sniffed.

"Stop it. You're dripping blood on the floor. Israel,
Israel, Israel! Why doesn't everyone just shut up about
Israel?"

"You don't like Israel?"

"I don't know Israel, none of us do."

"Soon."

I bit my tongue to stop myself from scorning his
dream. No matter how much I didn't believe, I couldn't
ruin it for my little brother because part of me wanted to
believe it too. At ten I wanted to ruin his innocence the
way mine had been ruined by wisdom, but at twelve I
wanted to join him in his dream. To hide within it like he
did.

But something deep inside me nagged at me and
filled me with doubt. Anton still believed that if you
wanted something badly enough, and if you were good
enough, well then you would get it. As if an all-year-
round Saint Nicholas existed to make sure we all got what
we wanted. Only I had begun to suspect that that wasn't
quite true. We were good people, and no-one wanted to
go to Israel more than us. And yet it wasn't happening.
And if I followed that train of thought—it meant that the
starving people in Africa, the beggars I passed on the
street on the way to school, well they didn't want food,

and a home bad enough? They weren't good enough? But as I watched the children of Africa on the television, with their huge distended stomachs and arms and legs that resembled thin sticks, I couldn't help but feel that no-one deserved good luck more than them. And yet it wasn't coming to them. So what right had we to expect anything too?

It didn't help that I was torn between Papa and Mama. Papa who never gave up on his optimism and hope for our future in Israel. And Mama who had given up a long time ago. I wanted to believe like Papa, because his hope kept him happy, whereas Mama was so obviously unhappy and bitter. I didn't want to be like that. And yet I couldn't quite be as positive as Papa was. I just couldn't.

~~

At school I was the sister of that crazy Jew. All my years of staying anonymous, of being just Russian, were ruined when Anton started at the same school with his knitted *kippa*. In the neighbourhood, I was the daughter of that crazy Jew. And even when I was just me, I was still forever branded with that word, "Jew." Even when I walked where people didn't know me from any other little girl on the street I still felt so conspicuous, as if people's eyes could bore right through me, and see the word "Jew" stamped on me. Sooner or later, I thought, they would find out.

I just wanted to be anonymous. Being just Russian was too much to ask, and it felt like a lie; so just to be anonymous, that would work. Only I could never feel anonymous. No matter how quiet I stayed, no matter how much I tried to shrink my features, no matter how much I retreated into myself.

One day my teacher asked me to stay after the others had gone. Was I in trouble? I ran my brain through the events of the day and couldn't single out at any point when I had done something that would have meant I was in trouble. I always sat at the back, said hardly a word all day, and kept myself as invisible as possible. Everyone knew who I was, who my brother was, who my father was, I had no intention of making them remember me beyond that.

"Dana!"

"Did I do something wrong? I didn't do it, or I didn't mean to do it."

"No, Dana, you didn't do anything wrong. I have this for you," and as she opened her hand I saw a silver chain.

"For me?" I asked confused beyond belief.

"Yes for you." And she fastened the silver chain around my neck. I looked down in disbelief and then I saw it—the tiny silver crucifix hanging off the silver chain.

"Do you like it?" she asked.

I did, I liked it very much. But all I could think about was Papa. Would he like it? Would he like me wearing it? I knew he wouldn't, one voice in my head told me that loud and clear. But there was another little voice inside me that wanted to wear the silver, sparkling, pretty chain. Plenty of girls in my class wore them. Jewellery wasn't supposed to be worn to school but everyone knew that that rule didn't apply to a necklace with Jesus on it. Girls wore their crucifixes proudly, over their green school jumpers, as opposed to hidden under them. As if they weren't afraid to flout the rules in the name of Jesus, although no-one would have ever told them off for wearing a crucifix.

How I envied those girls. I envied them their silver necklaces and the way they wore them so brazenly, so confidently over their school jumpers. My silver necklace with its silver star of David lay at home in Mama's jewelry box where it would stay, she said, until we got to Israel. How I wished I could have worn it proudly too.

And the girls with their necklaces, they chatted away to each other, borrowed each other's pencils and shared snacks at break times. They were a group I could never infiltrate, not in a million years.

But maybe, just maybe with the crucifix around my neck, I could. Maybe just for a day or two they would let me in on their whispered conversations and skipping games.

"Yes, I like it very much." And I smiled up at her.

"Good, you can go."

I wore it over my jumper through the school and all the way down the street to home. For once I felt as if I really blended in—just another Russian girl walking home from school with her crucifix necklace.

No-one at home seemed to notice it.

"What's that?" asked Anton

"A new necklace," I replied, and he left it at that.

"Want to play dens?" he said. " Come on, this is the den where the Israelis are hiding," and he pointed to a mound of pillows at one end of the sitting room, "and this is where the Arabs are hiding," he said pointing to a duvet under the table.

"No," I said too old for his childish games and I went to the bathroom to admire my new necklace in the mirror over and over again.

Nobody noticed until dinner when Papa got home.

He said the blessing over the food and then asked, "So how was school?"

Anton frowned and shook his head preferring to concentrate on the food on his plate. My mother looked at his bent head and sighed; she cast my father a dirty look.

"Dana?" he said turning to me with a hopeful look on his face.

Not wanting to disappoint him, I replied with a smile and, "Good!" And it had been at the end. Probably the best day ever.

Dinner continued and only as I got up to help Mama clear away the plates did Papa notice the necklace around my neck.

"Oh," he said happily, "You're wearing your Magen David," and he looked to Mama with a grateful look on his face.

"I didn't give it to her to wear," she cried. "Dana, did you take that necklace from my box without asking me?"

"No," I protested and then Papa saw it,

"That's not a Magen David," he said. "Dana, come here!"

And so I went, reluctantly, knowing what was coming next, and so scared that I would anger Papa and lose my lovely new necklace and with it the acceptance I hadn't even been able to feel properly yet.

He fingered the necklace around my neck. "It's a crucifix," he spat

"Did you give this to her?" he accused my mother.

She was at the sink and didn't turn around. "No, I didn't."

"Dana, take it off!" he ordered.

"But…."

"Take it off, now!"

The tears rolled down my face as my fingers stumbled over the clasp. In the end Papa did it, almost ripping the chain from my neck. He went over to the bin and threw it in. I couldn't stop the tears rolling down my face.

Mama handed out desert but only Anton ate. His eyes big and wide stayed on me the whole time as he scooped food into his mouth.

"Where did you get it?" Papa asked, not angry as I had expected, just disappointed.

"From school, from my teacher."

He sighed, " Why would she do that?"

"Maybe," said Mama, " because she wanted Dana to fit in. She wanted Dana to have some friends, to be a part of her class."

"And a necklace will do that?"

"Sometimes, Dimitri, you are as blind as an…as an owl! The necklace, Dana, why did you want to wear it?"

And she turned to me.

I wiped the tears from my face with my sleeve. "Because… because I wanted to be like the others. The other girls all wear those necklaces, and I thought if I had one too, maybe they would let me sit with them, or play with them," and the tears fell faster from my eyes as I realized that now the necklace was gone, they would never ever play with me. Or share their lunches. Or invite me over to their houses after school.

Mama looked at Papa as if to say, " I told you so," and Papa just looked sad.

"I am asking a lot of you Dana, I know that. And of Anton to. And I am sorry. I am sorry that there are people in the world who will judge you on your religion, on your skin colour, on your place of birth. But this is something we must do, Dana. We must not give in to them and let them win. Can you see how wearing that necklace would do that? It would mean that they are winning, and would tell them that they are justified in persecuting you because of your religion."

Mama sighed and began to clear away the dishes.

"I understand," cried Anton, "It's like the Arabs; we must not let them win. Otherwise they will take Israel and we will have nowhere to go!"

Papa smiled. " And you Dana, can you see?"

I wanted to see because Papa looked so hopeful. I wanted to make him happy. But really I didn't see. I didn't see why everyone else got to wear their silver necklaces and have friends, while mine ended up in the bin and I ended up at home alone again. Or why I was always at the back of the class afraid to speak, even though I knew the answers to all of the questions the teacher asked. Why I ate my lunch alone and huddled within myself for warmth when the wind ripped through the playground. The others huddled together; they had each other for warmth. It felt as if I had nobody. I gave him a smile and that seemed to be enough.

~~

As Mama tucked me into bed she whispered, "If you want the necklace I will get it back for you and you can just wear it to school, Papa would never have to know."

And part of me wanted to so much, but I couldn't do it to Papa—I couldn't disappoint him again. I wanted to be able to wear the necklace for everyone to see.

"No, thank you, Mama."

But I still cried myself to sleep at the injustice of the world. Or at least the injustice of my world.

~~

My mother had made *latkes* for dinner. *Chanukah* was just a few days away and Anton insisted that we had latkes with every meal in the week before and after the holiday.

There were photos and memories of when we were small, celebrating *Chanukah*—the house full of people; the candles always burning in the background; my father with his booming voice offering more wine, more latkes. My mother in a new dress. I remember small things and overall a warmth—bigger than any candles could generate—a security, a fuzzy happiness. That we had been saved, again.

As I got older I tried to re-create that feeling of safety but never quite achieved it. By the age of twelve I could see the pain on my mother's face as we celebrated the holiday. How she fried *latkes* reluctantly and spun the *dreidel* with Anton half-heartedly. I could see how forced my Papa's joy was and how Anton was the only one still basking in the comfort of a holiday spent amongst family.

And the people that filled the house in their holiday clothes, others labeled renegades like Papa? — Well, I saw the tension in their faces as well as manifested in their threadbare clothes. Yet more intellectuals whom the system had swallowed, choked upon and spat back out again. All of them waiting for visas that wouldn't come. Trying to live normal lives in the meantime. Trying to fake happiness in a holiday that had hope and the power of a miracle at its centre. How many of them wished for a miracle this Chanukah? How many Chanukahs had they been wishing for such a miracle? How many more would they have to sit through before their miracles came? How long before they stopped believing in miracles altogether?

At twelve I saw all that and the holiday was ruined. The doughnut in my mouth tasted like chalk and I hadn't the heart to finish it; so I passed it to Anton who swallowed it almost whole.

And I was angry at G-d. He, who had saved our people so many times, from near impossible situations and most certain extermination, seemed strangely absent from Russia in those years. He didn't seem to care about us. Didn't seem to want to know. No-one wanted to know.

Except for, as Papa insisted every night, the people of Israel. They wanted to know, they wanted to know us and they wanted us with them in the Holy Land. They were working to get us there as he spoke, we just needed to be patient, he said.

"How patient?" my mother cried across the dinner table, "How bloody patient do we have to be?"

Papa winced as she cursed, and winced at her lack of belief. He ignored her words, as he seemed to ignore her pain; in much the same way as Mama believed the people of Israel were ignoring us.

But Mama wouldn't let herself be ignored. She let it pass as we finished dinner, let it pass as I helped her wash and dry the dishes, let it pass as Anton and I had our baths, let it pass while Papa read us our separate bed time stories. Anton always wanted something straight from the Torah, I was happier with a fairytale.

And then when we were safe in bed and Papa was unarmed, without the protection of his children by his side, Mama stopped letting it pass.

"You're ruining our lives!" she hissed

The apartment wasn't huge. I could hear every word she said.

I could imagine Papa's shell-shocked expression as he turned to her.

"What?" he spluttered, caught off guard as she had intended.

"Our lives ruined." She spoke slowly, enunciating each word as if speaking to an idiot.

Papa was silent, as if he thought that, if he didn't answer, if he just walked past her to his comfortable chair and picked up a book, she would stop. Only that inflamed her more.

"Don't you care?" she screeched. " Don't you care that you are ruining our lives, that we are miserable?"

Papa faced the inevitable, "Miserable? Who's miserable?" he asked with genuine confusion.

"Us," Mama spat, "Living this life, waiting for non-existent visas to come, living our lives spat on and shamed and hated!"

I could hear Anton's feet padding down the hallway to my room. It was pitch dark and I was scared he would reach out to touch me before I was ready for it and frighten me in the dark. I held out my arms ready to grope for him in the dark. My heart beat faster and faster with the anticipation of fear as I did so. But still as my hands touched his arms, my heart and stomach leapt as if I had touched a ghost, or a monster—creatures of childhood nightmares. My arms helped him up onto my bed and he huddled himself up next to me, I draped my arm around him and held him tight.

"Are you unhappy?" Papa asked, as if the thought had never occurred to him before.

"Unhappy?" Mama screamed, "Are you blind? How can we be happy?"

Papa was silent.

"Tell me, how the hell can we be happy? We're living our lives in bloody limbo, not wanted here, and not wanted there. No-one wants to have anything to do with me, with you, with the children. And you ask me if I am unhappy?" she rounded on him. "Why not ask your children if they are happy? Haven't you heard them, crying themselves to sleep? Haven't you heard me crying myself to sleep?"

I could imagine Papa's head hanging lower and lower, with every excruciating word Mama spoke. "It's hard," he ventured, " I know that. It's hard for all of us. But it will all be worth it in the end. It really will."

I didn't have to see Mama's eyes to witness the scorn in them; I could hear it in her voice. "So you keep saying—and yet here we are, day after day, stuck in this hell hole, stuck in this rut!"

Papa had nothing to say to that. Everything she said was true.

Anton shivered, despite the heat of my duvet around us. I grasped my arms around him tighter.

Then just like that, as suddenly as she had started, Mama deflated and started to cry; heaving sobs that must have shaken her whole body. Papa standing over her awkwardly, unsure of what to do, how to approach her. He hated it when she cried; made him feel worthless; and her crying always sounded like something nobody could fix, nobody could make better. And I knew that she felt so alone—with a husband who couldn't bring himself to put his arms around her and promise that everything would be all right. He never got it, never realized that all she wanted was for him to hug her tight. To let her know that everything would be alright, even if he didn't really know that. She just wanted him by her. She would have done anything with him by her side. He just needed to let her know they were both on the same page, not—as she often felt—in different stories.

That's what made her so sad. Not that the rest of the world was shutting her out; but that her husband couldn't make her feel as though he wasn't. All that mattered to her was him. If he could make her feel strong and warm again, she would do anything.

That was why she was so sad. She felt as if she was losing him, and in the process herself.

~~

And then on the *Shabbat* before my thirteenth birthday everything changed. I came home from school at the same time as Mama came home from the shops. Anton was at a friend's, a Jewish friend. My mother went first. She unlocked the apartment door and pushed it open.

"Dimitri? Dimitri?" she called. "Are you there?"

The apartment was quiet, almost eerily so. It was dark and still. Papa was a man who had to keep busy and, if at home, was always at his typewriter or at his desk with a pen in his hand furiously scribbling notes on some new theory or idea.

~~

Mama never screamed, not even when they pronounced my father dead. He had hanged himself, with the tie he had had worn the day he graduated, so many happy moons ago.

~~

She saved her grief for a week later when our visas for Israel arrived. She ripped my father's into a million little pieces and threw them round the kitchen screaming,

"Happy now? Happy now?"

~~

I don't know why she didn't rip up our visas up too. She had become disillusioned with the idea of moving to Israel in the last years of Papa's life, and would have settled for her old life in Russia. She could have clawed that back with Papa dead. Or at least a semblance of it.

~~

"Are we going to Israel?" Anton asked, his face pale and white from the shock of having lost Papa. He had been hysterical since Papa died. Only now, a week later, had the hysterics become a cold, silent acceptance.

"Yes," Mama replied curtly fingering the visa acceptance letters in her hand.

"Really?" I asked.

"Yes," she shot back. "What is there for us here? What is there for you two here as the children of Jews? At least there you might have a future."

So we packed up the house and left.

~~

Looking back, I realize how much we owed Mama for bringing us to Israel. She had done it against her own better judgment, against her own wishes. She had left her family behind to bring us here to a suburb of Tel Aviv crammed with other Russian immigrants. She was so angry with Papa in the years after he died, and yet she did this for him.—She brought us here as he had so badly wanted to do. She did that for him. And for us.

I suppose I always felt I owed her for that. She gave up everything for us.

And, as I realized later, Papa had betrayed her. Israel had been his dream.—Living a Jewish life had also been his dream.—Mama had gone along with it because she had no other choice. And yet, ultimately, it was Papa who wasn't strong enough to see it through to fruition, and Mama who did. She made possible a dead man's dream, made possible a dream she never had. A dream she had detested. It takes courage to do that.

~~

For three days after we arrived in what he had supposed to be the land of ice cream, Anton locked himself in his

27

room, refusing to come out except when mother and I
were asleep. I would find him in the morning curled up in
a ball on the living room floor. I'd gently touch his
shoulder and he'd leap up like a frightened cat and run to
his room and lock the door before I could stop him. I
suppose it was delayed grief.

~~

"Anton? Lunch is ready, won't you come out and eat?"

"Where is the ice cream?"

"We can buy ice cream Anton, come out and we'll go
after lunch and buy some."

"Where is the ice cream?"

"In the shop Anton, just like in Russia,"

"But the ice cream, where is the ice cream?"

~~

And so the days passed, and the weeks, and the months,
and then finally the years. Sometimes when you stop in
the middle of the day you wonder how you will ever
make it through this day, let alone the rest of the week.
But then at some point you stop again and realize it has
been six months since you first stopped your day and
wondered how you were going to get through it. Stop to
think about it and time passes so slowly it almost stops.
Forget about it and it whizzes by so fast you don't know
where it's gone.

~~

My mother had never been close to Papa's parents. I think
she always knew what was expected of her as their
daughter-in-law, how she was supposed to behave
towards them, she just could never put it into practice.
She just could never see them as her family.

    She did what was expected of her from a distance.—
She sent them photos of us in our new lives. Of us in front
of our new apartment, of us all in front of Lake Kinneret
one hot summer when the North exploded with green life.
Sometimes I wasn't sure who she thought she was sending
the photos to—to my grandparents or to Papa. Sometimes

it felt as if she was sending them to Papa, as if showing him what he was missing out on, what he had lost, as if it was some sort of one-sided conversation with the dead.

I think my Grandmother realized the same thing and so she always wrote back saying how much Dimitri would have loved it there, how much he had missed out on, how we were living his dream and how happy that was making him, wherever he was now.

~~

Anton and I grew up. Mama grew older.

Anton and I made it our mission to assimilate into Israeli society as fast as we could. We stopped speaking Russian, except to Mama. Watched only Hebrew television, listened only to Hebrew music and radio stations. Devoured Hebrew newspapers and books, magazines and comics. We ate *hummus* by the bowlful—brought *shwarma* and *kuba*. We chose Israelis as friends, not Russians. Anton dated a succession of Israeli girls.

Anton assimilated quickest, within weeks. Hebrew seemed to trip of his tongue. Twelve years old and he was talking about what unit of the IDF he would join.

Looking back, there is no way Israel could ever have lived up to all our expectations; but what it meant to be living in Israel was more important than what we actually found there. Assimilation may not have been an immediate or even easy goal, but the point was that here it was possible, likely, almost guaranteed. Nowhere else could offer us that.

~~

The years passed; life went on. I finished high school, did my two years military service.

And then there was Elijah. He was what they call a Sabra. Born in Israel to immigrants from Marrakech. His mother could barely read or write and he'd managed to make a small fortune with a dot-com company that he had sold to an American giant before the dot-com bubble burst.

We would never have met in a million years had it not been for Anton who dated his sister. He came to pick up his sister, and while he waited for her and Anton to return from the cinema, I made him coffee. He hated the coffee, but he was polite and drank it anyway. And then for our first date he insisted on taking me somewhere for what he called real coffee.

It didn't take long for Anton to replace the sister, but Elijah and I kept dating. He took me to Abu Ghosh for *hummus*; I took him home for *bortsch* and dumplings.

He told me how he'd taught his parents Hebrew; and I told him how I'd come home from school to find my father hanging from the ceiling.

We talked about building a new life and a new country, free of our parents' hang-ups, pasts and prejudices.

We both agreed that here we could rid ourselves of the national and cultural stereotypes our parents had been carrying all their lives and which they had carried with them here, and in doing so we could pave our way as pioneers in a new land; a land where we were free to be anything we wanted.

~~

And then he called to end it all.

He said his parents weren't happy with our relationship. I wasn't Moroccan; my family wasn't religious enough, and I wasn't what they wanted for him long-term; I wasn't what they wanted in a daughter-in-law. He was sorry, but what could he do? They were his family.

"But we were pioneers," I wailed down the telephone. "We were supposed to be breaking free from our parents' prejudices, weren't we?"

He was sorry, really sorry; but his family had to come first.

~~

Two weeks after his call, what I had come to expect every month since I was fifteen didn't come, which only meant one thing.

~~

"What's up, Sis?"

"Nothing, Anton. Pass me the saucepan!"

It was an unspoken rule between mother and me that no matter what was happening, we always put on a brave face for Anton and shielded him from the truth. It started when Papa died and we'd just been doing it ever since.

We were washing the dishes, an after-dinner ritual we had made our own since moving to Israel. He passed me the saucepan and I submerged it in the scalding, soapy water.

"Sis?" Anton sat himself on the countertop, his feet drumming against the cabinets.

"Really Anton, it's nothing.—Pass me the glasses!"

He rolled the glasses along the counter top to my open hands. "So, you and Elijah are getting pretty serious huh?" he winked at me from his perch.

I ignored him, "Anton, the plate!"

He made as if he was going to throw them as Frisbees across the kitchen.

"Anton!" But I couldn't help but laugh with it.

"I haven't seen him here in a while," he said, pushing the plates along to me.

"He's busy, I guess."

"Is that all, Sis?" Anton's feet stopped drumming. "Seems he's been busy a lot recently."

"He has a lot of business to take care of."

"Sissssssss."

"What?"

"I bumped into Hofit at the club last week. She said he's with someone new—some daughter of some friend of their parents."

"So you know the deal. End of story." I rinsed the plates of their bubbles and placed them to dry.

"You OK?"

"Sure. It happens."

"Sure it does. But he was a good guy. You two were good together. It's a shame when it doesn't work out."

"A shame, but unfixable. Can we just leave it?"

"Sure! … You want to go get a drink?"

"Anything but alcohol!"

"OK, and I'll buy you a piece of cheese-cake too."

~~

"Hey Sis, you want me to find you someone new? I've got friends."

"No, I'm good thanks, Anton," I replied, stabbing the cheesecake in front of me.

"You don't look so good," he observed, cramming cheesecake in his mouth. Then, "Are you going to eat that?" He pointed at my cake.

I shook my head and he crammed my slice into his mouth too.

Was it me or were we surrounded by babies. Everywhere I looked, a baby. A baby in his pushchair, a baby eating *bamba*, a baby crawling under the table. Pram after pram seemed to go down the street and past our table carrying boys and girls of all descriptions. Fat babies, thin babies. Pretty babies, ugly babies. Big-eyed babies. Babies with lots of hair. Babies with no hair.

I closed my eyes. My palms were sweaty and something began to rise in my stomach.

"Hey, Sis! You OK?" Anton sprayed cake with his words. "Man, forget him! You don't need him!"

A baby cried, another cooed. A series of babies danced in front of my eyes.

Babies. Fear. Babies. Terror. Babies. Nausea.

"I…I need a drink, a cigarette, something, " I cried, opening my eyes.

"You? You need a drink, a cigarette? Damn it Dana, what's up?"

I shook my head, "It's nothing."

"Damn! Will you stop trying to protect me all the god-damn time. You and Mum are always doing this. I'm not five anymore. I can handle stuff, you know."

I was desperate; I had to talk to someone. I couldn't do this alone. "OK, but you must promise not to go crazy on me and start threatening to beat anyone up? Or kill anyone? Promise me!"

"OK, OK," came his reluctant reply. My timid Russian brother had been replaced by a tough, lean, Israeli, fighting, soldier-to-be.

I couldn't look at him. "I'm pregnant." It was almost a whisper and then silence.

Anton took my hand across the table. "Hey it's OK, I'm here."

And then I couldn't stop the tears from falling.

Anton took my face in his hands. "Hey Sis, it's OK. We'll sort this out together,"

"Really?" I sobbed.

"Of course! First I'm going to beat the shit out of that bastard Elijah and then we'll get through this together."

"No! You promised," I cried. "Any way he doesn't know."

"So tell him! Maybe it will change everything."

"I don't know."

"One telephone call, that's all it will take."

Anton—always the optimist.

~~

He said he was sorry, really he was but he was getting married. He didn't see how he could help. I mean, he supposed he could send money but how would he know the child was really his.

~~

"I'll knock his brains out," screamed Anton. "I'll make him wish he was never born."

"Anton, sssh, you'll wake Mama!"

"I don't care," he spat. "I'm going to kill that son of a bitch," and he cracked his knuckles as if preparing for a fight.

"Anton, stop, please!" I was tired, weary, "Killing him isn't going to solve anything. I just need to get it taken care of."

"Are you sure?"

"Yes! I can't bring a baby into this family. I want my own family—with an Abba for my children and a house....this way isn't right, it's not supposed to be. A baby should be wanted. I can't do this now, I'm not ready."

"Anything you want, Sis."

"But let's not tell Mama, OK? She'd just be upset and...."

"Make it about her."

"She'd just be upset. There's no reason for her to know."

~~

So simple, really. So clinical. A visit to the clinic. Unfriendly, judging nurses pretending not to judge but doing it anyway. The removal of a foreign growth. Then a day spent in bed and than what was never meant to be was gone.

I was relieved, glad to be free again, to forget Elijah and to get on with life.

~~

And then the dream.

It was a little boy. He might have been two, or maybe younger. He was hazy but I could see it was a little boy. My little boy. He stood in the corner of a room looking at me, and as I tried to reach out to him, he was gone.

~~

From that day on I was awash with guilt and regret; sorrow and sadness. I would have done anything, anything at all to have gone back and to have changed what I had done. How could something that had felt so right, suddenly become the worst decision I had ever made?

~~

So there we were. Anton had just finished high school and was looking forward to his months of freedom before he had to report to the army. And me? I'd done my time in the army, served my two years in an office in Tel Aviv as secretary to an officer and was now working with children at a private kindergarten not far from home which meant should Mama need me I could run home in a second.

~~

"Come on Sis, come with me! I've a new girlfriend to show you," Anton always had a new girlfriend to show me.

"Not tonight, Anton. Mama's unwell. I'm going to make her some soup and put her to bed. Maybe next time."

"You sure?" He was halfway out the door; aftershave filled the air around him. He had on a new shirt.

"Yes, go, have fun!"

"Love you, Sis."

"Love you too."

~~

He just went to dance and never came back. They say wrong place, wrong time. But for Anton there was no other place he could be but Israel. He was a young, Jewish male going to meet his new girlfriend at a nightclub—what was so wrong about that?

~~

His killer was no older than him. In another city, another country, another time, another place, they would have gone to school together, played football together, been eating ice cream together. But in this place at this time— one of them strapped himself with explosives, joined the line snaking into a nightclub and blew it up into the sky.

~~

The other was blown away into the arms of G-d? One G-d for all? One G-d cradling my dead brother in his arms while patting the other on the back? Two sides to one G-d? Or just no G-d?

~~

They say he died for Israel—for the Jewish state.

My mother spat at their feet. "Now he is dead," she said over the vodka bottle, "Now they notice him. —And before? —When he needed work what was he—a Russian, a second-class citizen? And now his blood is splattered on their streets they call him a hero? —We're Israelis when we are winning medals for them; when we're getting shot at guard posts for them; when we're dying in night club lines," her voice cracked and she sank to the floor clutching her chest. "And when we're not, we're Russians—stealing their jobs, their welfare and their Jewishness…." Her words trailed off.

~~

After Anton died, mother refused to have anything to do with anything she defined as Israeli. She stopped speaking the basic Hebrew Anton and I had taught her. She point-blank ignored our neighbours unless they were Russian. She would watch only Russian TV. She even talked about going back to Russia. It was an extreme reaction to an extreme situation.

~~

"To whom and to what?' I asked her. "There's no-one left there and the country is in ruins."

One December she started talking about putting up a Christmas tree.

"But we're Jewish."

"We always had a tree as children. It was your father who banned me from having one for you."

"Because we're Jewish."

She winced, "And that's when all the trouble started."

36

"mother, what are you talking about—we have always been Jewish."

"And look at the trouble it has brought us!"

"All families have troubles; we're not the only ones."

"But our troubles are because of that damned Jewishness!"

"Mother please! Please don't talk like that!"

"We should have converted, when everyone else was, we should have converted. Do you know where we would be now if we had? Safe in Russia, your father working at the University, Anton attending the same University, me with my friends...."

"You don't know that for sure and converting was never an option for father, nor for Anton—don't you remember how much their Jewishness meant to them?"

"Oh I remember; how can I forget when it killed them both and left me alone?"

~~

She refused to celebrate the holidays—wouldn't let me light candles for *Chanukah*, or banish wheat from the house during Passover.

It was only later, many years later, when my first baby was born, that I realized how mother suffered when Anton was killed. Only after I held my daughter in my arms and there descended over me a love so strong, so protective, so fierce—did I wonder how she managed to make it through the days after Anton was gone. How did she get out of bed, function—even do all the mundane things to get through the day—eat something, brush her teeth, get dressed. The sheer thought of losing my daughter took my breath away and only then did I realize what my mother had gone through in losing a child. And I wished more than anything that I could have had her by my side, to show her I finally understood and that I loved her.

~~

37

On the first Independence Day since Anton's death I went for a walk and found myself along the river in Yehousha Park. The park was full of families barbecuing, or doing *manga*, as they called it in Israel. Every available patch of grass was taken up with mangas, families, chairs and food. Some families had gone all out—boundaries of their plot marked by colourful string or balloons. Huge tables, dozens of plastic chairs. Hammocks swaying between the trees. Some had put up large canopies, others tents. Whole families gathered around, from the very old to the very young. Children played football, trying to score goals through a goalpost manned by their Abbas. The smell of barbecuing meat was everywhere. The sun shone down— hot and bright.

~~

Anton would have loved it. As a child he would have been running round like a crazy thing, playing football, scoring goals until he was exhausted.

~~

I got off the bus from Tel Aviv and walked down the street. Everyone else in the world—well in Israel—was with their family celebrating the day. Everyone; but Mama and me. She was upstairs in the apartment, busy doing anything that would make her forget what today was.

I turned into the path that led to the front door to our apartment block. The earth was parched around it, almost mud, and a few pieces of green struggled to grow through it.

"Dana!" called a friendly voice.

I turned around and there was Mr Peleg who lived one floor below. He had been a physician in Russia, in a famous teaching hospital in Moscow; since moving to Israel he had flipped burgers at a Burger Ranch. He lived alone since his wife had died several years earlier.

Then there with him was Mr Bernstein. He had been a concert pianist in Kiev and was now reduced to busking outside shopping centres. His wife was a teacher, something she had managed to continue doing in Israel.

Both of them were men who had lost their careers when they emigrated to Israel. Both had exchanged money, a certain degree of fame, and career satisfaction for their religious freedom, for the freedom to practise as Jews. My mother believed our family had paid too great a price for that freedom, but Mr Peleg and Mr Bernstein didn't seem to feel the same way.

I invited them both up to the apartment. Mama liked to spend time with others from Russia. Maybe they could help brighten the day up for her.

She welcomed them in, offered them vodka, which they gladly accepted.

Curious, I asked them both if they ever regretted leaving Russia and moving here, considering what each of them had given up.

Mr Peleg said, while his days of practising medicine were over, he now had dreams for his son who was much better off in Israel—as a Jew in his homeland—than anywhere else. The Israeli economy may not be the most successful in the world, he admitted, but he'd rather his son took his chances here than in Russia where the rich got richer and the poor got poorer and the Jews kept getting screwed. Here his son could walk down the streets without having to worry about getting beaten up; if he didn't get a job, he would know it was because he wasn't right for the position rather than the fact that he was Jewish.

Mr Bernstein agreed and seemed to think that you couldn't put a price on religious freedom. "In Russia," he said, "We were persecuted for practising our religion, so we stopped practising our religion. But they still labeled as us Jews, and we were still persecuted. We couldn't win either way."

"Although," Mr Peleg interjected, "Here we are persecuted for being Russian, so maybe there is no difference, either way we can't win."

"Persecuted?" asked Mr Bernstein. "No, we are not persecuted here. Persecuted is being hounded because of a belief you have; of being turned away from orchestras because of the religious label on your ID card; it's not being assigned decent housing because of your religion, of having your children come home from school black and blue because they share a classroom with a bunch of anti-Semites. Here they may be prejudiced against us, but that will change. In Russia things have never changed, will probably never change—they still attack us as we pray in our synagogues."

"No, here my son can marry a nice Jewish girl." —Here he looked at me and winked. —"They can raise a Jewish family and be a normal family who go to work, to school, rather than be the odd ones out, the different ones."

"I would rather have David and Anton alive than be able to light Chanukah candles," interrupted mother. She said it more to herself than to any of us.

~~

"Your mother is confused," Mr Bernstein confided to me afterwards, as I showed them to the door. "It is easier for her to believe that your father's faith killed him than that he killed himself—easier to accept that an ideal, and the fight for that ideal, killed him—rather than the fact that he just gave up. I'm sure he was a good man, your father.—It was a difficult fight we had to fight and there were many of us who didn't make it here."

"And Anton?" I asked.

"Well that was just unfortunate. We are Jews and our lives will never be easy. Our ancestors never had it easy, so why should we? Just because we now have our own state doesn't mean G-d is going to let up on his chosen people. We shall be fighting for our lives, and the right to be who we are for years to come. Anton was yet another victim in that fight."

What he said sounded so simple, so right; but so hard to accept. Because to Mama and me, Anton wasn't just another hero in the battle for peace, he was our son, our brother. He was a human being, who had lived and laughed and cried. Only he wasn't anymore. All that was left was a big gaping hole, where he and his life had once been.

I hid my grief, to protect Mama. It was as if there wasn't enough grief for both of us, she had sucked it all into herself and there was little left for me to wallow in. She grieved for both of us; I had to keep us together, to get us both through the long, lonely days in an apartment where Anton's presence still lingered—in the clothes that still hung in his closet, in his shoes that still cluttered the hallway. We couldn't even bear to throw his toothbrush away, as if doing so would mean finally admitting that he wasn't going to walk back through the front door—the smell of cigarettes on his clothes, the smell of a girl's perfume on his coat.

~~

It wasn't just Israelis Mama blamed, but pretty much anyone she could find a reason to hate, she did, no matter how ridiculous or minor the reason. That same night, just a couple of months after we had buried Anton, we sat, the television between us, filling the space left empty by our lack of words. Hundreds of Russian Jews filled the streets of New York to support the Israeli Independence Day Parade. Fireworks filled the skies of Israel, and the skies of New York in celebration.

Mama coughed and sputtered, "What do they know? Safe and rich in America. While here we are being blown up. If they love and support Israel so much then where the bloody hell are they? Why aren't they here sending their children to the army?"

She had a point. But it was a point I didn't have the energy or desire to argue. Criticizing them for their choice of migration destination wouldn't bring Anton back. Nor would it stop the bombers. If they had had other choices, who can blame them for taking them? Who would choose to live in a war zone? No doubt they sent money to feed Israel's hungry and poor, and they publicly supported us when so much of the world derided our foreign policy and our defensive attacks against the Palestinians. We needed that as much as we needed their American dollars.

~~

Israel had claimed the lives of my father, and my brother. My mother who had never wanted to move to Israel in the first place finally felt vindicated. And even more so when they diagnosed breast cancer.

I told her, "Israel didn't give you breast cancer."

"No," she said. "But they can't cure me of it."

And she was right. In a matter of months she was dead, buried beside Anton and my father's gravestone, which we had put up when Anton died—his remains were still in Russia but the sentiment was the same, my mother said.

Even the Doctors had been surprised at the rate at which the cancer destroyed her. She just gave up.

"I shall be glad when I'm finally dead," she used to say.

"Mama, please don't talk like that."

"I just can't believe that I'm going to die here," she sighed, "If only I could die in Russia!" She looked out the window as if hoping to catch a glimpse of her former homeland. "At least I shall soon be with Dimitri and Anton." And she closed her eyes as if imagining them waiting for her.

And me I thought? What becomes of me? She was my mother and of course I loved her. I loved the

42

memories I had saved of her—before father died, before Anton died. She was definitely miserable alive and so, I suppose, it only followed that she was better off dead. If it's possible for someone to be better off dead. I had always thought death was something to be feared rather than something to be welcomed. But mother was definitely ready to welcome it—she'd opened the door wide to let it in, and made coffee and cakes for it.

But regardless of what grief had turned her into over the years, she was the only family I had, the only person I really knew here. Without her it would just be me in an empty apartment. Me. Alone. With an empty space, where a family use to live. Not that we'd been much of a family recently.

There were moments when I envied her. To be the one leaving, rather than the one left behind. She would be going to Papa and Anton, only I would be left behind.

~~

She never once said, "Thank goodness I still have you; thank goodness you didn't go that night, that you didn't die too." But she never said it. As far as she was concerned, she had lost her family.

~~

To say there weren't many mourners at the funeral would have been an understatement. Me, Mr Cohen, my father's lawyer in Israel and his son, and a few elderly neighbours. Hardly worth the effort. It seemed such a sad and lonely end to what had once been a promising life. Mama had been young and pretty once, she had been born into a wealthy family and had married a very promising and very talented writer and academic. She had two beautiful children. And then my father's Jewish conscience attacked him and, as she saw it, destroyed her once promising life. She had a right to be bitter—I just wish she could have found some happiness in me rather than pinning everything on Anton, only to lose him too.

~~

43

"If there is anything I can do…" Mr Cohen took my hand.

He was one of the first people I'd met when we arrived from Russia. Mother never had the energy to discuss Papa's affairs, so I always did it. He had never seemed to mind doing business with a teenager. "No, thank you," I whispered.

"Well, let me know if there is. You know where I am. I'll see you next week; we can go over your father's things."

"Sure, thanks."

He gave me a warm smile, patted me on the shoulder and was gone. I felt about twelve years old again. At that age I hadn't thought life could get any worse. I had no friends, a stupid idiotic brother, and parents who didn't seem to like each other anymore, let alone love each other. But standing there saying good-bye to the few mourners who had bothered to come, I realized that life had suddenly got a lot worse.

~~

It was one thing to complain about what you had when you had a family behind you.

~~

Quite another thing to be standing alone with no family at all.

Chapter 2—Beruriah

My mother and her family were from Yemen. She came to Israel in 1949 with her younger sister and her uncle and his family. They came as part of the Magic Carpet Operation…and this is her story….It is her voice you hear now, and will hear until I tell you otherwise. I have heard her story so many times that every time I tell it I hear her voice reciting it to me, and so it only makes sense that she tells it for you too.

~~

Orthodox as his Judaism was, my father had assimilated so much into Yemenite culture that he was for all intents and purposes a Yemenite. It was just that he was able to justify his assimilation, with examples from ancient Judaism, when the Israelite way of life was very similar to the current Yemenite way of life. He never got that Judaism had changed with the times. He never got it because it didn't suit his purpose to get it.

I am never sure where he found the justification in ancient Judaism for my mother's black eyes and bruise-covered arms and legs. He didn't need to seem to justify that. He had however the justification for his wives. King David, King Solomon—who in ancient Judaic history hadn't had many wives? And who in modern Yemenite culture didn't have many wives?

There were six wives and then one died in childbirth and her children assimilated with us. And then there were six again because my father took another wife, younger than me.

It never mattered that father forbade us from playing with other children because there were so many of us, all so close in age that we always had someone to play with. And as we girls got older, there was always another baby to help look after.

When we first arrived in Israel others from Yemen used to describe how lonely life was in Yemen for a Jewish child, no-one to play with, and no school to attend. But life was never lonely for us.

My mother was the head wife but you wouldn't have known it. Everyone walked over her—from my father, to the other wives, to all of the children. She never protested when my father beat her, because her father had beaten her before him. She never protested when my father brought home yet another wife, because her own father had brought home wife after wife and her own mother had never murmured a word in protest or disapproval.

And she never protested as my father married her daughters off. From our ninth birthdays, when he could. It all depended on there being a male Jew available for marriage. Our numbers in Yemen were never healthy and it seemed, with each daughter, he had to wait longer and longer to marry us off. Even if he included in his husband-search widowers it still wasn't an easy task.

We are what our Mothers teach us to be, are we not?

At the age of twelve, my father's sister had been taken by a Muslim neighbour for a wife. Converting a Jewess to Islam was considered a holy act, a good deed. Married Jewesses were off limits, but unmarried ones fair game. It wasn't so much the loss of a sister that my father mourned but the loss of a Jew to Islam. To prevent the same happening, to prevent his daughters from disappearing behind a curtain of *burqas*, within his own family he made it his aim to marry his daughters off as early as possible, thus protecting them from a forced conversion as opposed to a miserable marriage. His grandchildren would be descendents of Isaac and not Ishmael.

And then one day my uncle, my father's brother, decided that he had had enough of being a repressed person, and of being a Jew in a Muslim country. He was tired of paying a poll tax that he paid just for being

Jewish, and he was tired of being told he wasn't allowed to ride a horse because of his religion, and he was tired of not being able to build his house higher than his Muslim neighbours'. He was tired of not being able to let his daughters out of sight, in case his Muslim neighbour forced them away, married them and converted them too Islam. "We have been Jews in Muslim countries for too long," he declared chewing on his *khat*. "Too long we have lived in fear of what may come next; too long we have been trodden on. Too long we have lived in the shadows. To Israel we will go."

"Then may G-d strike you down!" My father had never been one to mince his words, not with strangers and certainly not with family. "Only G-d can create a Jewish state and this imposter—this fake—won't last a second. Go, go to that land of heathens and you will soon feel his wrath!"

"Better the wrath of a Jewish G-d than the wrath of the Islamic bastard next door, who wants to take my daughter, or my sheep. I have to teach my four-year-old son how to shoot a gun, so that he may defend himself in this lawless land. No! Better he die from G-d's hand than under the hand of a G-dless descendent of Ishmael. We leave in three days at dawn, Avraham, after morning prayers."

~~

My father refused to go, and that in turn meant none of his children could go either. G-d would deliver them, not a group of secular Zionists. That was his thinking.

And then my aunt, my uncle's wife, decided she needed someone to help her with their children. My uncle had just one wife but ten children, the youngest being a baby still nursing. His wife he claimed couldn't manage with so many on the long trek from our village, Sook Al-Jadid to Aden. They needed help.

She wanted to take me and my sister.

My father said 'no'.

My uncle said 'please'.

My father said 'no'.

My uncle said we would be well looked after, that we were family and he was asking for help.

My father said 'no'.

My uncle said he would send us straight back. As soon as they reached the camp at Aden he would send us back.

My father said 'with whom'.

My uncle said my father could walk with us and escort us back.

My father said he wasn't walking all the bastard way to Aden only to have to walk back again—family or no family.

My uncle said his wife's younger brother would walk with them, to help, and would bring us back.

~~

To this day I don't know why my father agreed to let us go. We weren't even allowed to go to the well to fetch water without a male chaperone for protection, and we'd never left the village. Never. And yet here he was agreeing to let us go all the way to Aden, only to be returned by someone who wasn't a blood relation.

My sister always claimed that money passed hands. That our uncle paid my father for our help. But she was always ready to believe the very worst about father. I can't see how any amount of money would convince father to let us go all that way and back with someone he barely knew. But he did and that was that. It doesn't matter now why, because it was done.

~~

We didn't pack anything—only enough for the walk to Aden and the walk back. We had a bag between us— some water, some bread and that was it.

My uncle's family packed as much as they could carry—clothes, blankets, pots and pans. Every single piece of jewellery she owned my Auntie wrapped around her neck and wrists, only to cover it up with shawls and layers of clothing. My sister and I helped her sew it into secret pockets hidden deep within her clothes.

My uncle said goodbye to each of his animals in turn—he laid a hand on each sheep's head, on the back of every goat. They were to be my father's now.

My sister refused to look back at the village as we left it. She said we would be back soon enough; it wasn't going to change or disappear while we were gone. But I looked back. Some of our younger brothers and sisters had come out into the yard to say good-bye. They squealed and shouted, their arms waving wildly as we set off. There was no sign of mother or father.

Perhaps if I'd known then what I knew later, I would have stopped for a longer look at the village that had always been home.

But my sister pulled me roughly by the arm. "Come on, we're getting left behind!" And we had to run down the path to catch up with my uncle and his family.

Although a longer look wouldn't have shown me any more, or left a more lasting impression than the one I took. I hadn't known anywhere but our village, and knew only it. How could I ever forget it? There wasn't much to remember anyway. A lot of dirt and dust. Babies crying. Animals braying. My father shouting. Children fighting.

~~

To say that it was a tough journey was an understatement. The little ones got sick and their wracking coughs haunted our dreams. Every penny my uncle had saved he spent paying head taxes to yet another greedy country chief along the route to Aden. He begged, he cajoled; he emptied his purses again in an attempt to get us through each country on the way to Aden.

The days spent in Aden weren't much better, although we all sighed big sighs of relief to finally get there. Makeshift tents dotted the landscape for as far as the eye could reach. The whole camp swarmed with babies and children and wives.

Day and night the camp buzzed with stories of the Promised Land, and the angels of the sky that would deliver everyone there.

~~

And in Aden, our uncle's younger brother refused to go back. He had seen the airplane standing on the tarmac, he knew the stories of the air-lifts before—he knew what this angel was capable of. And he refused to go back. He wanted a place on the angel that would deliver the Jews to their homeland.

~~

"No, damn you. If you go, I go!—What is there for me back there?" He tossed his head in the direction from which we'd just walked. "I know what they have in Israel—electricity and shops and proper houses and a Jew can walk around like a free man. He doesn't have to hide behind a gun, or sleep on the floor with the goats."

And what could my uncle say? He too was leaving because he was tired of hiding behind a gun, and of teaching his children to hide behind guns. He was tired of living in fear of what was around the corner, of an Islamic government and population that could turn at any time. "But my nieces, who will take my nieces back?"

My sister shuffled her feet. "We can go back alone."

My uncle laughed, almost hysterically, "Your father would kill me!"

"How can he kill you, you won't be here, and he refuses to step foot in Israel." My sister was always the direct one.

"But two unmarried Jewish girls walking back to Sook Al-Jadid alone—never! You'll be married off before you even set foot out of Aden. And converted to them before this angel ever takes off." My uncle used the word angel as everyone else in the camp did, because it was named so in the prophecy. But he said the word as if he didn't have much faith in the machine, as if he wasn't quite sure if this angel would ever make it off the ground, let alone into the sky and then to Israel.

But there was no-one else. Everyone was gathered to leave Yemen, not to return. Men, women and children, their lives packed in the bags at their feet. Most looked terrified, others bent back and forth praying to G-d; praying for a safe journey.

"Let them come with us!" It was my uncle's wife. Ten children and still pretty. The day she met my uncle she told him she was the only wife he was getting—bible or no bible. She had promised her mother, who had been one of many wives that she would.

My uncle had agreed. "One wife is enough hassle," he used to say.

"With us? To Israel?"

"That is where we are going is it not?" She shifted her youngest from one hip to the other.

"Avraham would kill me."

"How can he kill you? You won't be here, and he refuses to step foot in Israel," my sister said again.

I looked at her in shock, "You want to go with them?"

She looked at my uncle's brother-in-law and said, "Why not."

And then my uncle looked at his brother-in-law, and then at my sister, and then at his wife. "Why do I get the feeling I have been taken for a fool?"

My sister's doe eyes feigned innocence as they returned his stare; Soloman stared at his feet and my uncle's wife looked back at him with a steely gaze.

"There is no-one to take them back. What can we do but take them with us? Better they come to a Zionist land than leave them at the mercy of the Muslims."

And then it was my turn to look at Soloman, and then my sister and then at my aunt. And I knew I had been taken for a fool too. I grabbed my sister's arms, my fingers pinching her flesh.

"Ow, ow, ow!"

"What are you doing?" I cried.

"Get off me!"

"What are you doing?" I repeated, releasing my grip only slightly.

She turned her back to the others and I did the same. "Please, Sara! I love him, he loves me. Going to Israel is the only chance we have of being together."

"And father?"

"He knows nothing, and if he did he'd have us both stoned. Please Sara! You know he wants to marry me to that old man. Please!" She was desperate, pleading—and then defiant. "I won't go back!" She turned to the others. "I won't go back! To get me to go back you will have to physically carry me back and who will do that?"

My uncle sighed and seemed to know when he was beaten. "You have been spending much too much time with my wife and it seems my brother-in-law too. Come on, let's go!"

~~

And so that is how we came to Israel. How we left Yemen. How we never saw mother or father or the others again.

~~

We boarded the plane, with eagles painted on its doors. My sister found out many years later that they did that to make sure we got on the plane; to reinforce the biblical prophecy in Isaiah, "They shall mount up with wings like eagles"; a prophecy that was repeated many times over on the long flight.—A plane full of old men, teenage brides and young children. The air was full of fear and dread, and hope and anticipation. I wondered what it felt like to be one of those who believed that this flight was the fulfillment of a biblical prophecy....It must have been pretty intense. All I could feel was fear over what my father would do to us when he eventually caught up with us. What punishment could ever atone for what we had done?

~~

My sister and Soloman took to Israel like calves take to their mother's milk.

They picked up modern Hebrew much faster than my uncle and I as we clung to our biblical version for much longer than we should have. I just thought that if I acted the same, kept life as similar as possible to what it had been in Yemen, well then I wouldn't have betrayed my family, or my father. The hold he had on me still, from so many miles away, was intense.

~~

For many months we lived in old military barracks, miles from anywhere, out in the harshness and heat of the desert. Then they moved us to *ma'abarot* or transit camps where we started our lives all over again.

"Like the Israelites!" my uncle cried, as we struggled to sleep in the heat of the tents. "This is our very own personal exodus," he cried again, as we tried to eke out what little rations we had for all of us adults and all of the children.

~~

We were no strangers to hardship. There had always only ever been just enough food to go around in Yemen, and clothes were passed from child to child until they fell part.

That wasn't the hard part. The hard part was adapting to life. To Israeli life.

In Yemen water came from a well. My sister and I used to go to collect enough for the family for the day every morning. Now water came from a tap, running all day and all night. You just turned the tap on when you needed some water, and turned if off again when you were finished.

In Yemen if we needed meat we slaughtered an animal. Here you went to a shop and brought it already dead, already skinned and boned. They wrapped it in a plastic bag and you took it home and cooked it.

The same with vegetables. We used to grow them ourselves, pull them from the earth and eat them straight away. Here you went to the shop, brought them and if you wanted kept them for days before eating them.

Our candles were replaced by electric lights, hand washing by washing machines.

Buses and cars and trucks thundered down concrete roads—a far cry from the horses and donkeys that carried us over the dirt in Yemen.

To me Israel was a strange land. A strange land where Jewish women had jobs, and fought in wars and openly took birth control. Where Jewish women got divorced and raised their children alone. Where polygamy was banned and openly frowned upon and monogamy the only recognized legal state of union for a man and a woman. Where Jewish women sunbathed on public beaches in bikinis and swam alongside men in the sea and swimming pools. Where children were taught in schools about evolution rather than about Adam and Eve.

I used to think how lucky it was my father never made it here with us. The shock would have killed him. He never would have coped with a Zionist Israel.

My uncle used to shake his head at the women in their cropped tops with their uncovered short hair and wonder aloud, "What is the world coming to?" But he accepted it as the price of a Zionist state. My father would have dropped dead on the spot; one look and bang he would have fallen down dead. That's how my sister put it. She used to find it funny, the thought of our father dead on the floor, dead from a glance at the bikini-clad women of Zionist Israel. But I could never laugh with her. I'd betrayed my family enough.

My sister and Solomon embraced it. My sister uncovered her hair, cut it short. Did away with her long skirts and blouses, opting for jeans and t-shirts instead. Solomon did away with his *kippot* and his black trousers, and even cut off his curls and shaved his beard.

Again my uncle shook his head and wondered what the world was coming to. His wife told him to hush; they were young and living life. This was why they had come to Israel; and if he didn't be quiet maybe she would burn her skirts and buy some of those jeans herself.

My father would have killed them both. I have no doubt about that. And he would have killed me for letting it happen.

~~

My sister and Solomon were married weeks after we landed in Israel. They both served in the army and then began their lives in Tel Aviv, far away from Rosh Ha'ayin, where my uncle, his wife, his children and I finally ended up. It was a mass of temporary tents at first, crowded with refugees from Yemen and then it became something more permanent. Proper houses sprang up, and kiosks, and backyard restaurants and coffee dens selling the black, strong coffee my father had loved so much.

I used to think of them at home, when I had a spare moment or two—as I rinsed clothes in the old metal tub, or stirred the rice on the stove, I thought of them, and wondered if they ever thought about us. I missed them because they were familiar, not through any independent idea of love. And because they seemed to me, still, more real than this strange modern land we now lived in.

~~

Eventually we would leave the tents. My uncle would manage to gather enough money to buy some materials to build a house. A house he and Solomon and my cousins spent many a day and night building.

People around us started to do the same. And suddenly houses started to spring from nowhere. We were building our own town. A town of Yemenite immigrants rising from the tents and the dirt."

~~

"And so, that was my mother' story. And also, I suppose the story of how I got here, in Israel. Me, Beruriah.

My mother's uncle chose my father for her. It wasn't very romantic, which I suppose was just fine because romance didn't suit either of my parents.

One night at dinner my uncle had asked, "So, isn't it time you were married?"

He was a little uncomfortable with the question. His daughters were still too young for marriage to be even an option, and he had hoped he wouldn't have to deal with this for many years yet. But he had a responsibility towards his brother—he had after all been an accomplice in his nieces' flight from Yemen—he had a responsibility to see them settled.

My mother had blushed and looked down at her plate.

My uncle's wife then looked at her squarely, "Is there anyone you would like to marry?"

My mother blushed and indicated no with her head. She didn't look up from her plate. She too was uncomfortable. She had never thought that this was something she would have to deal with. Since she was a child she had known her father would choose her husband and that would be it.

"Does that mean I need to choose someone?" my uncle asked.

"Looks like it," his wife replied. She had married for love and had thought that here in Israel my mother would have jumped at the chance to do the same, as her sister had done. She could not understand my mother's reluctance to embrace life in this new land where women were equal with men.

~~

My mother's uncle was a good man. It would have been easy to look at my father, whom my uncle chose, and based on that, call my uncle a bad man. But he wasn't. He was a kind man who loved his wife and children very much, and who always treated his family like he loved them very much. He went out with the best intentions of finding mother a good, kind, and—of course—Yemeni husband. My father was a charmer and had fooled many into thinking he was a good man. He charmed my uncle, and that was that.

He never had to charm my mother because she would marry him regardless. Her sister had married for love and look what it had got her—a dead husband and a baby to feed by herself. It was better to be married, to anyone, than to be like that.

~~

My father had been born in Yemen and he never really got over having to leave it. Most immigrants to Israel felt as if they'd gained a homeland. My father only ever felt as if he'd lost one. He never really got that every single Israeli had also lost a homeland but that it didn't matter because Israel was the ultimate homeland never to be lost again. Maybe my father was too much of a true Israeli, after more than two thousand years without a homeland he was unable to accept that Israel was Jewish again and this time for good. He never quite believed it. So he kept himself and us in no man's land. We weren't allowed to fully integrate into Israeli society but we couldn't return to Yemen.

~~

He was religious because of tradition not faith. Faith involves trust and trust comes from the heart. My father didn't have a heart; or he just didn't know how to use it or know what it was for. His heart wasn't evil; he just never used it. My father was determined to remain the Patriarch in a society that put equality before all else. And he

57

quickly found that the only place where he had any control was at home.

He used religion to control us—our clothes, our daily activities, our weekends, our futures. Our whole lives he dictated to us through the guise of religion.

Our religion demanded we cover our arms, he said. I didn't believe that he was listening to our religion. He demanded we cover our arms because he said so, not G-d. It was just fortunate that he was able to find something in the Torah that would justify our having to cover our arms.

He was never comfortable in the new Jewish state and never wanted us to be either. He was like my Grandfather, I think, or how I imagine my Grandfather to have been from my mother's stories. *My mother had come all the way from Yemen to become her mother.*

Take Aaron, my second eldest bother. At eighteen he refused to continue in his *Yeshiva*, or to work on the *Moshav*, as my oldest brother had done. He also refused to marry. Instead he joined the army.

"What kind of a man deserts his studies, his relationship with G-d, to take up a gun and kill?" roared my father.

"I have a duty to my country," came Aaron's calm reply.

"And your duty to G-d?" my father spat.

"I believe G-d would want me to defend his Jewish state." Again Aaron was calm. He'd made his decision, it had taken many months of soul-searching and it hadn't been an easy decision, he knew the reaction it would provoke and the family he might lose. But he was calm because he knew he'd made the right decision.

"His Jewish state?" my father was livid, his eyes bulged. "This piece of land founded by secular Zionists, you call His state?"

"You've never had any problems taking welfare money from those same secular Zionists." Aaron was defiant, the only person I had ever seen defy my father before.

"Get out," my father roared. "You no longer exist to me or this family! May G-d also strike you from his heart."

"But that's just it, father. You don't get to decide who G-d has in his heart. Only G-d decides that."

"Get out!"

And he was gone.

~~

My mother was too much of a coward ever to try and contact Aaron. In the end I went to my aunt who helped me find him. We learnt that he was OK, had done his time in the army and was working for a new IT firm. He had a girlfriend and was happy.

"I wouldn't try and contact him while you still live in your father's house," my aunt said during one of her moments of lucidity. "Be patient and wait until after you've gone."

~~

We never knew why my aunt agreed to be my father's second wife. She never said why. She never spoke much after Soloman died. She couldn't live without him and yet she'd promised him she'd keep on living after him if anything happened. Physically she was alive and well but that was it. She wasn't crazy as such; there were just no lights on, no-one home. Or maybe she was crazy, a silent kind of crazy—why else would she agree to live with my father like that?"

~~

My mother never really reconciled herself to what she considered to be the abandonment of her family by her and her sister. If you left your family behind she used to think what did you have left? And so what kind of a person did that make you? My aunt suffered no such guilt and—free of a domineering father and the confines of an

Islamic country—she was more than happy to build a new family in a new land.

"It's time to build our own families, to start again," she told my mother as she adjusted the top she'd brought just that morning in the market. She turned to admire her legs in her jeans. All this was before Soloman died. After Soloman died, my father ordered her to cover herself, to share my mother's long skirts and head-dresses, and she agreed. With Soloman, had gone her will to fight.

But my mother didn't think it worked like that. You couldn't just cast aside your family by geographically moving away from them. You couldn't just abandon them and the thousands and thousands of years of history that came with them.

Maybe she saw my father as punishment for that. Who knows?

~~

On Independence Day, not long after Aaron had left us, I went for a walk and found myself along the river in Yehousha Park. The park was full of families barbecuing, or doing *manga*, as they call it in Israel. Every available patch of grass was taken up with mangas, families, chairs and food. Some families had gone all out—boundaries of their plot marked by colourful string or balloons. Huge tables, dozens of plastic chairs. Hammocks swaying between the trees. Some had put up large canopies, others tents. Whole families gathered around, from the very old to the very young. Children played football, trying to score goals through a goalpost manned by their Abbas. The smell of barbecuing meat was everywhere. The sun shone down—hot and bright.

~~

As children we never had the money for *manga*; nor really the money for the food to go on it. Plus it would have meant associating with secular Israelis, something my father was reluctant to allow. My brothers would go

60

anyway and would always manage to *blag* some meat of a sympathetic *Ima*—usually one whose boys were long grown up, or serving in the army, or traveling through South America, and she would see some of her own boy or boys in my brothers and her heart would melt. They used to boast about the juicy, thick meat they had eaten—full of spices and flavour. My mouth watering, I told them to shut up or I would tell on them, that they had eaten non-kosher meat, which would certainly mean a beating—or two—depending on how long my father remembered what they had done.

~~

"Why do they hate us?"

"I don't know. I don't care."

"We're Israelis too, aren't we?"

"Of course we are, stupid!"

My cousin Lilach looked hurt. It didn't take much to hurt her. Some children lose their parents and develop a thick skin, a hard shell that nothing can penetrate; others became as soft as jelly. Lilach was as soft as jelly could get. "So why do they hate us? We are Israelis, they are Israelis—the same." Lilach thought out loud.

"Does it matter?" I was impatient with her. I didn't like being hated either but I also didn't want to give our tormentors my pain.

"But I thought they left Yemen so we wouldn't be hated." Lilach had a really annoying habit of thinking out loud, especially when upset.

"Who are 'they'?"

"Ima and Abba."

"They did."

"But they hate us here too," and it was true.

"Does everyone hate us?"

"No." But I wasn't sure. I knew the Arabs hated us, but they hated all Jews, not just the dark-skinned ones who spoke Arabic, and that's why our grandparents had left Yemen. But now other Jews, European Jews mainly, seemed to hate us too.

"Who doesn't hate us?"

Again I wasn't sure, "The Americans maybe."

"So maybe we should go there, where the Americans live."

"It's called America, stupid!"

And she was stupid—stupid for thinking that you could just decide to go to America and then go. How would you pay for it? It costs thousands of *shekels* to go to America and we didn't even have one.

"Is it nice there?"

"Where?"

"In America."

"How do I know?" But I thought it probably was. Maybe America was somewhere where it didn't matter what G-d you worshipped, or where your parents were born, and what language you spoke at home, as long as you were willing to work hard to make money and live.

"Maybe we could go there."

I scoffed.—My father was right. Lilach had no hold on reality, just like her parents.

Anyway if we went to America who would look after all the babies?

I was beginning to wonder if mother didn't like babies a little too much—they kept coming, exhausting us all and making our money last even fewer days. I had told her once that maybe she should stop them coming. She had replied, rather wearily, that it wasn't up to her. It was up to G-d and my father. I wasn't sure what my father had to do with it, he never showed any interest in the babies. Mother looked tired so I left her and braced myself for yet more babies. I didn't know that there were even more yet to come.

~~

When Soloman died, my aunt tried to support Lilach on her own. But she found it impossible to find work, with no high school qualifications, she found it hard to find anything that would feed, house and clothe the two of them. She tried for a couple of years and then got sick. In the end she brought Lilach and herself to live with us. My father insisted that he and my aunt live as husband and wife, even if the law wouldn't technically allow them to marry.

My aunt didn't fight it. A Palestinian grenade had extinguished the fire in her and so she became my father's second wife. Which meant more babies, something I secretly cursed G-d for. I did wonder if father had anything to do with the new babies too, but I didn't dare curse him, not even in secret.

~~

Things only got worse in school; for now—not only were we Sephardim, who spoke Arabic, and didn't eat *schnitzel*—but our father had two wives—or as good as had two wives. In our Yemenite community no-one batted an eyelid, but school exposed us children to a secular world—a secular, Ashkenazi world, where polygamy was illegal and weird.

~~

I was nervous. No; terrified. Terrified that at any minute my friend Abigail's parents would throw me out of their house for being all wrong.—For being from Yemen.—I was terrified that I would do something wrong, say something wrong and they would ask me to leave. The house was so quiet—no screaming babies, no crying toddlers, no shouting from the neighbours above and below. Everything was so tidy, so neat—everything had its place. No holes in the sofa, no peeling paint on the walls but pictures and paintings instead. Comfort. Warmth. Everything matched.

And the space! Everyone had their own bedroom— and no-one had to share a bed with a younger sister or two.

~~

"There must be something we can do."

"Do what?"

"Someone we can call, someone who can help that child."

"Dinah, please! It's none of our business."

"But you saw her!—She looks like she's half starved, and those clothes…."

"Dressing a child badly is not a crime, nor does it constitute child cruelty."

"It's what the clothes represent that worries me."

"And what do the clothes represent? That there's no money for better clothes? It's not a crime to be poor. You can't take a child away from their parents just because they are poor."

"Forget the clothes. Her father has two wives—two! And there are god knows how many children…. To have two wives is a crime."

"If he is actually married to them, yes but I bet you he isn't, not officially. They just live together as man and wife."

"Same thing."

"But not a crime. Not technically."

"It's not right."

"It's not our place to interfere."

"But that child—did you see the way she came in here, those eyes. She has obviously never seen anywhere like this—and this is hardly *Herzeliya Pituach*."

"So, encourage Abigail to bring her here as much as possible. We can feed her, give her clothes, free rein over the books and television. But that is all we can do. It is not our place to interfere with how others choose to live, especially those who live according to their culture."

"What are you talking about?—We're all Israelis!"

"Dinah, please; even you are not that naïve."

"But that child is no better off than if her family had stayed in Morocco."

"Yemen."

"What?"

"Yemen; her family are from Yemen. And of course she's better off. Here she goes to school, she hasn't been married off to her uncle or cousin and she's not going to have to carry a gun to protect herself from an Arab neighbour. Change doesn't happen overnight, it can take generations but I bet you her children and their children will have better clothes, more opportunities. That's how it works."

"One god and yet not one people at all."

"Not yet, but one day."

"It just doesn't seem right that a Jewish child should go hungry in a Jewish state."

"Dinah, my love, you would have made a fine kibbutznik, a fine Zionist!"

"Don't turn it into a joke. I'm serious. What kind of a Jewish state are we, where we let our own go hungry?"

"A capitalist one."

"Well, it's wrong."

"So, one at a time. We can't save them all but we can help those who are on our doorstep, starting with a hungry teenager your daughter brought home for dinner and who wants more potato salad."

~~

So this is how real Israelis live, I thought to myself. Abigail's father didn't grunt at his children. He kissed their foreheads, looked them straight in the eye and asked about their days, and then showed interest in their stories.

Abigail's mother wasn't permanently weary, her head was never bowed and she couldn't pass her children or husband without planting a kiss on them somewhere or dragging them into a hug.

The only physical contact in our home came in the form of slaps, blows and punches. As a very young child I once thought that women wore long skirts, like my mother, and covered their arms to hide their bruises.

Those without long skirts and bare arms had no bruises to hide.

Dinah had no bruises to hide. My mother had too many.

She used to say it wasn't his fault. That he was frustrated in a Jewish state that was just too secular for him to understand. He was frustrated that he had nothing here—that his family's land, home, livestock were now somebody else's.

Eventually I started to hate my mother for trying to make me believe that. I hated her more for that—for trying to *make me accept* his behaviour—than I hated her *for accepting* his behaviour. She was a big enough fool without trying to make me into one too. I wanted to shout at her, to hit her even—to make her accept reality, "This is not Yemen, somewhere you don't even know! You were born in Israel. Israeli women don't have to put up with this!" And more importantly, "We don't have to put up with this!"

I didn't dare take any of my anger out on my father, so I took it out on my mother instead, for being so weak.

I loved G-d, he had created me and the world and Israel. I read the bible like a storybook—but where did it say that beating ones wife was allowed?

But my father was weak. He knew it too. That's why he picked only on the weak—my mother, my aunt and Lilach. He beat me once or twice and each time I refused to cry and so he never tried again. The more they cried, the more likely he was to single them out next time. Most of the time I wished him dead, or at least that he would leave the house one day and never come back.

Chapter 3—Amelia

So I am related to them.—Which makes me related to the founders of a state.—And not just any state, but only the most controversial state in the whole world! I guess as a kid it used to impress me, but now I would quite like them to go away and leave me be. When we are in public my mother says we have a name to uphold, whatever that means. We have an image to portray—that we are worthy of our name. Big deal! To me it's just a name and one I changed as soon as I could. I have enough drama in my life without having to lug the baggage of that name with me too.

When I changed my name in an attempt to be free, my mother, of course, cried....

"Why, why, why?"

"Why what?" I was impatient. I had friends to meet and my mother's dramatic monologues of nonsense could go on for hours.

"You were born with the name of heroes, with the legacy of heroes!"

"My god, do we have to be so dramatic mother? It was like years ago, get over it. It's no big deal."

"No big deal? People died, people fought, people struggled so you could be free, so our people could live in peace. And all you have to do is respect that, by wearing your name with pride, with dignity, as they did."

"Do we have to do this now? I have to be at the mall in ten minutes."

I left her crying. She probably took a valium, or two. It was, she said, the only way she could cope with my teenage angst and rebellion, which—she always added—my older sister had never experienced. My sister had also never changed her name; that is until she married her millionaire and went to live in Herzeliyya where she promptly turned into a baby-breeding machine. A baby-breeding machine that played tennis and lunched. My father never made a fuss about the valium; that was his way of coping with her. He was away a lot anyway—business here, business there. He had let Mama give us her surname. He claimed it was because it meant so much to Mama and because she had no brother to keep the surname and the legacy alive. I believed that for about two seconds. When Lucille was born my father's business was in trouble financially.—Mama's papa bailed him out with a loan that he took several years to pay back. That loan saved his business and his reputation. You work it out.

~~

My mother's dramatics left me late for a date with friends. Not that anyone would be there at the agreed time. There was traffic—when wasn't there traffic into Tel Aviv?

Galgalatz played music through my car radio.

mother would be at home now retelling to herself the story she had shoved down my throat a million and one times.

My great-great-grandfather was present at the first Zionist Congress in Basle in 1890 something, and shook hands with some dude called Theodore, and they'd discussed something about forming Israel or some crap like that.

This had then prompted my great-great grandfather—mother's great-grandfather—to emigrate to Israel in 1905 before Israel was even founded....So he didn't exactly emigrate to Israel; he emigrated to Palestine. He helped start a *kibbutz* where my great grandfather was born and he helped defend it from Arab attacks, and he survived disease and epidemics and bad weather and crops failing and whatever mother wishes to add to the story. My great-great-grandmother worked for the Jewish agency when it was established in the 1920s,

1928, 1929? The dates stick in my head only because mother has repeated the same story everyday of my life.

Then my great grandfather, my mother's grandfather joined the Irgun underground, he was a bit of a rebel—so at least there is someone in my family I can slightly relate to. And he was one of the parachutists trained to be dropped into Europe, only he wasn't one of the ones that eventually made it there. So he had to busy himself with helping Jews from around the world get to Israel, illegally—again someone else after my own heart. And his wife had been this tiny but really brave woman from Germany and they had worked together, in the name of love, and Zionism to save more people….blah, blah, blah!

Then my grandfather, mother's father, was some bigwig in the army during the Six Day War, and the Yom Kippur War and led many men into many victorious battles—something like that.

~~

"Hey have you seen this?"

I half turned my eyes on a pair of shoes in the shop window that I just had to try on.

"This!" Ifat had stopped at a kiosk and had taken a newspaper from its rack and was engrossed in something in its middle.

"What is it?" My eyes still on the shoes, I had a skirt at home they would match perfectly, and it had been almost two days since my father's credit card had had an airing. It would be getting bored sitting in my wallet not doing anything.

"Look!"

Reluctantly leaving the shoes for a minute I turned to Ifat. The middle page of the newspaper was taken up by an old man surrounded by three women. The headline screamed"New Jewish cult master takes advantage of innocent women."

"What is it?"

Ifat's eyes turned to the page; scanning the script she recited. "... Some guy that says the ancient Israelites had more than one wife, so why can't he.... Something about the right way to G-d. Blah, blah, blah.... What a pervert! He has like seven kids from these women and look! She's no older than us! Blah, blah.... Something about how worried their families are, trying to rescue them. Blah, blah.... Insane, no?"

"Mm, insane."

"Oi are you going to buy that?" the kiosk man shouted from his perch behind the counter.

"Does it look like we are going to buy it?"

"Then clear off!"

"Ass!"

"Jerk!"

~~

Driving home with the shoes on the passenger seat next to me, as a joke I tried to imagine mother's face if, for example, one of her daughters had married a polygamous, ageing man with white hair and a beard and as a consequence ended up on the middle page of Israel's most popular newspaper? I knew it would be priceless; all the Doctors in Israel, Europe, and North America wouldn't be able to prescribe enough valium to keep her quiet or sane. I chuckled at the thought and then turned to the shoes next to me.

~~

"Darling, what did you buy?"

"Shoes," I grunted, throwing both the shoes and my jacket onto the sofa."

"Darling, no, not here!—In the cupboard, please!"

I ignored her and turned my attentions to the kitchen where I knew there was chocolate cake with my name on it. I came out with the cake between my fingers.

"Darling please, get a plate and a fork! This is not a Sephardim household!"

I ignored her again.

She gave up, briefly. "So did you have a nice day?"

"Was OK." I watched her flinch at my choice of words, or lack of.

"You bought shoes?"

"Mmm." I turned to the television and MTV.

"From where?"

"Shenkin."

"Oh darling, really? How many times have I told you not to shop there. There really is nothing of any quality to be had there."

"Leave me alone!" I shouted.

She flinched again, there was a time when shouting at her would have knocked her over, but that was when she needed only half the bottle of valium, now she was on a whole bottle a day, she coped a little better. "Who were you with?"

"Ifat."

"Oh no, not again, Darling! Why must you always choose the strangest friends?"

"What's wrong with Ifat?"

"So scruffy darling! And what did you say her father did—a bus driver?" mother shuddered.

"He's a taxi driver and who gives a shit what he does?"

"Your Grandmother would be turning in her grave if she knew the people you socialize with darling."

"Fuck off!" I said it right up close, right into her face, and stalked off up the stairs to my room.

Let the bottle of valium handle that, I said to myself, as I slammed the door to my bedroom.

~~

I opened the door to a dark house. The light on the answering machine was flashing. I pressed it.

"Tali, it's Mark. I'm not going to make it back tomorrow after all. There's more to do here than I realized and I have clients wanting to meet me all week. You'll just have to handle Amelia on your own. Send her to

71

Lucille, or let her stay with a friend. I'll try and get back for Friday and we'll deal with her then. Bye."

~~

Deal with me? I wasn't going to let anyone deal with me. I picked up the phone, "Ifat? Want to go get drunk?"

~~

On Independence Day, just a few days later, I went for a walk and found myself along the river in Yehousha Park. The park was full of families barbecuing, or doing manga, as they call it in Israel. Every available patch of grass was taken up with mangas, families, chairs and food. Some families had gone all out—boundaries of their plot marked by colourful string or balloons. Huge tables, dozens of plastic chairs. Hammocks swaying between the trees. Some had put up large canopies, others tents. Whole families gathered around, from the very old to the very young. Children played football, trying to score goals through a goalpost manned by their Dads. The smell of barbecuing meat was everywhere. The sun shone down— hot and bright.

~~

Manga in the park was not something our family did. It was too far beneath mother—too many uncouth people, too many screaming children. Eating outside, on her lap, was never her thing. father of course never had time for manga—who can eat when there is business to take care of and more money to make? And Lucille would but not when everyone else was. She took the children for manga on random days when no-one else would be there.

~~

"Because people identify luck and happiness and ultimately success with money if someone has a lot of money we call them "lucky," and "successful," and assume that they are essentially happy.

We all know, often from personal experience, that real happiness isn't found in money and the things it can buy. We all know that happiness is found in family and friends and what we have come to call the "simple pleasures of life"—laughter, a good meal, a child's first step, a wedding vow.

~~

You could be married to a banker who furnishes your mansion with Chippendale furniture and your body with the brightest, sparkliest diamonds ever and the biggest bruises you will struggle to hide behind the glitter of the diamonds.

Or the husband with the large expense account, top of the range cars and oh the mistresses.

A new diamond for each new broken rib?

How many designer handbags does it take to fill the void of an empty home and empty heart?"

The above was an article from a magazine I had recently bought, I carefully cut it out and left it on her bed, right in the middle of Papa's pillow—he hadn't slept on it for days, weeks.

She never mentioned the article. She crumpled it up and left it in the rubbish bin. I saw it lying there when I went to throw my banana skin into it. I was pretty sure she read it; her face was streaked with tears that morning, the morning after—although there weren't many mornings when her face wasn't streaked with tears, her eyes red and puffy and swollen. I only hoped, that morning, that my article had been the cause—although she used to shout, most mornings, as the valium wore off, that I was the cause of the tears. And on the rare occasions when my father decided to try and be a father and shouted at me down the phone, he blamed me for her tear-streaked face and rantings. I shouted back at both of them that they only had each other to blame and that I hated them both. This always prompted fresh tears and sobbing from my mother, and always made my father hang up the phone. It was always weeks before he called back.

~~

It didn't seem to matter how many times I screamed at her, "Papa isn't ever coming home!" She wouldn't listen.

Instead her shaking hands struggled with the top of yet another bottle of valium.

"He's found someone else!" I cried, stomping over her beloved carpet in my army boots.

The bottle slipped to the floor and she stared at it, a lost look on her face.

"HE HAS ANOTHER WOMEN!" Who cared if the neighbours heard, they all knew already. Everyone knew.

She bent down to grasp her bottle and brought it up to her lap with shaking hands that again struggled to open it.

I grabbed the bottle from her, twisted the cap and dumped the tablets onto her lap. "Go on, ignore it!" I challenged her, "Ignore what is right in front of your own face. Ignore what everyone is talking about behind your back."

Her eyes were sad but fixated on the tablets in her lap, "I love your father," she whispered.

"Oh get over it!" I scoffed, "How can you love someone who doesn't have a shred of respect for you?"

She plucked a tablet off her skirt and brought it to her mouth. She closed her eyes and swallowed it. "He loves me," she said, more confidently now, her eyes still closed.

"Yeah, you and the rest of Israel and Paris combined!" I retorted.

~~

They met in high school, were teenage sweethearts. It's enough to make you want to puke. He was Mama's first and only one. Again enough to make you want to puke. She wasn't his only one, not by any means. But what is love, if not blind? Mama wasn't just blind; she'd sewn her own eyes up and blocked her ears. They both wanted a home and a family, like good Jews should, and so they got married and had it all.

Papa just couldn't give up the game. He was an attractive man and knew it. If Mama didn't find out, his conscience didn't bother him. No-one was being hurt; so why not?

After all we lived in a society that viewed adultery as a common if not necessary trait of a successful man. Generals did it, politicians did it. What kind of successful, powerful man didn't?

~~

There was the mother of my best friend in the third grade; my teacher, Miss Frank, in the fifth grade; one of our neighbours, when I was in the sixth grade; Lucille's piano teacher; and God knows how many more. He didn't seem to care how close to home or to Mama each conquest was. He seemed to know that Mama's love for him, her need for him, made her as blind as a bat to it all. He was a first class jerk, or as I like to call him, asshole but he was a charming one. He could have charmed the pants off a lesbian. Hell! Perhaps he already had.

Chapter 4—Rachel

"Now you take care, honey; call us if there is anything, anything you need. And be careful who you talk to...."

"Mom PLEASE...." Ever since Leah Schwartz had visited Israel and run away with an ultra orthodox guy and cut off nearly all contact with her parents, my Mom had began to voice her objections to my traveling through the Holy Land alone.

~~

"I'll come with you, how about that?"

"Mom, how am I supposed to find myself with you breathing down my neck?"

~~

"Would all passengers on El Al Flight LY028 to Tel Aviv please proceed to gate 45 for boarding!"

~~

I ignored the in-flight safety spiel on the TV in front of me. Jack, my best friend, told me once that the chances of surviving a plane crash are next to nothing, and that airlines played the safety video only to make it look like there was something you could do to save yourselves should the plane go into freefall. He said it wasn't worth spending the two minutes of your life on, when you could be reading through the crappy in-flight magazine in front of you, or checking out your neighbours for the flight. My Jack batted for the other team, as my father liked to put it, he thought it made him sound "with it" and cool, and checking out his neighbours in any given room or mode of transport was one of his favourite things to do.

~~

My neighbour was a businessman engrossed in *Newsweek*. Checking out my neighbours had taken ten seconds but there was still a minute and fifty seconds left of the safety video to run and so I turned to the crappy in-flight magazine.

~~

When people asked why I was going to Israel I had told them it was to immerse myself in Jewish culture. This was after all what they wanted to hear and to an extent it was true. Growing up in the American Midwest without a kosher store in sight, let alone many other Jewish people, it was easy to just be American.

~~

That was the way my brother had gone; and at thirty he'd pretty much given up on Judaism. Something that disappointed my Mom a little; but not really my Dad at all. It was also something they accepted as a consequence of living in the Diaspora. It was the price they had paid for staying in the States. They had had friends who had emigrated to Israel mainly to ensure that their children would marry other Jews instead of other Americans. But to my parents it had seemed a little extreme to uproot us, my father's business etc. to live in Israel—a country they had never really ever planned to visit, let alone emigrate to. My father gave money every year to organizations that helped Jewish children, the Jewish elderly in Israel—he was a good Jewish donor like many other Jews in America. But he only ever made it to synagogue on Yom Kippur and only then if it didn't clash with work, or a tennis game.

I signed myself up to Jewish school, ran out of the basement of the Schwarts's house every Sunday. At first it was just me and the Schwartz kids, and then kids started to trickle in from neighbouring towns and villages.

~~

My parents didn't seem to mind that my brother's new wife wasn't Jewish or even that she was Catholic and they didn't blink an eyelid when we visited their new home with its Christmas tree standing proudly in the corner. They just didn't seem to notice it; or if they did, they didn't care.

~~

This was all during my mid teens when I had decided it was cool to be Jewish. Cool because we were the persecuted, the oppressed—you couldn't pick a year in history when we hadn't been the ones picked on, beaten up and killed in our droves. And as a teen supporting, and even being a part of the oppressed, was cool. It fitted my teen angst perfectly.

~~

And I decided on that particular visit to my brother's new home, that he and his catholic wife now shared, that I would care.

~~

"What is that?" I asked determinedly feigning ignorance, as if I had never seen a Christmas tree in my life.

My parents, knowing what was coming, chose to ignore me. I'd already berated my mother that morning for serving bacon for breakfast and for then trying to serve me chicken sausages (specially bought for me and my new-found kosher diet) that weren't kosher after I had just finished off a bowl of cereal with milk.

My brother however decided to take the bait. "You know what it is, I believe your friend Jack has one every year. You know the Christmas tree that his mother always has a present under for you." My brother was made confident by his new marriage and had decided that I was no match for this.

"But Jack and his family are Christians, we are Jewish. I don't know, Ben; correct me if I'm wrong, but we don't celebrate Christmas. Do we? Mom, do we? Have you been denying my Christmas all these years just for the hell of it?"

Jack's new wife, Maria, was eager to impress and tried to offer me a plate of cocktail sausages on sticks. A snack Rachel?" she asked tentatively almost as if she expected me to throw the whole plate in her lap.

"Are these kosher?"

"Jeepers, Rachel! You know they're not!"

"Then I'm sorry, Maria; but I can't eat them."

"What the...."

"No Ben, honestly, it's fine—maybe something else, a chip, a pretzel?" She was nice, Maria, and patient. Must have had something to do with her coming from a very large family. It seemed she had an endless supply of teenage sisters and so wasn't fazed by my new act.

"Well technically if they aren't kosher approved, which I'm assuming they are not, then I shouldn't really."

"I swear to god, Rachel, you are this close to being thrown out of our home."

"What is it?" I taunted him, "The bigger the Christmas tree, the easier it is to hide your Jewish behind, behind?"

He looked ready to jump across the room at me, to pull my hair as he had done when we were children and I had taken one of his books or toys without asking.

"Ben please, it's just a phase she's going through, leave her be."

"Just a phase Mom—being Jewish is just a phase? Am I the only one that remembers we are actually Jewish?"

"Rachel that's enough! Any more from you and it won't be Ben who's throwing you out, it will be me!" My father never had much time for teenage angst—he hadn't had it when Ben went through his I'm a teenager and hate everyone and everything stage and had spent the majority of his teenage years in black and silver chains; and he didn't have it with me.

While my mother rushed around attempting to find kosher food in our very non-kosher town, even going so far as to have food ordered from New York via the internet, my father refused to play ball. If I refused to eat dinner because the steak wasn't kosher and Mom had added milk to the mashed potatoes then as far as he was concerned I should and could go hungry. "If she's hungry, she'll eat," he insisted. But Mom had worried enough already about the eating disorders that seemed to be eating away at a large number of the teenage girls in our town that year and she did all she could to make sure I ate. A Chabad Rabbi came from New York to make our kitchen kosher. We had two different sets of cutlery and crockery—one for meat and one for dairy. She berated my Dad constantly for mixing the two; for pouring milk into a parve glass, for cutting kosher beef salami on to a dairy plate. She marked the bottom of each plate with a permanent pen mark. Red for meat. Blue for dairy. He still forgot and she was constantly replacing them. But then I forgot too. Which made me feel bad. Because Mom never mixed them.

~~

But relations between Ben and me remained strained.

~~

"So, Rach, how are the college applications going?"—It was Ben's birthday and he and Maria were at our place for dinner. An uneasy truce existed between us; we were family after all. And Maria chose great birthday and holiday presents.

I ran my finger through the icing on the top of the slice of cake in front of me. "Fine."

"So don't keep us in suspense, where are you applying to?"

"I want to go to Gratz College."

I saw my parents exchange glances. "Where?"

I repeated the name of the college again.

"But I've never heard of it, what is this college, where is this college?"

Mom started collecting dishes from the table, "It's a Jewish college, Rachel wants to go to a Jewish college."

I thought my brother would explode. "A Jewish college! Why the hell would you want to do that? With your SAT scores you could go anywhere! You can't be allowing this to happen—Mom? Dad?"

"It's a phase, right, Rachel?" my Dad turned to me. "There's plenty of time to apply for proper colleges too."

"Thank God for that, you know I can put in a good word for you at Harvard."

Harvard—my brother's Alma Mater. I toyed with my cake, "Do they have Jewish studies?"

It was like setting a match to dry kindling. "Jewish studies!!!! What the hell do you want with Jewish studies? What are you going to do with Jewish studies?"

I wanted to say, "Not become a pompous ass lawyer like you." But I figured he was close enough to a heart attack as it was. Maria had only been married to him for six months. It wouldn't have been fair to make her a widow so early on.

"Something!—Mom can I be excused?"

"Well, if you're sure, honey. You don't want more cake?"

"No, thanks."

~~

Then later as I emerged from my years of teenage angst my reason for being Jewish and staying Jewish centered around one event—the Holocaust. Something, funnily enough, I learnt about, not from my Jewish parents but from my Catholic teacher (we lived in a very Catholic town, that's why my life is littered with them).

As a child the Holocaust had been something hazy and blurred—almost like a newsreel running through my mind. Shots of emaciated people staring through barbed wire; women, men and children emerging from cattle trains with stars on their coats and suitcases in their hands; the letters A-U-S-C-H-W-I-T-Z above a gate. I knew it was something awful that had happened, that six million Jews in Europe had died and that then the Americans had come along and saved everyone.

~~

And then Mrs O'Brien came along and made it all real. Each month for a year we studied a different time of genocide from around the world—we did the war in the former Yugoslavia; we did Rwanda; we did Apartheid in South Africa; and then we did the Holocaust.

And then I realized that no-one was actively trying to erase me from the world because I was Jewish, there was no Hitler and his minions to send me to a death camp or the gas chambers but that in assimilating, my Jewish self was being erased. Judaism had survived the ghettos, the Gestapo, the concentration camps, the death camps and the gas chambers—but it was losing against the all-American way of life which didn't mind if you were Jewish *per se* but preferred it if Judaism was a part-time thing, may be a once a week thing.

~~

But it made my Judaism a quieter thing, something more personal. Something with more dignity—the dignity, for example, that the victims of the holocaust had been denied. But a dignity which they had tried to maintain, as they found a way to light Shabbat lamps in the very darkest times of the Concentration camps. Judaism became a personal thing for me, rather than a label as a person. And then I realized that being Jewish and not visiting Israel, the Jewish land, was like being Catholic and not loving the Pope. (I also realized that I had been living amongst too many Catholics for far too long.)

~~

So I told my parents that I didn't want a big eighteenth birthday party or fancy presents and that an air ticket to Israel would do fine. I would go, find myself, and then come back ready to start college in the fall as a newly empowered Jew.

~~

My father said sure—a big party or a ticket to Israel, either way his wallet was going to feel it; however I wanted to spend the money was my choice.

My Mom's reaction went from interested to slightly hysterical, although in all fairness to her I announced my plans to visit Israel the same week Leah Schwartz had called her parents to say she was pregnant for the third time in five years.

~~

"So who are you going with? A lucky boy maybe?"

"No boy, Mom, just me."

"Just you, honey, are you sure? There's no-one you want to go with?"

"Who, Mom? Who in my class is going to be interested in a trip to Israel?"

"Anyone! It's not just for Jewish people. They have great beaches, great food, great shopping.....so I hear, just like anywhere else."

"Mom I'm going to find my Jewish self, I can't do that with someone tagging along."

"Tagging along? Who would be tagging along? A friend wouldn't be tagging along."

"Mom, if I promise not to run off with some ultra orthodox guy I meet out there, get married and tell you I'm never coming home, will you leave me alone?"

"So why not go with a friend, someone from Jewish school—Hannah? Sara?"

"Mom if I promise not to speak to a single orthodox guy, will you leave me alone?"

"And if they talk to you? That's how it starts—you remember Leah Schwartz...."

"Mom, please!—I can take care of myself."

~~

That ended the conversation for that day but I knew it hadn't stopped the thoughts and the worry gnawing through my Mom's mind every time she thought of me traveling to Israel alone. Yes, I was going to find my Jewish self; but I had no intention of getting myself married off and having to live the rest of my life in long skirts, under a wig, and pregnant with another child every year. That may have been where Leah Schwartz found her

Jewish self, in the depths of Bnei Barak, but it was not where I was going to find myself. I was sure of that.

~~

The food was overcooked. The pasta was hard and crunchy round the edges and had to be peeled from the sides of the metal container with some force.

Blockbuster sequels I'd always wanted to watch, until they were forced in front of me, suddenly had no appeal; and I flicked from one to the other as often as I flicked through the slightly boring, advert-laden, in-flight magazine.

Every other passenger on the plane seemed to know each other—at least they chatted and stood by each others' seats as if they did.

A middle-aged women took a squawking baby from an exhausted looking young Mum and jiggled the baby up and down the plane aisles, people cooed and laughed at the little thing as she went; its mother trying to rest but not quite being able to relax as her baby was passed from the arms of someone's mother, to someone's grandmother and back again.

~~

The plane doors had been open for less than thirty seconds and already three-quarters of the plane's passengers were making their way to passport control.

"Ladies and Gentlemen, we'd like to thank you for flying with us today. We know you always have a choice and we'd like to thank you for choosing us. We'd kindly like to remind you to stay in your seats until the aircraft has come to a complete stop."

No-one seemed to be listening. No sooner had the plane's wheels hit the tarmac than people around me jumped up and started opening the overhead lockers, dragging out briefcases, trolleys and bags of duty-free whiskey and cigarettes.

I scrambled for my things—one shoe under the seat in front of me; my book wedged down between the seats.

I grabbed my knapsack and joined the queue of passengers shuffling down the aisles to the exit.

So here I was. Tel Aviv.

The arrival hall was bright and busy—confusing to my eyes, still tired from my journey and still getting accustomed to a new place. People clustered at the barriers searching for friends and family. Some stood with their dogs by their side. (They let dogs into the airport? I thought at first I might have been hallucinating—lack of sleep can do that, right?) Someone passed my shoulder to meet a relative only to be showered in rice and what looked like candy.

Groups of Orthodox passed me—the men in black, the women in black, their trolleys piled high with wig boxes and expensive suitcases And children—so many children—a baby gurgling in its stroller, a toddler chewing on its dummy, two older children sharing a packet of chips. The little girls already in their long skirts and long sleeved shirts. Someone else pushed past me holding the Torah scrolls on his shoulder, others rushed past to follow the Torah.

The bright lights stunned me as I looked frantically for the Kleins, who had promised to meet me and put me up for a few days.

I saw them before they saw me—something about their size, their loudness (even though they had yet to say anything) made me know they were fellow Americans. It seemed eight years wasn't enough to wash them of their American gleam and replace it with an Israeli layer.

"Honey, over here!" Mrs Klein beckoned me over.

"George, get her bags!"

"Honey, you look beat."

"I'm OK; the flight was OK."

"Honey you look beat!" she repeated. "This way!" she said, steering me towards the car-park.

I took my first breath of Israeli air—mainly car exhaust fumes!

~~

I ignored Mom's warnings and called Leah. We had sort of been friends, in the way that you are forced to be friends with the children of your parents' friends. We played together when we had to, but never really would ever have chosen to be friends ourselves. But I was intrigued—Leah had always been the most popular girl at school, she always had the latest fashions on, never went anywhere without her lip gloss and had changed boyfriends on a weekly basis. She was always late for Jewish school—if she ever turned up—and always managed to get out of Jewish camp every summer. What had made the all-American Leah run away with an ultra orthodox guy?

~~

I went to her place. She said she was pregnant again and not up to dragging the children on and off buses. The taxi dropped me off outside her apartment block. So this was B'nei Barark. The word 'grotty' sprung to mind. I once had a Jewish pen-pal from London who had taught me that word. I had used it once in an English essay and Mrs O'Donaghue had told me off for using a made-up word.

But B'nei Barak was grotty and grim and all one colour. Not one colour but all dark. Blacks, and browns and grey as if the sun knew not to infiltrate its religious streets for fear of disturbing the sacredness, the religion of the place.

Lines of washing hung from windows. All sorts of people—from toddlers to old women—ambled past in their black skirts and covered arms. The air stank of poverty, I could feel it closing in around me—from the clothes people wore to the exteriors of the buildings no-one had enough. So many snotty, sniffling noses and black velvet *kippot* on the heads of the snotty boys. Big sisters with babies on their hips, already in training for what would one day be their fate; a new baby every year.

Another set of clothes and shoes passed down to another brother or sister.

~~

But there must be happiness here I thought. Behind the doors of these crumbly buildings there must be something beautiful—a vase of fresh flowers, the mischievous grin of a toddler, a loving kiss between husband and wife. Roses grow in manure.

~~

I walked up the crumbling stone steps to the entrance of Leah's apartment block. The intercom didn't seem to work and I let myself in through the half open door. The lobby stank of cooking—from somewhere in the building a baby cried, and then another. The lift didn't work so I prepared myself for the walk up five flights.

~~

Leah answered the door—her swelling stomach visible through her black dress. Two heads popped from around her legs—the little boy with his long curls, his back *kippa*; and the little girl with chocolate around her mouth.

Leah beckoned me in and shooed the children away. She showed me to a worn couch, foam spurting from its holes. "Sit, I'll just be a sec."

I could hear her shouting at the children in Hebrew, her American accent still plain to hear.

"So now they are out of the way—how are you?" It sounded like Leah, but it sure as hell didn't look like her.

"I'm good." From somewhere in the apartment I could hear screams.

Leah waved her hand, "Ignore them, kids!"

"They are gorgeous," I ventured—isn't that what you are supposed to say when you first meet someone's children?

"Sometimes," Leah half-heartedly agreed. "They're exhausting too!" She picked at the foam from the shabby couch. "So, how's home?"

"Oh you know, the same! Everyone asks after you."

"I bet they do!—Am I still their main source of gossip?"

"Sort of. They eased off you a bit when Betty O'Reilly ran off with some guy from the navy, but when they moved back to town happily married, they went straight back to you."

Leah laughed. "I wanted you to meet Jonathan but he won't be home until late. The Yeshiva keeps him busy."

"Oh, that's a shame! Perhaps some other time."

"Yeah, perhaps." Again screams erupted from somewhere in the apartment. Leah heaved herself and her unborn baby off the couch in the direction of the screams. More shouting in Hebrew.

"So, another baby?"

"Yeah," Leah seemed uninterested. "Jonathan loves children."

I wanted to ask, "And you"? But it didn't seem appropriate—we had never been that close and it would have been too much of a challenge. You don't challenge someone who has left their family to start a new, radical life in a new country.

I didn't stay long. Leah seemed to spend most of the time screaming in Hebrew at the children.

As I left, she wiped her hair from her face. "No wig in the house," she explained. I knew that Leah's Orthodox community and her new found faith commanded she cover her hair with a wig in public or at home when men other than her husband were present. There was no such commandment when hosting me. "Enjoy yourself!" she said.

"Any message for the folks at home?"

Leah thought for a minute, "Just 'Hi,' I guess."

~~

I didn't get it, couldn't understand it—why Leah had given up the comforts of an all-American life for that. For a small apartment in a dingy neighbourhood. Why she had swapped college for three babies in five years and

88

mopping floors and washing dishes. Why she had swapped jeans for long skirts and the all-American husband for a religious student who didn't earn a dime. Love? But what a sacrifice to make for love.

~~

I didn't get it for quite some time.—Until I'd been in Israel a couple of weeks.—I'd dipped my toes in the Kinneret, plucked olives from their trees growing along the roads winding through the Golan Heights. I'd driven past the mammoth border that was to keep us in and them out and in the process protect us all from ourselves. I'd stood in Rabin Square and said *Kiddush*. I'd covered my head and arms at the Western wall and watched the men in black pray. I'd lost myself in busy bazaars bursting with souvenirs from every corner of the Arabic and North African world. I'd walked along Shenkin, dodging the very fashionable and the not so fashionable. The Israeli dress sense took some getting use to. I had admired local art in Jaffa and stood at its peak surveying the whole of Tel Aviv. I had cracked sunflower seeds between my teeth and loaded my *shwarama* with chips.

The more I saw, the more I experienced, the more I walked the more confused I became. How could I ever hope to find my Jewish identity in such a place?

A place where Iraqi Jews did it *this* way, and Romanian Jews did it *that* way. While the Russian Jews did *this*, the French Jews did *that*. Where the Moroccans did that and the Poles did this.

I was struggling to find myself in a Jewish land where *shwarma* was as Jewish as *latkes* and *gefilte* fish. Where Jewish Israeli-born children spoke Arabic with their Syrian—or Lebanese—or Iranian-born grandparents. Where the ultra orthodox and secular populations seemed to hate each other, and argue amongst each other, as much as the state of Israel fought against the Palestinians. In a country where the ultra orthodox threw stones at the secular for breaking the Sabbath. Where old Jewish immigrants looked down on new Jewish immigrants.

Sometimes I couldn't help but think that it would have been easier to have found my Jewish self in our catholic town rather than in a Jewish country where Jews drove on Shabbat, where some supermarkets sold pork next to kosher chicken and where it was possible to order a bacon sandwich or shrimp cocktail in a restaurant.

I had thought Israel was going to be the solution to my confusion—not another cause of it. I felt let down by this so-called Jewish country. I felt as if I'd been the victim of false advertising.

I had come from somewhere where I had to fight tooth and nail to be and stay Jewish; where I had actively to act and be Jewish. I thought coming to Israel would take that away. In Israel being Jewish would be effortless. But half the population didn't seem to be acting Jewish (except on Shabbat and holidays); while the other half were so Jewish, it was scary.

~~

All this confusion made me wonder, and brought me back to Leah again. Maybe she had the solution after all. Even in Israel the only place to find a Jewish self was amongst the Orthodox. It was the only way to be a full-time Jew.

Not only that; but it made everything simple. From what to wear…to what to eat…to choosing a career. It took away the pressures of modern life, the freedom of choice and decision-making, and with it the burden of having to make the best or right choice. There was a comfort in being told what to do, how to live—in having a set of rules to follow…a set of rules for every aspect of life.

~~

There would be no right or wrong decisions to make. Take choosing a college. I'd had my heart set on Gratz since I was fifteen. I couldn't imagine anything more perfect than spending four years in a completely Jewish

environment, with other Jewish people studying Judaism.
And at eighteen it was a dream I still held dear, albeit one
I knew my family wanted me to drop.

~~

On Independence Day I went for a walk and found myself
along the river in Yehousha Park. The park was full of
families barbecuing, or doing *manga*, as they call it in
Israel. Every available patch of grass was taken up with
mangas, families, chairs and food. Some families had
gone all out—boundaries of their plot marked by
colourful string or balloons. Huge tables, dozens of plastic
chairs. Hammocks swaying between the trees. Some had
put up large canopies, others tents. Whole families
gathered around, from the very old to the very young.
Children played football, trying to score goals through a
goalpost manned by their Dads. The smell of barbecuing
meat was everywhere. The sun shone down—hot and
bright.

~~

I couldn't help but wonder how they had managed to get
their whole families in the same place together, enjoying
each other's company, for a whole day. The last time we
had been together as a family was at my Bat Mitzvah,
which no-one really wanted to be at. Ben sneaked off
after an hour and a half to meet Maria; and Dad kept
muttering about a tennis game he wanted to get to, was
going to miss, couldn't miss. I was almost relieved when it
was all over—it was exhausting trying to keep everyone
together, trying to second guess when they would decide
to leave and preparing myself for it so I wouldn't care
when they did. Things had been slightly better at Ben's
wedding but it wasn't long after the cake was cut and
shared around, the champagne flutes toasted and clinked
again, that Dad loosened his tie and began to talk about
getting back – to work, to tennis.

~~

People were always so busy with their own lives. Not that they shouldn't be, but it was almost as if it was a sign of how great and fulfilling your life was if you didn't have time in it for a friend or realities because you were just swamped already that day, that week, that month, that year.

It was far better to be with people who didn't have anywhere else to be, anywhere else to go, or anyone else to meet. People who couldn't run, couldn't hide behind a PDA, a full schedule, yet another work commitment. People who knew that all that mattered was family.

~~

I tried to explain it to Leah one afternoon in the park. She'd managed to sneak out on the pretence of giving the children some fresh air.

The older two ran from the swings, to the slide, to the climbing frame like a group of banshees. The new baby slept in its pram. Leah sat with one foot on its undercarriage and one eye on her eldest two, ready at all times for falls, bumps and fights.

"Having a family always there, that's what this is all about?"

She took her eyes off the children to look at me. "Yeah....But you can have that without having to live like you do now. Look at me, my family is always around— kids hanging off me day and night, in-laws in the building across the street. Believe me, having a family permanently around is not all it's cracked up to be."

"So where is Jonathan now?"

"He's studying."

"And tomorrow where will he be? And the next day? And your parents where are they?"

She looked at me strangely, "Oh Rachel, come on! You can't have your family physically around you all day every day—people have to go to work, to study and to do their own thing."

"She looked at me with another puzzled look on her face. That's what you need—a family physically around you twenty-four hours a day?"

"Perhaps. Or at least a family that puts its members before work, study and the mundane. What can be more important a commitment than family?"

Leah looked at me again, this time a worried look was on her fact, "Wow," she said softly, "You are more screwed up than I thought."

"Oh, thanks!"

"No, listen. Families are the most important thing we will ever have and yes I agree, in a lot of cases people should be spending more time with and in theirs. But families are made up of human people and human people aren't perfect. We make mistakes; we don't always see the happiness right in front of our eyes or realize what is truly important straight away. But that's just us being human. Different families show their love and commitment in different ways. It's not all about always being in the same room together. And sometimes being part of a family means making sacrifices. Of course I hate that Jonathan gets home late every night and leaves early every morning; that I'm with the kids alone most of the day. But he loves what he does and to him it's his purpose in life and more importantly he believes that he's the only one for this task. If I stopped him doing that he'd be miserable. He'd be in the same room as us everyday but he'd be empty, unhappy and we'd all be unhappy as a result. He loves us and we love him, and we have great times when he's home...."

The sun began to set behind the trees casting an orange hue across the sky. Children were pulled from climbing frames, plucked off swings, hoisted from the tops of slides and bundled into waiting cars.

Leah held the hands of her eldest and I followed alongside them with the baby still asleep in his pram.

As we reached the bus stop the sky turned a deep indigo colour as the sun disappeared to make way for the night.

"This is my favourite part of the day," said Leah. "When the sky goes that gorgeous purple colour, it doesn't matter how busy my day has been, how hard it has been— that colour reminds me again how beautiful the world is and how lucky I am to be a part of it. How lucky my whole family is to be a part of it."

We sat on the bench and waited for the buses that would take us home.

"I bet your Mom told you never to get on a bus in Israel, didn't she?"

"Of course."

"Mine too." Leah stroked the hair of her daughter as she lay with her head in her Ima's lap. Leah laughed softly. "If only they could see us now!"

I smiled. "Why did you run?" I asked her.

Still stroking her daughter's hair, she replied, "Because I wanted to belong somewhere. I mean really to belong. I didn't want to be a Jew in America, an American in Israel or even just an Israeli in Israel. I wanted to be an Israeli in Israel with religion as my identity. And I wanted my children to have that. Israeli teenagers are as confused about their religious identity as we were in the States. The way I see it, religion is what defines as us Jews, so why not embrace it completely? I wanted my children to have that identity. And I was lucky. I fell in love with Jonathan and that meant all of this anyway." She pulled at her long skirt and then at her daughters. "It's nice to belong," she said, looking at the sky.

"That's all I want," I said.

"I know," she replied. "You'll get there, you just need to work out if and how you want it. It's not always in the first place you look, or even in the most obvious place. You have to feel as if you really belong. Don't be fooled by others trying to make you feel as if you belong there."

"You got wise in your old age, Leah Schwartz," I laughed.

"Did I? They say pregnancy kills brain cells, not the other way round," and she laughed too.

"Will you promise me something?" Her face and tone were instantly serious.

"What?"

"That you won't bring children into the world until you are sure you really belong there. You know how badly we sensed it growing up, how much it affected us. Just wait. Until you are sure."

"But that would mean...."

"I know, birth control, and I know I am supposed to be against it, and I would never use it myself, at least not now, never again. And don't get me wrong; I love my kids, they've changed my life and only for the better. But it's not all just changing nappies, feeding them and waving toys around. You are responsible for how your kids turn out. You have to make sure you are not bringing them into an environment that might harm them and screw up their future. Everything you expose them to will help decide who they will become. If you bring them into a screwed up environment, you have to be prepared for them to be messed up later and you will have to take responsibility for that."

Leah's use of cursing was enough to make me listen to what she had to say; strange as it sounded, coming from her newly orthodox mouth.

~~

Buses and cars sped past, their lights guiding them through the darkness. Israelis loved white cars; why was that I thought?

~~

On the bus ride home I went over Leah's words.

~~

And from then on I saw Leah a lot. She was housebound with her new baby and so I went to visit her as much as I could.

~~

Leah sighed, "They will never completely accept me," as she let her baby son wrap his finger around her finger. She kissed his tiny knuckles, "I may be Jewish but I'll never be Jewish enough for them. Silly isn't it? One G-d and yet never one people. I thought, you know, when the children were born that they would get over it and accept me more but no....they're different with our children than they are with their other grandchildren. Less attentive, less bothered. They never wanted us to marry—they had someone else chosen for Jonathan, someone from a 'proper' Jewish family; but their Rabbi intervened. He said it would be a *mitzvah* for Jonathan to convert me, and that if they weren't careful they might lose Jonathan altogether if they tried to fight him, and so they gave in."

She sighed again, "I love him. Really I do." Her tone was tired but her eyes were fierce.

I nodded as if to say, "I believe you."

"If the children need something, shoes or something important and we can't afford it ourselves, they refuse to help out. My parents are wealthy, they live in America, let them help out. At first they wanted me to cut all contact with my family. Now they are keen for me to stay in touch with them—no doubt because of the money." Leah looked sad, "I want them to accept our children; so what else can I do but obey? And we do need the money."

My face must have said, "So why stay?"

"Leave? No I could never leave, this is my life. But it would be nice sometimes if it wasn't so hard and just a little easier.

"The first Independence Day Jonathan and I were married, I thought I'd surprise everyone—decorate the flat, buy some cakes to celebrate. Jonathan's parents were furious. His father pulled the flags down and threw them in the rubbish!" Leah shook her head in disbelief, "Why would a Jew throw their country's flag in the rubbish? They screamed at me, called me a Zionist. I had no idea it was a bad thing to be a Zionist. I had no idea that only G-d could create a truly Jewish state and that for that to happen we needed the Messiah to come first. I thought a Jewish state, no matter who made it, was a good thing for all Jews. They won't celebrate the birth of Israel, but they'll take her handouts," Leah said, bitterly. "Why are they here if they don't see it as real?" Her harsh tone made the baby in her arms jump and look up to his Ima with wide open eyes. She kissed his cheek tenderly and he closed his eyes in contentment. "I thought when we moved into our own apartment that things would be better, that we'd be freer. But they found us this flat, in their neighbourhood, trapping us into their way of living. Just last week we were at a birthday party for a friend of Benjamin's. They didn't want me to take him. His friend is Orthodox, but a different Orthodox to us. I was insistent. Benjamin had been invited to his friend's party; he wanted to go; he's four years old; and he was going. So they went on and on about how we mustn't eat anything; mustn't drink anything. So I said 'OK,' anything to get them off my back. How was Benjamin to know? So he ate a piece of birthday cake. I tried to explain why he shouldn't have, but those big eyes of his looked up at me, so innocent, and I thought who cares, he's a child, G-d can understand that surely? So they asked us when we got back had we eaten anything, I said 'No,' and little Benjamin couldn't lie. They screamed at him, they screamed at me. They are still talking about it—a piece of damn cake!" and she shook her head in disbelief.

~~

"It won't always be like this," Leah vowed. "When Jonathan has finished all his studying, when he's a Rabbi, we're going to go and run a Chabad centre somewhere in Asia, you know, somewhere where there are a lot of

Jewish people who will need us. Somewhere where we can do some good for the lost Jewish people of the world, for those far from home," she smiled. "That's our plan."

I smiled back at her, unsure of what to say, wanting to let her know I believed what she said, but not sure if I did.

"People think," said Leah, "That the main issue we have to face is making peace with the Palestinians. But that isn't true," and here she looked sad, "We have to make peace with each other first."

~~

Leah looked out of place along the very secular Dizengorff. Almost as if she belonged to a different place or time and had stepped out of a page from the Torah to find herself in modern Israel where mini skirts were more popular than those that grazed the floor. She was awkward, as if she knew she was out of place.

"Stupid isn't it." She said after declining my offers to sit in a coffee-shop for lunch. "A couple of years ago I was one of these people," and she looked around her at the confident Israelis striding past with shopping bags, and baby strollers and dogs. "And now...well now I'm nothing like them!"

"How about a crêpe?" I asked as we passed the crêperie.

"No, thanks," said Leah.

"How about some shopping?" I asked as we descended the slope down from the fountain that seemed to attract more pigeons and homeless people than Tel Aviv residents or tourists, and looked towards Dizengorff centre.

Leah gave a small smile, "Sure."

We handed our bags to the security guard who patted them down and waved us in.

We wandered in and out of shops. I made Leah choose a present for her new baby from Fox and we spent ages riffling through the little outfits, choosing something that he would be the very first to wear.

And we watched the world around us—people sat and smoked under "no smoking" signs; walked their dogs through the crowded shopping centre; sat trying on shoes in Zara with their dog sat beside them; Grandmas pushing babies in their strollers, huge groups of them on a senior citizens' play date.

Even Leah had to smile at the Israelis represented before us. "Israelis!" she said, not without another smile.

The shopping centre was crammed with pre-Shabbat shoppers. The smells from the Friday food market wafted up from the ground floor. Couscous, meatballs, burekas, schnitzel, noodles, cakes, fresh limonana. Munching and crunching. Chewing and tasting. Home-cooked food for a Friday feast.

~~

Tel Aviv is dusty in the summer. The heat brings out all the smells of the city—the dust, the rubbish, food cooking. Parts of the city look as if the street cleaners have been on strike for a very long time; other parts look as if they have never even seen a street cleaner.

Dirty, smoky, hot buses straddle pedestrian crossings and scooters terrorize pedestrians as they speed down the pavements.

A delivery-van driver argues with a traffic warden over the ticket he has collected on his waiting van. He succeeds in his mission and drives off with a, "*Toda, toda*," out of his window to the forgiving traffic warden who loses many battles on these streets—and wins a few when drivers miss him by seconds.

The religious mingled with the secular, although the secular far outnumbered the religious. Long skirts mingled with jeans. *Kippots* mingled with baseball caps. Long sleeved shirts mingled with halter-neck tops. Wigs mingled with hair extensions.

To belong. Never to feel out of place. Always to fit in. Always to be wearing the right clothes, always to be doing things the right way. Never being in the wrong clothes, never doing things the wrong way at the wrong time.

~~

The lights atop Azrielli flashed out; and on the other side white clad sedate crowds lead each other to the Kabbalah centre. The shutters were down on all the shops. The roads were quiet and mercifully still. A Shabbat calm descended over the city. I watched it all from my hotel balcony. Lights twinkled out from homes, as people sat down to a Shabbat meal together. Was it too much to want the same?

Chapter 5—Dana

I was lost. The hospital seemed to be made up of a labyrinth of corridors and blank white doors. Was I even on the right floor? Mama was on the fourth floor and yet this was, oh no, the fifth floor. It was the maternity floor. Babies squealed and cried behind blank doors. The beginning and the end I thought, all within one building. Babies being born, people dying. People all on the edge of life. What a place to work. What a place to be lost in.

A door opened and a man walked out. I walked past him and up the corridor, only to have to go back on myself as I came to a dead end.

"You look lost," the man said.

"Um yes, I'm looking for the lift."

"And in life?"

"Sorry, I don't know what you mean!" Who was this man?

"What are you looking for in life?" How did I know, I wanted to shout. Right now I was trying to find my dying Mama, wasn't that enough for one day?

I made to leave and turn in another direction; any way that was far away from this nut would be fine, even if it didn't lead to the lift.

"Maybe I can help."

"No, thank you," and I walked away.

The hospital seemed devoid of any staff until I bumped into a friendly nurse by the nursery who pointed me to the lift doors and I stumbled into them and up to the right floor, the right blank door and my dying Mama.

~~

She died that night. A last sigh, a last call for Anton and then she was gone. So that was it. I was alone. No family. An orphan. Only I'd felt like that for such a long time I don't think I really felt any different. But still, now it was final. Official. I was alone.

I went to the canteen, not yet ready to face a house full of ghosts. I sat and played with a cup of water.

That man again.

"You still look lost."

I ignored him; dealing with a nutcase was the last thing on my list of things to do today.

"Will you come with me?" he asked, "I can help you find what you are looking for."

He sounded so sure. So certain. It had been a long time since I'd been around someone like that.

He led me to the same floor we had met on. He opened a blank door and led me in. He pointed to a bed and then left.

A baby lay in its plastic hospital cot, its new face barely visible above the white blanket it was swaddled in.

A woman lay in the bed—her tired eyes followed me as I stood awkwardly by the door, suddenly conscious of where I was—in a room with a stranger. A stranger who appeared to have just given birth. That made things worse. Surely giving birth is a personal time, for family only. What was I doing here? I felt like an idiot.

"Hello," she said.

"Hello."

"Are you lost?" She beckoned me over to the bed.

"Perhaps."

I sat, perched on the end of the bed, anxious not to crush her legs. She brought the baby to her breast and stared at me.

"Will you join our Family?"

They'd been searching for me, Beruriah said later; searching for a second wife to join them.

~~

I said yes because I had nowhere else to go—just an empty apartment where my family—or at least part of it—had once lived. A new family was a promise of children, of love, of security. Who didn't want that?

~~

I went back to the apartment to collect the last of my things. Stripped of its furniture and possessions, it looked so bare, so naked and as if we'd never lived there at all. Almost as if we'd never existed. If you looked carefully and you knew where to look you would find faint evidence of the lives lived there—my brother's name carved into the back of a bedroom door.

So amazing that one small apartment could hold so much. This had been our first home in Israel—the land we had all dreamed about for so long. Here we had had birthday parties—cake crumbs on the floors, balloons hanging from the ceiling. Here Anton had brought home his first girlfriend, and the second, third, fourth, fifth, sixth...until even mother had stopped counting and remembering their names. Here I had brought Elijah home to meet the family and here I had cried when he broke my heart. Here mother had whirled herself around to father's old records, on her good days; and here she had cursed his name a thousand times over. It was here they had called us to tell us that Anton would never come home, and here mother had begun to die.

But now the apartment was no longer ours. How quickly it had cleaned itself of us—a clean slate ready for a new family, and their miseries and happiness.

"Let it be more happiness than misery," I whispered as I shut the door behind me." And more happiness than we had," I thought.

Not that it was all bad but it could have been better. But it had been my family and when it's your family you take everything as it comes and that's the deal. Only it wasn't just a deal—it was my family, my father, my mother, and my Anton.

~~

I sometimes had my doubts about joining the Family. Fleeting ones that flitted around at the back of my mind. For the most part I ignored them—batted them away with other thoughts, thoughts about how this was the best thing for me, how I finally belonged, had a family.

And then when Tamar was born—so tiny, so soft and pink—I banished the doubts for once and for all, and they no longer bothered me.

Nothing else mattered. With her birth I'd achieved everything I'd ever wanted to achieve. I didn't realize it until they handed me my baby, or maybe not even until she was a couple of months old, but by her first birthday I knew that nothing I ever did in the future would ever make me feel as successful and as fulfilled as she did. Nothing else could compare.

And then the years of my life were marked off by my children's birthdays. I only realized that another year had passed when my children turned yet another year older. Another year in their lives marked another year in mine. That way the time just seemed to fly by.

All that mattered was my children. No suicide bomber would take them, no cancer of their lungs. Every second I was with them, and they with me. As babies they slept in my bed, I couldn't bear to have them out of my sight and most nights I lay awake watching their tiny chests heave up and down. I was scared—scared that if I fell asleep they wouldn't be breathing when I woke up. I carried them with me all day. And now at almost one, five and six I still had them in my bed.

Israel took my father, my mother and Anton but it had given me Yuval and Tamar and Isaac. They were all that mattered—not him and not the Family. They just provided the shelter from the outside world where we weren't safe. In the Family we were safe, untouched by crime, and danger.

~~

I didn't love him; I was no fool. But what was love? And what did it get you? It had brought my Mama nothing but heartache—a dead husband, a dead son. I may not have love but I had comfort and security and stability. And in turn my children had that too. So there weren't always enough pairs of shoes to go around, and the clothes they wore had once been someone else's and sometimes we lived off rice and hummus peas, and tea and biscuits, but we still had the security of the Family. And I had my children. They made it all worthwhile. I lived no longer for myself, but for them. Their needs, their happiness came first, and making them happy made me happy. I didn't need anything else.

As for what would happen when they grew up and went off into the world, well I would deal with that and with my future then.

~~

Beruriah came to me and said that he wanted to talk. She said she would watch Yuval, Tamar and Isaac who was still then a baby at my breast. I swallowed nervously and told them I would be back within minutes. I could feel their eyes on my back as I left and I knew they would sit like that waiting for me to return.

~~

"We need your help Dana, the Family needs your help."

"Anything!"

"Money, we need money. Feeding the Family is one thing; but with winter coming, the children need coats and we need heating."

"But what money I have, I give."

"I know that, Dana; and the Family appreciates it. But it isn't enough. For the good of the Family, for all its children, we need more. You must go and speak to your Father's publisher. There must be more money you are owed. You must go—for the Family."

~~

It was the first time I had been outside in many weeks. The bright sun was harsh on my face and I shied from the people walking the streets—they seemed too harsh and cold. Paranoia filled my brain, weighed me down, made each step a giant one, an impossible one.

~~

His office was comfortable without being plush. Well it was a little plush—rich carpets, old antique rosewood desks, books that stretched from floor to ceiling.

He caught my roaming eye. "My wife's choice!" he explained.

"Oh, your wife—how nice!" I replied not daring to meet his eyes.

He looked at me and smiled, "My ex-wife. Different ideas about interior design was just one of our many differences."

"I like it."

"It's too pretentious for me. It's wanting the firm—and me—to be something it's...we're not." He smiled, "Coffee?"

"No, thank you. I don't like to leave the children for long....Why don't you change it?" I asked.

"Because my clients seem to like it. My ex wife wasn't always wrong. But my always wanting her to be wrong made us all wrong.

There were no pictures on his desk—no snaps of smiling children, chubby toddlers or tiny babies.

"No children!" he said, as if reading my thoughts. They were supposed to be our next step but we just couldn't make it, not together." His usual perky tone was replaced by something resembling sadness.

"It's better," I insisted. "It would have been so hard, the divorce, if you had children."

"Yes, perhaps. But it would be nice to know that children will be a part of my future." He looked wistful for a second before he was his own self again, "And your children, how are they?"

"Good, thank you."

"Enjoying school, they are old enough for school aren't they?"

"Oh, they don't go to school; we teach them at home."

"No school?" he looked shocked as if I had told them we boiled them alive and ate them for breakfast. "Really?"

"Yes, really!" My tone was sharp—a fact he noted straight away.

He looked sad, as if he deeply regretted upsetting me, "Dana, I'm sorry. I didn't mean to offend you—I was just surprised that's all." He seemed genuinely sorry but I hated that he had judged—hadn't people been doing that of me all my life? "It's probably for the best," he said hurriedly, "That they don't go to school.... I mean what with the teachers always on strike, they'd spend more time at home anyway," and he smiled quietly at his joke.

"My father's books, are they still selling well?"

"Yes," he said; his eyes still sad, "In Hebrew, English and Russian."

"Good," I said, determined to keep the conversation on business. "Is there anything I need to do?"

"No," he said, resigned to the business nature of our current conversation. "Michal will give you your cheque."

"Thank you!" And I made to leave.

He stood up and came out from behind his desk, and made as if to take my hand, "Dana, I'm sorry. I offended you! I didn't want to do that."

I pulled my hand back. "It's fine."

~~

But afterwards, as the bus trundled down the highway, I wondered what it would have been like if I had let him take my hand—would it have sent a tingle down my spine? I banished the thought as soon as it came, "Dana, pull yourself together!" I admonished myself.

Chapter 6—Amelia

He found me wandering down Shenkin one Thursday afternoon. I was bored out of my skull; waiting for Ifat to finish work so we could go and get drunk, or high. I scuffed my feet along the pavement, bored even with the shops that lined the street.

I stopped briefly to watch a performance of the Breslev Hasidim, their long curls bouncing up and down as they danced to the booming house music from their speakers. They danced like they were high as kites; they had to be to stop in the middle of the street and dance like that in the middle of the day. Or they were just crazy. Either way; not normal.

Man, you had to admire them their confidence, even if it was drug induced. Ifat seemed to think it wasn't drug induced but instead powered by their belief....that was some strong belief that could get them doing that crazy dancing. I'd like some of that. I'd pay for it too.

But even they were the same old shit; different day. How many times had they stopped traffic on this street? And how many times had I stood here, outside the same dam shops, watching these same crazy dancers do their thing.

I was bored and fed up. I'd left the house early, to get away from Mama and her constant nagging and whinging. "Blah, blah, blah." She'd wanted me to meet the son of one of her tennis buddies and had been close to tears when I had refused. I didn't give a damn. I couldn't care less if he was wealthy, educated—it was just more bullshit. And underneath it all, what would he be? A well dressed bore; who just wanted a trophy wife to bring out on holidays and work functions and charity balls. Well, she could forget it. I wasn't interested.

I looked at my watch, still another hour before Ifat finished work. I could go for coffee, but I did that every single bloody day, in the same coffee shops. Eating the same salads, day in, day out.

Tel Aviv suddenly felt very small and claustrophobic. Maybe I needed a holiday. Not Thailand, every Israeli and his dog my age went to Thailand or South America. No, maybe somewhere else....Africa maybe...I wondered if I could convince Papa to pay for Ifat and me to go to Africa. We could go on safari and sleep with the elephants, or whatever it was you could do there. Maybe run away with some tribesmen and wear plates in our lips or hoops on our neck. That would soon send Mama running for her bottle of valium.

I smiled at the thought and began to locate the nearest travel agency to Shenkin street. No harm in asking about flight prices.

I went to cross the street and saw him smile at me.

"Pervert," I thought to myself. What else could he be? An old man leering at me like that, he was old enough to be my father.

I crossed the road impatiently, barely waiting for the little man to turn green.

He smiled at me again as I reached his side of the street. I ignored him. Why did I always attract the weirdoes, and not the nice handsome, buff ones?

"Hello!" he said, suddenly by my side.

"Uh, Hello?"

He laid his hand on my arm to stop me and I shook him off. "Can I help you?" I almost shouted.

"No, but maybe I can help you."

"Whatever—look weirdo, stay away from me or I will scream so loud, every policeman in Tel Aviv will be here in a second."

"No, please, I don't wish to harm you. You look lost, I want to help you."

"Oh, actually I'm looking for the closest travel agent to here. Do you know where it is?"

He shook his head and smiled, "No not that kind of lost. I mean spiritually lost. Lost inside."

"You crackpot," I thought and then said aloud, "Well OK then, thanks for the help," and I made to walk off.

"Will you meet my Family?"

"Why?"

"Because I think we can help you."

And then he explained the deal. He had two wives. Well he was legally married to one, but lived with them both as his wives. Some shit about it being God's way, blah, blah, blah. He was always looking for more women to join his Family—something else about predestined soul-mates, blah, blah, and blah. And he wanted me, me? To join them! I nearly laughed out loud. Nobody had ever wanted me to join them ever. Nobody wanted me to be in their group for a project at school, or sports team because I refused to participate or do my share of the work. The same went for in the army. And yet here he was asking me to be a part of his crackpot Family.

"Just come for dinner," he coaxed, "Meet my Family, and then decide."

But an idea was already forming in my head....screw running off with the African tribesman, now this would really screw Mama up...if I stayed in Israel, on her doorstep; but lived with this man and his wives, like some Bedouin slave. I'd like to see her explain that to her tennis buddies and country club mates.

"Sure, why not."

I quickly texted Ifat, "Gone for din with some guy call u l8tr."

Ifat texted back, "OK be safe x."

The bus stopped on some nameless street in Rosh Ha'ayin. Rosh Ha'ayin! Who ever would have thought that I would ever make it out here? Wasn't it practically in the West Bank?

~~

The house was a dump. It had been his first wife's great-uncle's and he had left it to his wife, who had left it to her niece, who had left it to her sister, who had left it to Beruriah—that was the name of his first wife.

~~

The back garden—or perhaps yard is a better word for it—was a mess of dry dirt and tangled weeds. Rainwater collected in puddles in the winter, and the dirt dried and cracked in the summer. Grimy, once white, plastic chairs of varying sizes and shapes shared the space with a rusty metal table and an assortment of rusty bicycles, all again in varying sizes; each having seen several owners and each to serve several more before retirement was an option. A garden hose served as the children's main source of entertainment during the heat of the summer and relentless sun of cloudless days. From the garden the kitchen was accessible by sliding glass doors. The kitchen was the heart and stomach of the home; where *kuba* was made alongside borscht, alongside schnitzel and hotdogs. Here the *challah* for *Shabbat* was baked and here cakes and cookies went straight from the oven into waiting open mouths and hungry empty tummies.

The table was old, and flanked either side by its wooden benches made smooth by the weight of many bottoms. The oven wore the stains of a thousand dinners and holiday meals. Coffee, we made in a pot on the stove. The fridge groaned and shook in its antiquity.

From there was the living room. The absence of a television, DVD player and play-station made it defunct and rather pointless. Its only decoration was a bright oil painting of the desert of Yemen. A well-worn Persian rug once garishly red and blue, now sadly grey and brown. Plastic protected the sofas and several hard chairs flanked them.

Stone stairs led up to the second floor. His room, our rooms and the children's rooms. The children slept in bunk beds, and in the one cot repainted every year for the latest arrival.

From the yard the mass of tangled grass and weeds rose steadily upwards covering first a slope and then a hill, from where you could sit on a clear day and look out upon Rosh Ha'ayin and the fields to the south and west. The efraim mountains on the east. Geographically we were in the heart of Israel.

He took me up the hill beside the house and there was Petach Tikva, one of the first settlements in Israel, and there the West Bank, perhaps one day to be one of the first settlements of the Palestinian state.

The red-roofed houses of Rosh Ha'ayin spread before you and that was it.

~~

If Mama could have seen the house she would have died. She was all I thought of as he showed me from room to room. Her reaction to the tired furniture, old paint was what I saw and felt. It was perfect.

It was only afterwards that I realised that this was the family from the article that Ifat had shoved under my nose that time we were shopping. Which made them well known, which made my staying with them even more perfect, because it would mean that Mama's public shame and humiliation would know no boundaries.

~~

"I'll stay," I said when he finished the tour.

He did look slightly shocked, "Great," he replied. "Let's properly meet the others."~~

There was Beruriah. This was her house. She would be a pain in my neck, I could see, as she shook my hand. Her face was hard, her body soft and plump. She looked pregnant, or like she had just given birth. I learnt later that Beruriah was always in a state of pregnancy or having just given birth. She was some human form of a breeding-machine.

Then there was Dana. Her eyes were sad, but her smile was kind. She shook my hand warmly and welcomed me to the Family. She was the one who showed me to my room, and the bathroom, and introduced the children. What a lot of sniveling snotty brats this family had.

~~

I called home, told Mama what I had done, and then got on with it—my new life.

~~

In the newspaper article that Ifat had found and read aloud that day in Tel Aviv, he had had three wives. But—and I counted that night at dinner—he had only three, including me. Where was the girl from the newspaper?

I asked him that night. He said it had been Beruriah's cousin. She had died giving birth to her first child. She had gone into labour at home, here in this house, and before they could get her to hospital she had bled to death. Right here, in this house, he kept saying. It was just so creepy. I mean who would want to advertise the fact that someone had died in their house? And to me, of all people, who had just moved into it and expected to live there. The baby died too, he added. As if the baby was nothing but an afterthought, which I guess it was, having not even taken so much as a breath in the world.

~~

Ifat called, wanted to talk. Could we meet? I told her I'd have to ask permission first and she snorted down the phone.

They said I could go, if I kept it brief, to tell my family what I needed to tell them. I didn't bother explaining that technically Ifat wasn't family. She was close enough.

~~

"We fly to Thailand on the 15th—Bangkok, Koh Samui wherever else takes our fancy. It's not too late to get you a ticket; I know your Mum would pay. Come on, like old times—we'll go get drunk, take things we're not supposed to, meet gorgeous foreign guys."

"I don't need gorgeous foreign guys. I am his wife, and I have a family."

"His wife?! He's old enough to be your father!—No your grandfather!—What is wrong with you? HE'S OLD, HE'S UGLY, HE'S SLEEPING WITH OTHER WOMEN, HE'S USING YOU, HE'S A CRIMINAL. HE'S DISGUSTING."

~~

People were beginning to stare.

"I have to go; the Family are always together for dinner."

"That's it? OK, OK you've made your point—you've made your Mum more upset then you ever thought possible. You have all the attention now; it's all on you—just go home."

"Home? To that drug-addicted woman living in the past? You must be joking!"

~~

She stormed out, leaving her salad and coffee untouched. I caught the stares of people as she left—they always go first to the skirt, which makes them think 'orthodox,' then they see my uncovered head and arms, and then the tattoo; and then the confusion sets in. I love to see it. The rest of the Family call me childish for enjoying it so, for enjoying getting a reaction from strangers. They sound like my mother.

What I love most is the disgust—if I can get people to move or run away in disgust, then so much the better.

Beruriah hated it—the way I tried to call attention to our lifestyle. "Why do you care what strangers think or know of us? What matters is what G-d sees, and what our Family sees." That was Beruriah. Head wife, or so she thinks. Even though he calls me to his room more often than he calls her; more often than anyone.

"You are not my mother!"

~~

She spoke to him, I know she did. No-one else would have. Whatever she said, the next time I rushed to kiss him in public when the Family were out together, he stopped me, held me at arms length.

~~

"Not now."

"But why? Who cares, we don't, and we are doing nothing wrong by how we choose to live? Not hurting anyone?"

"No, my child; but we are misunderstood and all the Family wants is to enjoy the day, like everyone else. Let's not ruin it for everyone by making a scene."

"So what better way to end the misunderstanding than to show the world how we live."

I went for him again but he pushed me away firmly.

Beruriah walked by—screaming brat in her arms. "Amelia, we need some help with the lunch; go with Dana, she'll tell you what to do."

I wanted to scream—who on earth did she think she was?

~~

But screw Beruriah, who cared what she thought, which is why I grabbed the hundred-shekel note left on the table for the bill and ran. Fast as I could, my skirt billowing, the cries of the waitress following me down Dizengoff.

~~

Then Lucille wanted to meet. I told the Family I could probably get money out of her, for the Family of course, and they let me go.

So we met. She suggested Cordelia's in Ramat Ha'Sharon. I said, "Yes." Mama's friends went there and I was more than happy for them to see. She said, why did I care and she didn't want Mama hurt anymore. So we went to the old port and sat on the waterfront. It was cold and windy and everywhere was half deserted

115

"Come on Amelia, no bullshit. I known we've grown apart since I got married, and the children—but we're still sisters. Let's talk, no crap, just us—OK?"

She sounded so like the sister I used to know that when she called and begged we meet up I couldn't say no. Even when she refused to let me come to her place, because the children would be home.

~~

"It's not you *per se* Amelia. It's just they will want to know why the tattoos, why they don't see you any more. And I just don't have the energy to try and explain to a seven-year old and a nine-year old why their Auntie has joined a cult."

I shrugged my shoulders—I had enough little brats to deal with at home. Only my nieces weren't brats; at least not all the time. And they weren't dopey-eyed or snotty-nosed—they were pretty cute, and always dressed well.

~~

"He's got her a Doctor, you know."

"Who?"

"Papa has, for Mama."

"So?"

"So she's finally getting some help, she's really trying."

I shrugged my shoulders again.

"I know things have been shitty since Dad pretty much moved to Paris and we all neglected you and Mums dreadfully, but things are changing."

I looked down at my schnitzel, "So?"

"So can't you meet her half way, go home for a visit, see how she's improving?"

"May be."

"So how are things?"

"Fine."

"You don't sound fine."

"No? I'm living with philistines who speak Hebrew like Arabs, who eat like Arabs, who think like Arabs."—

116

At least that's what I wanted to say, but I didn't. "Everything is great; why wouldn't it be?"

"No second thoughts?"

"About what?"

"About your new unorthodox way of living?"

"No." My eyes met hers in a challenge of defiance

"OK, OK I'm sorry I asked." She took a sip of diet coke. "You know they'll give you anything if you go home."

"Who?"

"Our darling parents."

I shrugged my shoulders.

"Come on, you don't fancy a trip somewhere nice—the States, the Caribbean? Or a new season designer shop shopping spree?"

I ignored her. Of course I wanted all that—since stealing the food money I hadn't been allowed to touch as much as a shekel.

"Tell me what it's like?"

"What?" I speared some schnitzel and brought it to my mouth.

"Sleeping with…him."

I smiled. "The same as sleeping with anyone, you don't do anything differently just because one of you is slightly older, it's still basically the same."

"How can you? He's the same age as Papa."

I shrugged my shoulders.

"I have a friend who is a therapist and she thinks you're doing this as part of a search for a father-figure.— Papa was never there when you were growing up and so you're looking for a father figure wherever you can find it."

"You've been speaking to someone about me?"

"Relax! She's a friend, I just asked her a question or two. It means I care."

I shrugged my shoulders. "If they made that an Olympic sport, you'd win gold for Israel."

117

"Actually she read the article about you all in the paper."

"Mmm...I need more coffee." I turned around, trying to catch the waitress's eye. The coffee shop was full—the young and single sat clustered around tables with other like-minded friends.—The pick-up joints of Tel Aviv I thought to myself; more so than the bars.—Couples sat at their table, with their dog or baby depending at which stage they were at in life. Every-one watching each other and the world going by.

"She seems to think you are all looking for father-figures, not just you."

"Hi, yeah, can I get another coffee—lots of milk."

"Like the Russian one."

"Dana." I turned my attentions to the Labrador sitting at the table next to me. We used to have a dog just like it when I was small. I use to take him to the park to chase a ball. Mother gave him away one day when I was at school—too much hair she said, too much work.

"Yes, her.... So her father committed suicide, right? And the others—their father was some dictator, no?"

"I'm not really interested in your psychobabble right now." I turned instead to the gaze I felt upon my back, "Can I help you?" I glared at the woman. She held her baby tightly as she looked at me. I watched her taking me in—the tattoo, the long skirt. She ignored me and kept walking but she couldn't help it; she kept looking back. There was pity in her eyes.

"So why do you feel the need to join them?"

"Huh?"

"Come on, Amelia! They're all society's misfits—they had abusive parents, dead parents—what do you have in common with them?"

"Uh...maybe the awful parent part."

"Please! So Papa is never home and Mama is a little hysterical but they never beat you, you never had to come home to one of them hanging from the ceiling—so why?"

I fiddled with the teaspoon by the side of my cup. "Does it matter?"

"But you must know what it is that has made you cut off your family, give up university, friends and a life, for whatever it is you have now. You must have a reason for doing that."

"I don't know."

"You don't know?' her voice was raised. "For God's sake Amelia, grow up! So life is shit sometimes, and it doesn't always go the way you want it to. So sometimes parents screw up and make mistakes, sometimes they even go off the rails for a while—but are you really going to make that an excuse for every bad decision, and every mistake you make?"

"You said you wouldn't lecture me, we would just have coffee you said."

She sighed, "I know, I'm sorry. I'm just trying to understand why you would give everything up just to piss Mama off? I mean is it really worth it?"

"Leave me alone." My tone was a warning; any more and I would walk.

"OK, OK I'm sorry. Let's have another coffee, OK?"

As she called the waitress over, I looked across at my sister—her perfectly manicured nails, the diamonds sparkling on her left hand and in her ears, the cashmere shawl sitting perfectly on her shoulders, the perfectly applied make-up. Was this really the same person who had shown me how to steal chocolate from the local kiosk on the way home from school? The same sister, who showed me how to climb a tree, beat someone up and dance like Madonna? What had happened to the sister who gave me my first puff on a joint, my first can of beer and sworn me to eternal secrecy on pain of death? What had happened to the sister who when asked the name of the last guy she had slept with replied, "Oh god what was his name again?"

Did I want to be her, what she had become? Wealthy husband, large house, new cars, darling children who took every class going, the nanny, the black Labrador puppy, tennis lessons. The lunches at Reviva and Celia, the charity committees, the parent-teacher evenings. The cocktail parties, Sundays in the park, the school run in the mornings, holidays in Europe, the Caribbean.

She'd turned into Mama, just without the valium, the absent husband and the delinquent teenagers. Or maybe she had all that. Expensive clothes and make-up plus a fake smile could hide a lot of pain. Mama had been pulling it off for years.

Maybe we had no other choice than to turn into our Mamas? Was it predestined? They say families get stuck in a cycle of poverty. Was ours stuck in a cycle of rich but absent husbands, loneliness and insecurity? Was there any point in fighting such a fate?

Ultimately that fate didn't make us any different from "repressed women" in third-world countries—or second and first world countries, for that matter. So we could vote and work and wear as little or as much as we liked and yet we were just as dependent on men for our happiness and quality of life as the women behind the veils, forced to marry their cousins, were.

We were all prisoners of disastrous relationships as much as someone forced into marriage.

And what were the chains, the bars imprisoning us in these relationships? Love of course. Take my Papa for example. He came home from Paris once a month, if that. It was common knowledge that he had some fancy woman holed up in Paris and yet Mama still loved him. Not only that, but she was miserable, dependent on drugs to get through the day, had ruined her life pretty much and yet she still loved him. She did it all because she loved him. What kind of bullshit was that?

We're no better off than the women of the Torah. Take Sara, she's unable to have a child so what does her husband do? Swear his loyalty to her and only her, promise it will be them together forever regardless of whether they can have children or not? Oh no! He goes and sleeps with their servant and then when he's finished with her allows his wife to throw her and her son out of their house, effectively making them homeless and destitute.

This same man takes his only son, the son his wife thought she could never have, and prepares to sacrifice him—does he even ask his wife, tell her that he plans to kill their one and only son that she waited so long for? Oh no of course not, why would he do that? That would mean actually thinking of his wife, and maybe putting her first. All men are bastards, even the biblical ones. Men hadn't changed in thousands and thousands of years, so what else was new?

So why bother with love? The Family was one place where there was no danger of me finding that—not amongst a bunch of lovers and an old man. I had nothing to gain and thus nothing to lose. Perfect.

~~

She waddled towards me. Fat arms, fat legs, her fat stomach swelling out in front of her. How could she do it? I thought. How could she have so little respect for herself? Has she seen what she looks like? Every frigging year, another bloody baby keeping me up at night. Hasn't she got enough dopey-eyed, snotty-nosed kids running around?

"Amelia, have you seen Dana?"

"Nope."

"She's supposed to be helping me do the food shopping and I just can't make it." She started rubbing her stomach. I started to feel sick, but saw a great opportunity to have some fun. I was bored, stuck in the house all day—no internet, no MTV.

"I'll do it."

She looked at me suspiciously. I had never volunteered to do anything that involved helping out.

"Come on, you can trust me." She couldn't. But I was desperate to get out, and the more of a reality it became the more desperate I was to escape.

"I don't know…."

She was wavering, I could tell. It was hot and I knew the last thing she wanted to do was drag her fat stomach around the supermarket.

"I'll be good, get everything we need."

"Maybe we should look for Dana."

"I can go and be back in record time."

Dana had asked her to give me a chance. To see what I was capable of, if given responsibility.

"OK, but I'll write a list. This has to last us until the end of the month." It was no mean feat feeding six adults and fifteen kids on a government stipend. And didn't I know it—I was sick of rice, sick of vegetables and no meat. Sick of their food! We never ate out, never had take-away. I was craving pizza, and a burger and a huge salad in a glass bowl from Café Netto with crumbly cheese on top.

~~

Mother used to take me to Café Netto when I was a kid, before my father started working so much; and before her best friend was a bottle of valium. We used to go on Friday lunchtime—just us. Café Netto was my choice. I always craved a salad in a big glass bowl. Mother never ate, but she would sit across from me sipping elegantly from her glass of mineral water; her make up immaculate; her nails perfect; her clothes expensive; the overpowering smell of her perfume assailing me across the table.

She used to say, "Order anything you want!" I devoured salad, bread and always cheesecake afterwards. I'd talk about school and friends and everything really.

And then my father moved the majority of his business to France, where his parents were, and practically moved there too. Mother couldn't handle it and the lunches stopped.

I hadn't thought about them for a long time—what was the point? But for some reason I craved them more than anything.

~~

I threw the list out the car window as soon as the house was out of sight. I had the money for two weeks food in my pocket and I was going to enjoy it. Admittedly it wasn't much, not anything like the allowance I use to get, but it would do.

~~

"Amelia? How's shit, where have you been?"

"Later. I need some stuff," The phone box on Shenkin offered no privacy whatsoever.

"That's it?—No sight or sound of you for six months and you ring up demanding drugs?" Ifat was obviously somewhere more private. Or maybe not. She didn't tend to care what others thought.

"I'm not demanding. I'm asking, begging."

"And if I managed to get you something, will you promise to talk?"

"For as long as you want."

"So, meet me at my place in an hour."

"An hour, are you sure?"

"Are you doubting my networking abilities?"

"No?"

"An hour!"

It only took me half an hour. I sat on the steps outside the building, its front yard strangling under the weeds that populated it. A huge flag fluttered from the roof of the building opposite.

What memories…one flag I thought.

All through high school, it had been a popular history/social studies lesson question—what did that flag mean to us.

~~

"Amelia?"

"Uh."

"Our country's flag, what does it mean to you?"

I returned to the half-finished doodle on the notebook in front of me. I shrugged my shoulders, "I don't know."

Mrs Perlman sighed, "Try, Amelia, please! Our country's flag, what does it mean to you?"

Mrs Perlman was nice. She tried hard; so for her I tried to think. What did it mean?

~~

Another argument at home.

"What is this?" cried Papa, going out to the terrace to snatch the flag off the railings. He brought it in and threw it on Mama's lap.

She looked up in shock.

"It's our flag," she replied, her eyes welling with tears.

"I know that!" he thundered. "What is it doing out there?" and he nodded at the garden.

Mama held the flag in her hands. Fat tears dropped onto it.

"Do you know what that flag represents?" he cried, looking at it with disdain.

Although wet with tears, her eyes were as defiant as they could be. "Everything my family did to build this country!" she asserted.—He could mess with Mama all he wanted but not her family. They were sacred.

His tone was calmer, as if out of respect for her dead ancestors, whom he had never liked anyway. "It represents the stranglehold the orthodox political parties have on this country and its government," he continued calmly, "a stranglehold that holds us back economically, socially…a stranglehold that prevents peace from ever becoming a reality. And that prevents this country from ever building a decent economy."

Mama sniffed, "It doesn't mean that to me; it's special to me," and she hugged the flag to her.

Papa shook his head. "Just keep it out of the garden."

~~

"I'm waiting, Amelia!" demanded Mrs Perlman, whose voice was trying to be firm but whose eyes were trying to coax something out of me.

"It's pretty," was the best I could give her, "the blue and white look good together."

She looked disappointed. Who could blame her? She knew who my great-grandparents were and now I guess she couldn't get how I was related to them. I didn't get it either.

~~

Ifat slapped me on the knee and beckoned me inside. She patted her bag confidently and smiled at me. I smiled back. She pulled my arm, "Come upstairs, man do you have shit to tell me!"

I headed for the lift but she shook her head and pointed to the stairs. I groaned and she smiled.

"Damn broken lift!" I cried through clenched teeth, as I tried to get my breath back after dragging myself up four flights of stairs.

Ifat didn't mention the last argument we had had the last time we met. But she didn't need to. It was forgotten by both of us. Isn't that what sisters did? Forgive and forget everything?

~~

"Want something to drink?" Ifat called, as she headed for the kitchen.

"Water!" I sank into the sofa.

"Diet coke?"

"Just water," I replied, playing with the cigarette burn in the fabric next to me. Magazines and overflowing ashtrays covered the table in front of me.

Ifat plonked the glasses onto the table, although not before sweeping a pile of old newspapers and magazines onto the floor.

"Nice to know some things never change!" I smiled as Ifat threw the baggie at me and I shook it up to hold it to the light.

"It's not my mess," she cried surveying the room, "Tal just got out of the army and was here before heading off to India."

Tal was Ifat's younger brother. Ifat had made me snog him once as a drunken dare and I don't think he'd every gotten over it.

"Shame I missed him," I said.

"Not sure he would feel quite the same way," laughed Ifat, remembering the same memory.

~~

"You want?" I asked her starting to open the bag.

Perched on the coffee table, Ifat shook her head.

"No? Well I guess some things do change—have you got a card?"

Ifat threw a Bank of Harpoalim ATM card from her pocket at me.

"Any reason why not?" I asked as I poured a larger than average amount of lovely white powder on the mirror that Ifat had placed in front of me.

Ifat raised her eyebrows at my generous pouring.

"Making up for lost time," I explained, chopping away as I did so.

"So," I asked again, "Any reason why not?" concentrating as I did so on dividing the pile into neat lines.

"Shouldn't I be the one asking the questions?" Ifat demanded." After all you're the one who disappeared into a cult."

"Not a cult," I insisted, as I rolled the 20-shekel note from my pocket as tightly as possible. I smiled to myself

126

at the thought that this was actually the grocery food-shopping money. If only Beruriah could see it now!

"So why?" I asked again, looking straight at Ifat.

She rolled her eyes at me but smiled at the same time. "Because I have a new job, a good job and I don't want to lose it."

"Mazel-Tov," I said, "Congratulations!" bringing one end of the note to my nose and the other end to the carefully aligned powder.

"I'm trying to live a normal life," Ifat continued, watching me take a snort. "I'm trying to get out of this dump, to stop always being so confused in the head!"

"Nothing wrong with being out of it," I said as the powder blasted up my nose and then straight up into my brain, coursing around my body as it did so. I lay back against the sofa for support as my whole body tingled; and elation, excitement and energy pushed me physically and mentally into what was going to be a fantastic drug-induced afternoon.

"I don't want to be so confused anymore," said Ifat as she looked across at me and I closed my eyes, enjoying the physical rush just that little bit longer. "I just want a normal life," she went on, assuming I was listening, "a stable job, a nice home and car. Maybe a husband, children...." She spied the shock on my face.—"Yes, children !" she continued.—"Why not? I'm tired of being part of this idea that to experience life fully you have to do and try every crazy sodding thing that comes along.— The idea that if you want a good job, and a family and to make money then you must be boring and stupid and not really living.—I'm tired," she sighed. "I'm tired of chasing extreme experiences. I'm ready to find happiness and yes contentment in the little things."

"I get it," I replied. Ifat was watching me, waiting for me to say something.

God, did I feel alive!—alert as hell, eyes wide open! But, more important, I could feel—every little emotion and feeling was mine to feel and enjoy.

"Cigarette?" I asked.

Ifat rummaged under a pile of old newspapers on the floor and threw me a half empty packet of Parliaments. "Forget it!" she said. "I'm not talking to you when you're like this."

"Why?" I said, my legs jiggling. I'm ready to talk." And boy, was I ready to talk!

"Go on then!" Ifat goaded. "Tell me about your life."

I smiled. "Really?" Nobody could hurt me now.

Ifat threw a magazine at me, laughing as I ducked. "Just tell me!"

I shrugged my shoulders, "There isn't a lot to tell. It's basically the same as what you want, I guess… normality. You know it's just being part of a family with kids who do the same shit day after day and have fun with each other doing family shit," and I leant forward to take another hit.

"Normality?" Ifat threw another magazine at me, narrowly missing my treasure.

"Watch it!" I cried with genuine fear.

"Normality!" screeched Ifat again. "What kind of normality is living in some cult with one man and god knows how many bloody women?"

"Not a cult," I insisted, as fire coursed through my body.

"OK, so not a cult but it's certainly not normal either."

"So what? Do you want to hear?" I said. "I did it to piss my Mama off and to get my Papa's attention."

"Is that why you did it?"

I brought the note to my nose again, "I guess, in part." I didn't need the coke to be open with Ifat. We'd known each other since the army which wasn't a long time in years, but a long time in memories. "But it wouldn't have taken even half of that to piss Mama off, nor could

128

anything be extreme enough or bad enough to get Papa's attention, so I don't know. I needed a change, something resembling a family, something as close to normality as I could stand."

"But this is the family you always dreamed of?" Ifat wasn't demanding, just curious, and trying to understand my decision, rather than judging it.

"Maybe. Why not? It's how people used to live, how a lot of Arabs and Bedouin still live; so why not?"

"You have some serious issues," commented Ifat matter-of-factly.

"Honestly," I said, "The life we live in the house is as normal as any other family. Our make-up is just a little different, that's all."

"So you're happy?" asked Ifat, eyeing her coke-covered mirror.

"Because I'm doing this, I'm unhappy?" I demanded to know.

"No, but it means you're not content. People who are content in life do not do drugs."

"What is your new job as, a drug counselor?" It was an awful joke, but Ifat managed a smile and wagged her middle finger at me at the same time.

"You know it's true," she said.

"So, you're content?" I asked.

"Getting there," she admitted. "And part of getting there for me means none of that," and she wagged a finger at the mirror.

"Is it possible to be content, but momentarily bored?" I asked.

"Probably," said Ifat. "But boredom doesn't drive you to coke." And then as an afterthought, "Why are you bored?"

I shrugged my shoulders, "Not in general, just today, I fancied a change."

"You need a project," Ifat advised, "…something to keep you busy and fulfilled day to day."

"A baby?" I asked dead-pan.

Ifat's face registered nothing but pure horror. "God, no! You can't inflict you on a poor innocent baby!" She hesitated before asking, "You're not, are you?"

I grinned back a "no."

She looked visibly relieved, "No, not a baby! An interest, a passion…."

I pointed to the powder in front of me and she shook her head.

"Not that! It'll bankrupt you and kill you," and she made as if to take the mirror away. I swatted her hand away.

"How about a job?" she suggested.

"A job?"

"Yes you know one of those things normal people, who don't have Daddy to support them, get."

I ignored her sarcasm, "A job doing what?"

"I don't know!" Ifat said, with some exasperation, "A job doing something you like, something you are good at."

Again I pointed to the powder and she gave me a stern look.

"But that would mean working for someone else," I complained.

"Well, yes."

"Some asshole who is less intelligent than me but who has the right to act superior just because they've been kissing someone else's ass for longer."

Ifat laughed, "Not all bosses are assholes. And you have to start somewhere. Then one day you get to be the superior asshole."

I tapped the tightly rolled note on the table as if contemplating the option of getting a job.

"How about working for your Abba?" Ifat said quite calmly.

"Are you crazy? Work for him? Why would I do that?"

"Because you'd have a ready-made job, a ready-made great salary. Why not?"

"Because he's the biggest superior asshole of them all."

Ifat smiled wickedly, "I always liked your Abba."

"Of course you did," shooting her a look of complete disgust. "Women always like him, especially the stupid ones." And I leant over to sink a punch into her arm. "Anyway he's the world's biggest flirt, as well as the world's biggest asshole. Working with him would be a nightmare. I'd be constantly reminded of his latest conquest."

Ifat returned my look of disgust. "Fair point," she agreed, and then, "So you're screwed, unless you get off your ass, out of that cult and accept the reality of life— both the shitty parts and the good parts. Enough running from life just because you got lumbered with a neurotic, drug-addict Ima and a cheating bastard Abba. A shitty childhood is no longer a valid excuse to screw up your life. Move on! Get over it! We all get handed shitty cards in life, at some point; that's just life. I'm tired of thinking that a crappy childhood gives me the right, or the need, to expect a shitty adult life. So Ima died when I was four, and Abba spent my childhood trying to drink himself to death; but that was then, and this is now. I'm tired of making up excuses for doing nothing constructive with my life and I'm sick of using my crappy childhood as an excuse. Aren't you?"

"Perhaps," was all I could say. Suddenly my coke-induced clarity had gone and I wasn't sure if I was ready to let go of the past and accept the future. Not even a bag of coke was powerful enough to make me do that.

"How's Ziv?" I asked trying to change the subject.

Ifat took the hint, she knew when to leave me be. "Gone."

"Gone?" I said shocked, "But you guys were together for ages, and I liked Ziv,

"Two years. He didn't want to move on. And he wouldn't stop taking that shit." An accusing finger pointed itself in the direction of my stash. "And he wouldn't even consider doing something other than serving coffee. So I told him it wasn't working." She said it as calmly as if it had been the easiest decision she had ever made. But she couldn't fool me. Ifat was infamous for her tough outer shell.

She cracked just a little. "I don't know. He started to get resentful. He started spewing bullshit about how I thought I was too good for him. I denied it at first until I realised maybe I was too good for him after all.

Ifat took a long drink of diet coke, "And then he slept with someone else."

"Really? The asshole!"

Ifat smiled, "Yeah, I thought the same until I realized I didn't actually care who he slept with, as long as it wasn't me."

"But what a piece of shit! Who was she?"

"I don't know, his dealer's sister I think. I didn't, no don't care. She's welcome to him! He was happy wasting his life away being high 24/7 and I was tired of that."

"If you say so."

"I do."

"He's still an asshole."

Ifat smiled. "Something like that, yes."

"How about me?" I asked, "Do you want me to go?"

Ifat smiled, "No you can stay. I care about what happens to you."

I smiled back. "Wanna go get coffee?" The walls of Ifat's dingy apartment were closing in on me. I needed people, bright lights, lives being lived, cars racing past, if I was going to truly enjoy this high.

"How's your Abba?" I asked, strangely desperate to talk, to sympathize with others, to feel again.

"Yeah! Good, I think. He's been sober for a month, which is a new record."

"Wow."

"Yeah, wow. But I'm not holding my breath. I don't think it'll last. He won't let Ima go. And until he does that, he won't stay sober. He won't even get rid of her clothes. It's been twelve years and he still has the same furniture in exactly the same places as when she died."

"Wow!"

"I used to think it was kind of romantic. How he still loved her so much he couldn't bear to throw anything out. But enough is enough. He's so goddamn miserable and drunk all the time because he can't let go."

Thoughts crowded my head, too many to articulate into words.

Ifat looked at me and no doubt guessed my mental confusion. "Come on, let's go out!" and she reached out for my hand.

~~

"Do you remember our biggest fear?" asked Ifat as the waitress showed us to our table and we sat down.

"Mmm...not getting laid enough," and I pulled out a cigarette from the crushed packet in my jeans.

"Being ordinary." Ifat declined the cigarette I offered. "Being like everyone else. Getting up day after day, to go to the same shitty job, and then coming home day after day to the same person."

"Yeah."

"So we took as many drugs as possible to avoid being ordinary—we refused to study or do anything that everyone else was doing."

"Sure, we had a lot of fun," I said, pulling the menu towards me, I wasn't hungry or thirsty, just desperate for something to engage my racing brain.

"But I thought about it and I tried to find out why we were so scared of life anyway? I mean, maybe happiness is truly found in the little things you know. I don't know, there just has to be more to life than getting high every night. I think of Ima and of what she would have given to have lived and what she would have done with her life if she had lived—and it made me think how cruel it was, to her, for me to waste my life. I want her to be proud of me but more than that, I guess I want to appreciate and respect the life she gave me. I know I was only young when she died, but I saw it in her eyes, heard it in her voice—she didn't want to die. She was desperate to live. She would have taken any kind of life just to have been able to stay alive. I have my life and I just can't waste it anymore," Ifat sniffed.

I gave her a brave smile and offered her my cigarette. —She smiled and took it from me, "Enough sympathy," she said through her drag. "I've had so much sympathy since Ima died. Enough. I just want to get on and live my life." She handed me back my cigarette.

"Fair enough," I agreed.

"Now you," she said folding her arms across her chest.

"Me?"

"Yes, you. Come on, I've spilled my guts. Now it's your turn. So, what's really going on with all this cult crap?"

"Not a cult," and we paused to order drinks.

"Amelia!" Ifat was exasperated.

"OK, OK, I surrender," and I put my hands up. Ifat swatted them away and I took a deep breath. This was Ifat after all. She was like a sister. Hell, she was my sister. So we didn't share the same blood or the same uselss parents, but she was my sister.

"Honestly, I don't know. I needed a change and this came along and I sort of just fell into it."

Ifat shook her head, "You just fell into it," she parroted.

I fiddled with the fork in front of me, "It sounds stupid I know. But I couldn't be at home with Mama anymore. I would have killed her, or myself."

"You could have come to me, or gone to Lucille's."

"I didn't want to bother anyone. I wanted to find my own solution. I wanted to try something different—to get out of Ramat Ha'Sharon and that whole circle of ladies who lunch and play tennis and pop valium."

"Well, you sure did that!" And Ifat smiled.

"This isn't forever, I know that. I guess I wanted to shake Mama up a bit."

"And get your Abba's attention."

"Yeah maybe that too," and I smiled back. "I don't know, it's not so bad. Sometimes it's kind of nice. We have fun; we talk a lot about stuff."

"Hey, you don't need to explain anything to me. As long as this is what you want and you're OK. So long as that's your choice!"

"Thanks," and that was why she was my sister.

"But remember that I am here—always," and she reached out a hand. I took it and squeezed it and we smiled together.

"Thanks," and I meant it more than she could ever know. And yet I couldn't take her up on her offer of help just yet. There was still something keeping me with the Family. A desire to keep shocking those around me? Yeah maybe. A desire to separate myself from everything I knew in order to get away from all the shit there? Yeah, maybe. Because I liked living with the Family? Really?

"So you need some time to figure out your shit," said Ifat, as if reading my thoughts. "I get it. It's easier to do it away from everything you know, I understand," and I was amazed that she did know. She seemed to know why I did stuff, better than I knew why I did it.

~~

It was late by the time we left Café Aroma. I could feel my buzz slowly wearing itself away—leaving my fingers, my toes and at last, I knew, my brain. It was ebbing away like the tide leaves shore, and trying to stop it would be as fruitless and pointless as trying to hold back the tide.

I had to get away from the world, from the people who had stimulated and excited me earlier...before it started to feel as if they were all staring at me, analyzing me.

Ifat huggged me tight, "If you need a place to stay....Money....Anything, call me....OK?" She hugged me again and I promised, while hugging her back, that I would let her know if there was anything I needed.

If I hadn't been so busy trying to fight what I knew was going to be the mother of all comedowns, I would have been sad leaving Ifat. She was the only friend I'd ever had and it had taken me eighteen years to find her. I would have been even sadder, if anger hadn't taken over, if I'd known then that that was the last time I would see Ifat.

Just a month after our last meeting she sent me a letter through Lucille:

Hey, Amelia!
Don't hate me. I just want you to know that I love you as I've always loved you. On the plane over here all I could think about was how I'd promised to be there if you needed anything and yet here I am a million miles away, or so it seems.

You remember my brother, Gilad. You remember how we use to laugh at him driving his ice cream truck across America? Well he's done really well and now has several trucks, and needs help managing them. He's family, he needs my help.

And I want normality. I can't get that in Ha'aretz. There are too many crazy memories and too much craziness in that place. I know America is hardly sanity central but there are pockets of normality here. Israel is so small, everything is in your face, I'm trying to escape that.

136

So I know I don't have a place for you in Tel Aviv anymore. But if you ever need somewhere to bed down in Miami, then all you have to do is call ☺

Think about it, maybe a clean break is what you need.

Love and kisses, Ifat

PS Stop letting your Ima and her craziness get in the way of your life, and your future. Just let it go!

I ripped the letter up and threw it in the bin. Who needed to keep a reminder of yet more betrayal. It would be harder to score from now on. That's all Ifat's leaving meant. Not that it mattered really, as, since that night with Ifat and returning with none of the grocery shopping and no groceries, they banned me from leaving the house alone and with any money. I tried to argue that most of the money was mine, seeing as it came from my Papa, but that just made them give me some shit about what was individually ours was also the Family's….blah, blah, blah!

~~

They let me out to see Lucille, but only to collect my donation to the Family. Beruriah didn't like it, but she had to accept it. The money I brought back was desperately needed.

~~

"It just seems so unnatural," said Lucille. "I mean, the thought of sharing Tal with someone, it's just something I can't comprehend."

I leant across the table to take the bowl of cheese from beside her arm, "Because you love Tal."

"And so none of you love him?"

"I don't think so," and I smeared the cheese on my bread, "I don't, Dana doesn't, Rachel is too confused to, and Beruriah is just doing her duty."

"But still, to agree to live like that? It isn't normal."

137

"Not now maybe, but once it was. Abraham, Jacob, Saul, David, Soloman, they all had more than one wife."

"Oh come on Amelia, they lived thousands of years ago."

"So?"

"So society changes, takes on different ideas of what is right and wrong. I thought modern Judaism had banned polygamy anyway."

"It did—Rabbi Gershon or someone. But he was Ashkenazi, a lot of the Sephardim, including Beruriah's Family and him didn't accept the ban."

"Really?"

"Really," I claimed, taking another bite of bread and cheese. Lucille fiddled with a bowl of olives. "Something about the ban only applying to where this Rabbi who banned it lived, and to the year that he banned it. I don't know anything about him trying to apply Christian morals to Judaism."

"Wow!"

"What?"

"Here you are talking about Jewish history. The fights you and Mama used to have about doing your homework, and yet here you seem to have just soaked it up."

I shrugged my shoulders and stole an olive from under Lucille's nose. "Beruriah kind of chants it all the time, as an explanation for how we live. If people ask. Same as she chants on about polygamy being the best way to have as many children as there are stars, something like that."

Lucille hook her head. "I love my children, but two is enough. Maybe three at a stretch."

I shook my head, "None will do me just fine."

Lucille took a sip of water, "Why are you so bitter, Amelia?"

I dragged on my cigarette and closed my eyes as the head rush hit me. A month without a cigarette and here I was reacting like a teenager taking their first puff. "I'm not bitter!"

"Come on, Amelia! You are the most bitter person I know!"

"So?"

"So I don't get it! I know family life hasn't always been heaven but it wasn't that bad."

"You never felt bitter, too?"

"Of course I did, all the time. When I realized what an asshole Papa was, and how stupid Mama was for staying with him. When I realized that people assumed we had it all because Papa had so much money. When no-one would take Mama's side, tell her the truth about Papa and help her. But I couldn't stay bitter. I would have been miserable all the time. I had to get past that to be happy. Don't you want to be happy?"

"Of course."

"So let it go. Just let it go. Let them all go."

"You make it sound so easy," and I stubbed the cigarette out into the ashtray.

"It isn't easy, but it is do-able. You have to try."

"I have to go."

"Already?"

"Yes. I just came to get money. You knew that. Did Papa send it?"

"Yes…although he is threatening to cut you off if you don't come to your senses and go home."

"Tell him I'll go home when he does."

She smiled, "Let it go," and then, "Do you want a lift back?"

"Sure!"

"Where's your car?"

"Beruriah has it; she took the kids to Kadima."

"Where?"

"Some youth-group thing."

~~

"Drop me off here." I said as Lucille's BMW reached the start of the street.

"Let me take you to the door."

"No, here is fine." The BMW would cause a stir in the street that I didn't want to have to explain.

"See ya!"

"Amelia?"

"Yeah?" I was halfway out of the door.

"Just think about it! Think about letting it all go!"

"Sure!" and I slammed the door behind me.

I waved as she drove off and she beeped her horn in reply.

Chapter 7—Rachel

The beach seemed full of bronzed, fit people playing *makot*. Walking along the promenade I seemed to hear more French than Hebrew—it seemed the French had discovered Tel Aviv as their new playground. A lifeguard called across his speaker system for an iced coffee. People jogged along the promenade—from the very healthy to those desperately trying to be healthy.

Old women threw bread from old plastic bags for the scabby pigeons that flocked around stale crusts and what seemed to be old pieces of pizza. Old men sat in the shade under peaked hats, chewing on sunflower seeds. Children paddled at the water's edge or jumped through the waves. Young couples kissed as they shared a sun bed and a packet of *bisli*.

Jaffa rose in the distance and the sea stretched out and out and out. Air force jets flew overhead, a reminder I guess, of where we were.

The beach swarmed with people. Every chair, sun-bed, spare inch of sand was occupied by someone. Rows of people stood, swam, and sat in the sea. The clunk of balls hitting *makot* racquets filled the air. Hebrew mingled with French, some English and Tel Avis' second language, Russian.

The sand was hot; it burnt the soles of my feet as I scanned the sand for somewhere to sit. A piece of sand by the water beckoned and I hurried over to it before an Israeli family could claim it was their own.

It was morning and the beach swarmed with children enjoying their freedom before the fierce, unrelenting sun would force them inside. Dogs swam in the sea in blatant disregard for the 'no dogs on the beach' signs. But nobody seemed to care, or be prepared to enforce the rule.

The sea invited me in as I spread my towel onto the sand and stripped down to my swimsuit. I was hoping that the hordes of people would hide me in my near naked state and I wouldn't have to worry about being studied and rated, like a piece of meat.

Rearranging my swimsuit bottoms so as to hide my unshaved and rather neglected bikini-line, I headed for the sea. It wasn't particularly warm but got warmer as I swam. The water was shallow for quite a way out and with my toes resting on the seabed I watched the activity on the beach with considerable interest.

The water's edge was the domain of the yoga enthusiasts, the joggers, the walkers and the babies. Further up the sand men and women fresh from the army, or off an El Al flight from Bangkok, tanned their bodies, or kissed their lovers.

Whole families gathered around bottles of Nestea and packets of *bisli*. Someone's grandma pulled out fresh pita from a bag, someone else olives, and someone else hummus.

The Sheraton, the Hilton towered above the people and the beach. Next to them, the fantastically located French embassy, where staff could enjoy their lunch on the beach every day of the week, if they wished.

A lifeguard in his wooden tower called out across his speakerphone, "Shalom Avi, Shalom Eli, so nice to see you here again, my friends. I take it this means you haven't found jobs yet."

It felt strange to be here alone without any clear purpose. There were others here alone but they were jogging, or in mid yoga pose. I envied them their purpose in life. All the confidence and poise I was able to keep up, when in a group, shattered into tiny pieces once I found myself alone, and I was instantly awkward, both in body and mind.

I tried to get comfortable on the sand—shaking a ton of the stuff off my towel as I did so. Only to end up with even more sand on it.

~~

Three women. One man. A gaggle of children. Spades, buckets, squeals and yells.

One of the women laid down mats, another helped the youngest children take off their shoes.

The third woman headed straight for the seat—her pink bikini in contrast to the dark skirt and blouse she had just removed.

One of the women, her eyes shielded from the sun by her hand, followed her with her eyes and shook her head as she did so.

The woman in the pink bikini kept on walking to the sea, followed by some of the older children.

The man sat on one of the mats, his shoes still on, as he took out a book and started to read.

One of the women, the one who had shaken her head, heaved herself down onto the sand, her body full of baby—her eyes on the water.

The other busied herself with the smallest children, and with a baby she put to sleep in his stroller. She helped fill buckets to make sandcastles and other such magnificent structures.

My eyes and mind were drawn to them and I couldn't look away. One man. Three women. So many children. It didn't make any sense. Was the man the grandfather? Or one of the fathers? If so where were the other fathers? Were they coming later? Or just busy today?

It didn't help my confused thoughts that the children all looked strangely similar—the same big, brown eyes, the same gangly thin limbs. Were they all cousins? But none of the women looked related to each other in any way. Were their fathers all brothers? But if so where were they?

The children fawned around the man as they would their father and he gave each the same affectionate pat on the head. Each he treated equally. But why?

~~

"Oh," I said aloud. That was it. He had fathered each child. Really? Yes, now the woman in the bikini, dripping wet from the sea, fawned over the man; she had her arms around his neck and she laughed. The older woman scowled as she pulled sandwiches out from the bag in front of her and handed them around. The other woman pulled two children close to her and handed them pieces of sandwich as the baby in the stroller next to her stirred in his sleep.

But even with the mystery solved I couldn't look away. What a sight—and here in broad daylight on the beach, right in front of me. I was watching a story that should be on *Sixty Minutes*.

Several times the man caught my eye and each time I looked quickly away, blushing as I did so and cursing myself for being so blatantly nosey. But each time I waited until I was sure he had looked away and I stared again! What was wrong with me! Each time I cursed myself and looked away, but each time my eyes were drawn back to them all again.

The man stood up, brushed the sand off his trousers and began to walk.

Began to walk.....to me!

"Oh shit!" I said under my breath. My heart raced. Were my palms really sweating? Why was he coming over here? I frantically asked myself. Was he coming to me? Yes there wasn't anyone else along the path he was walking. It had to be me. Or was I being arrogant, or paranoid by assuming that it was towards me he was headed.

My heart jumped up to my throat as he stopped in front of my towel,

"Shalom."

"Shalom." My Hebrew was passable. I'd made Mom hire me a private tutor (not an easy or cheap thing to arrange where we lived) and I'd spent night after night on online Hebrew-language websites.

"You are alone?" he asked

"Mmmm, yeah."

"So, please—join us?"

"Sure." 'What?' I asked myself. 'Where had that come from? Was I really agreeing to join this man and his Family? Mom would have had a heart attack.' Yet here I was following him over to his Family.

The older two women greeted me with a hello and a smile and then turned to their respective children. The one in the pink bikini merely grunted at me, gave me a sharp look and walked back in the direction of the water.

"Sit!" suggested one of the women.

And I did.

"Dana!" she said, introducing herself and holding out a hand.

"Rachel!" I said, taking it.

"This is Beruriah," Dana explained. "And that's Amelia," she said, nodding her head towards the sea.

I smiled nervously and let my fingers play with the sand beside me.

I declined an offer of a sandwich but gladly followed Dana and some of the children to the sea, where we splashed and played, and dare I say it, had fun.

As the sun began to set and the families began to pack up their things around us, Beruriah looked at me squarely and said, "Come to dinner!" And so I did.

It got late, and I stayed the night and the night after that and the night after that. I felt safe and secure and warm and I didn't want to miss anything the Family did next. I had nowhere else to go, nowhere else to be. It seemed natural to stay and so I went with that.

Dear Rachel,

It has taken me a long time to know what to write which is why this letter has taken so long to get to you. I wanted to call you but I decided I could never put everything I wanted to say in a telephone call. I was also worried you may not answer, or hear me out. I know that may also mean you won't read this, but at least I tried.

We miss you honey. The house is awfully empty without you. Rufus lies by the front door morning and night as if waiting for you to walk through the door at any moment. Sometimes I feel like joining him, he looks so hopeful every time the doorbell rings, or when he hears a key in the lock—only to look so dejected when it's just the postman, or your Dad, or friends. I know just how he feels.

I spoke to Leah. She's in contact with her folks again which is great news. The Schwartzs are even planning a trip to Israel to visit her and the children. She says she has tried to contact you, and she was able to get us your address. Her in-laws and their community have forbidden her from contacting you anymore. She wants to help but says her hands are tied.

Your brother was ready to jump on the first plane and come rescue you but the police told us that as you are over eighteen there is nothing we can do. It is very difficult not to be able to help you honey.

We want you to know that we love and miss you. We'd love to see you soon. If there is anything you need— money, a ticket home, please call us. Or even if you just want to say Hi, we'd all love to hear from you. Will you try honey? For us?

Mom and Dad

PS Your brother wanted to add a note at the end.

Dear Rachel,

Not sure how this note will find you. Well, I hope. Just wanted to let you know that you have to stop trying so hard to "find yourself." Everything doesn't have to be so extreme. I know you always thought that I went out of my way to hide my Jewish self, to deny it both to myself and to everyone around me, but that isn't true.

I didn't go out of my way to marry someone not Jewish. Maria and I fell in love; and she just happened to be not Jewish. I didn't search out non-Jewish girls on purpose; it's just the way it was.

I also haven't gone out of my way to stop living a Jewish life. I just got lazy and let it slip. It wasn't as if Mom and Dad ever enforced it very much. Maria grew up very differently—in a house where religion and tradition were considered very important and followed very closely, so we celebrate her holidays because she makes the effort; we don't celebrate ours because I don't make the effort. Again it's not something I purposefully chose to stop doing. It just happened—each year you celebrate a little less until you just don't bother celebrating at all. It's assimilating, without really knowing you're doing it.

I'm just saying, you don't have to run away and join a (the word was crossed out, but it looked like cult) religious group, to find yourself. It can be more subtle than that, more true to who you are.

"You have done it before, haven't you?"

"Well…no."

"No? How old are you? Anyway it doesn't matter. You'll have to now; you can't live here and not, it's like payment or something."

"Payment?"

"Yeah; payment for living with the Family," Amelia laughed. "It's not payment for me. I enjoy it—regardless of how old he is!"

"But don't look so worried," she added. "It's always pretty shit the first time—so people say. But there is one thing you might want to think about."—She quickly looked around as if making sure we were alone.—"And that's getting pregnant."

"Getting pregnant?"

"Yes, that's what tends to happen after you do it—God, what do they teach you in America? Anyway, I can help…stop you getting pregnant, understand?"

"But…the Family?...God?"

"Oh, screw the Family! It has enough screaming brats to feed without us adding more…and I am personally not about to get that fat for anything. And God? He has enough people to worry about without worrying about those that weren't or might have been."

"But how?"

"Holy Moses! Don't you know anything? I thought America was the land of free love, drugs and rock n'roll, and I'm teaching you about birth control!"

"I'm from a small town"…it was almost an apology… "a small Catholic town. Birth control didn't really ever come up."

Amelia shook her head, "So do you want?"

"Well, I guess….."

"You guess yes?"

"Where did you get them?" I dared ask.

"They're my sister's; she gets them from her Doctor. It's not as if it's illegal or anything—well, apart from in Queen Beruriah's kingdom of course. But then there isn't a lot in Queen Beruriah's kingdom that isn't illegal."

Amelia was contemptuous, and arrogant in the knowledge that she was in some way thwarting Beruriah and her 'rules'.

~~

But wasn't that part of the deal—joining the Family to add to the Family? And what was Judaism, what was anything without the family? Wasn't that what I wanted, why I was here? A family that would always be there. And wouldn't children be that? So why the hesitation? I don't know, it seemed like cheating. By doing this, wasn't I holding back, refusing to commit fully to the Family? And if so, why was I doing it?

~~

"But won't the Family find out?"

"Not if you're careful, they have no idea that I use it. Anyway they're from Yemen, they don't even know it exists."

"Can I think about it?"

"Sure it's your choice, your loss."

~~

"Rachel?"

"Yes?"

"It's Leah."

"Leah?"

"Yes. Look, I have to be quick. If my in-laws know I'm calling you, I'll never live it down. Are you OK? I promised your Mom I'd ring, to make sure you were OK."

There came the sound of glass smashing in the background.

"Amit, what are you doing?" shouted Leah.—"I'm sorry, G-ddamn kids!"

"I'm fine."

More smashing glass.

"Amit!—Are you sure?"

"Yeah. I'm fine. Really."

"Will you call your Mom? I can tell her you're OK, but maybe she'd appreciate it more coming from you."

I hear crying in the background, "Amit, leave Hannah alone!"

"Sure I'll call her."

"Great, she'll be so pleased. I have to go, but take care, OK?"

"Amit, put that down!"

"Sure, bye Leah."

~~

"I'll take some."

"Some what?" Amelia teased.

"You know what."

"You sure? God could strike you down at any minute."

"That's not funny and yes I'm sure."

"Keep then well-hidden," she said, handing me a silver pack. "I'm pretty sure no-one in this house would know what the hell they are, but you never know."

"Thanks for this."

"No worries; happy to help."

"What are you two up to?" demanded Beruriah, poking her head around the door.

"None of your damned business," replied Amelia.

Beruriah shook her head, "Dana needs help with the washing. Please go help her."

"Sure," I replied, as Amelia muttered what sounded like the makings of a curse under her breath.

"Evil old witch," she cried under her breath, as we left the room.

I didn't mind as much. Beruriah was the first one after all and the eldest. That gave her the authority. Plus I was feeling horrendously guilty about the little magic pills in my pocket and would have done anything she had asked to appease my guilt and my sin.

And yet the guilt didn't stop me washing each little pill down with water every morning. Furtively, secretly, during my share of bathroom time. I thought they would be hard to swallow, each little pill, like trying to get a stone down. But they weren't. They slid down easily, morning after morning.

———

Chapter 8—Amelia

"You will take each and every child with you to Meir Panim, to eat this week!" Beruriah was furious. She slammed dirty dishes into the soapy water in front of her.

"Is that my punishment?"

"No, not your punishment. You spent all of our food money, so we have no money for food. The only way the children will eat this week is if you take them to Meir Panim." And she slammed plates into the sink.

"So I will get some more money for food."

"Or I could," cried Dana. "Is Meir Panim really necessary?" She looked uncomfortable with the idea, "I mean if we can get some more money, do we really have to take the children there?"

But Beruriah was adamant. "Amelia will take the children to Meir Panim to eat."

"So that is my punishment."

Beruriah's eyes flashed. "You will learn," she cried, turning away from the sink and facing Amelia across the table, "that your actions have consequences, not just for yourself but for others too. You obviously don't care about the consequences for yourself, but it's time you realized the consequences your actions have for others." She paused for breath without taking her eyes off Amelia. "You spent our food money. The consequence of that is that you and the children will have to eat at Meir Panim all week. You will hate it. But because of your thoughtless actions we have no other choice. I hate for the children to have to suffer because of your selfishness." Beruriah relaxed her gaze on Amelia and her shoulders slumped as if she was suddenly tired and defeated, "But that is something your conscience will have to carry."

Beruriah made me walk with the children to Meir Panim. As if it wasn't bad enough that I had to take them to the soup kitchen, now I had to walk in public with them all.

Dana had begged Beruriah to let her come too, but the fat old hag refused to let her come and here I was, in broad daylight, with a goddamn gaggle of scruffy brats. In broad daylight where everyone could see us.

"I'm hungry," cried Sara, Beruriah's eldest.

I ignored her.

"Me too," whispered Tamar, Dana's eldest.

"Shut up!"

And Tamar shuffled back to Sara who took her hand. "You're not very nice," she shot back at me.

I ignored her. "Come on," I cried to the younger ones at the back.

Dana's second youngest, Yuval, began to snivel about being too tired to walk. I ignored her too.

"She's tired!" called Sara.

"So?"

"She can't walk any more, you have to carry her."

I scowled at them both but Sara started back defiantly.

Yuval was a dead weight on my hip, her thumb stuck in her mouth.

Meir Panim was full of sniveling, scruffy kids. Lisestte would have fainted dead away at the sight of them. There wasn't a DKNY shirt or prada shoe between them.

Children with snotty noses, dirty cheeks, and hair that needed brushing tied up into scrawny ponytails. Children with big eyes, skinny arms and a permanent look of hunger. Two boys started beating the crap out of each other in the corner until a volunteer went over to pull them apart.

Everyone sat down and the volunteers brought around bowls of hot food that they placed amongst the children. The majority threw themselves onto it.

"God," I said under my breath. "What a place!"

I pushed the children I had been made to bring ere down into their seats, and then backed myself into a corner, hoping to make myself invisible, not wanting to be seen here.

Sara helped the little ones take food from the big bowls in front of them and handed them their forks. She looked over at me backed into my corner but made no gesture, noise or even look of recognition. I tried to push myself back further, hoping the wall would swallow me up and transport me to safety out in the street again.

Hurry up I thought as the children spooned god knows what into their mouths. Tamar looked upset, she was a fussy eater and would currently only eat food that was white. Sara handed her a piece of bread with the crust removed and she pushed her bowl away and carefully nibbled on it.

"Can I get you something?" a volunteer asked as they walked past wiping their hands on their aprons.

"No," I said hurriedly, thinking, "Get away from me, I am not here, just ignore me!"

"OK!" And on they went, occupied with feeding the hungry and the poor.

God, it was a depressing place! So many of the children seemed to have come alone, dragged here by older brothers and sisters. Where were their parents? What it must mean for the parents to concede defeat and to send their children here because they can't afford to feed them? Maybe the parents were at home cringing with embarrassment and shame. Poverty was not a state I relished or enjoyed. God why did these people keep having kids if they can't feed them? Or clothe them? Most kids complained when their parents wouldn't or couldn't buy them the latest play-station but what did these kids have to complain about? My Abba can't afford to buy me dinner. God!

This certainly wasn't the vision of the "equal for all" Jewish state my great-grandparents had in mind as they picked olives on their kibbutz, that's for sure. What a load of crap. While their descendants, my family, lived in the best neighbourhoods in Israel, drove the best cars, ate in the best restaurants, shopped in the best shops—these kids were eating donated food in a cold, draughty room in clothes someone no longer wanted their child to wear; and would go home to cold houses and wake up to no breakfast.

"Sara," I hissed, "Are you ready to go?"

She shot me a look that was intended to hurt.

"Come on, it's cold in here."

"We're still eating," she called back not bothering to keep her voice down. People looked round. I shrank back into the corner.

God, why did they have to eat so slowly? I could have sworn they were doing it on purpose.

Finally they were done and I pushed them out of the door and into the crisp, cold night air.

"Come on, come on, it's freezing," and I hustled them down the street wanting to be rid of the responsibility as quickly as possible. Relief flooded through me as I realized that I had done it—I had taken them there and now it was over.

"That was horrible," said Tamar quietly, as she slipped her hand into Sara's.

"Was OK," replied Yonathan. "At least we're not hungry anymore," and a few of them nodded.

I grimaced—poor bloody brats!

~~

"Was it awful?" asked Dana, as we sat in the kitchen that night. Beruriah was showing Rachel how to sew, in an attempt to mend some of the children's clothes.

I shrugged my shoulders, "It was OK."

"Did Tamar eat anything?" asked Dana anxiously.

"Some bread."

Dana looked worried, "She's so fussy about what she eats. I'm so worried she'll be hungry."

154

"She'll be fine," interjected Beruriah. "It will do her good. Teach her if she is hungry enough she will eat anything," and she passed the threaded needle to Rachel, who looked at it with a combination of confusion and fear.

"Can I go tomorrow, Beruriah, and borrow some money off Papa's next cheque?"

"I'll go!" I cried out, before Beruriah could reply. "I mean I'll get some money...from somewhere."

"Thank you Amelia," came Beruriah's gracious reply.

She had to be gracious now. Without my money, she and her brats would starve.

Dana gave me a small smile, "Thank you. I just can't bear the thought of the children having to go back there."

And I couldn't either—with or without me.

~~

I guess it upset Dana the most. When I'd come home without any money, and without any food, her eyes had welled up with tears and her voice had cracked as she tried to understand what it meant.

We sat around the dining-room table, the children in bed. It was like facing a bloody inquisition—Beruriah at the head, Rachel and Dana beside her, and then me banished to the end of the table.

"Tea?" Rachel offered.

Dana just sat, watching the tears drop down on her lap. I said nothing, stared ahead defiantly. Beruriah would not let me out of her sight, her eyes were dark in their attempt to intimidate me. Good luck with that, I wanted to say.

Rachel started to make tea anyway, it kept her busy I guess. She was awkward, unsure of what to do or say.

The water began to boil furiously on the stove. Rachel watched it as if her life depended on it.

"What we are going to do?" wailed Dana. She couldn't stop the tears. "We needed that money for food, for bills. Without it what will we do?"

I guess at that point I was supposed to feel bad, only I couldn't really see what all the fuss was about. "It'll be OK," I guessed I was supposed to say. So I said it, in an attempt at appeasement.—Anything to get Beruriah's she-devil eyes off me!

Dana's emotional state however suggested my words were a lie, and even I didn't really believe them. "No, No it won't," replied Dana quietly. Even in her obviously distressed state, she refused to lose her patience with me or my pathetic attempt to cheer her up. Even I could admit to the pathetic-ness of it.

Rachel poured boiling water into four cups and slowly placed them on the table in front of us. No-one touched them.

"No money, no food!" Dana said, almost out of nowhere, pulling my attention away from the tea in front of me. It was as if she was explaining it to a child, which I knew Beruriah thought I was. I guess she didn't mean to patronize, I knew that. She was just trying to impress on me what it meant."

"There must be some way to get some money," offered Rachel, as she cradled her cup of tea, which was unusually brave of her, to offer an opinion like that.

"From where?" Dana asked, her face a desperate mess.

Dana thought aloud for all of us, "No bank will lend us any, the government allowance is already spent, and we have nothing to sell."

And there it was. Even here within the Family, where money was always chronically short, I had never been faced with the reality of nothing.

Having very little was one thing. Having absolutely nothing was suddenly a million times scarier.

~~

Coming back from brushing my teeth I heard Dana and Rachel's muffled voices coming from within their bedroom, I stood outside listening.

"Do you think we have security without financial security?" Rachel asked Dana. "I mean where is the safety-net between us and starvation?"

"Starvation?" queried Dana, shocked at the severity of the word.

"I know, I know! It sounds silly," admitted Dana. "Starvation in a modern country in the 21st century!— Maybe starvation was the wrong word."

"Perhaps," replied Dana, clearly tired and fading into sleep.

Rachel kept on, "I mean it's one thing to envy people with millions, those with private jets and the designer handbag lifestyle. It's quite another thing to envy those with a normal salary. Those with enough money to go to the supermarket every week and fill a trolley; those who can afford their monthly car repayments and to fill it with gas; those with the money for new shoes as and when they need them; those with money for trips to the cinema at the weekend and dinner afterwards; those with money for a holiday once a year; and those with enough left over each month to save."

"Mmm," mumbled Dana slowly succumbing to the power of sleep and the sleep-inducing drivel of Rachel's words. I stifled a yawn.

"So where is the security?" Rachel demanded of someone.

Dana didn't reply but Rachel kept on anyway. Talk about not being able to take a hint! "I mean is the Family enough?" she continued in a quieter voice. "At home I had the security of my family and money. Sometimes I wonder why I gave that up. Giving it up for love would have been one thing, but have I done that?"

"Forget it!" I wanted to tell her. "The only security is in money."

"Maybe if I had the security of true love," she continued to drivel on, "Well, then the concept of security from money wouldn't be an issue. Or maybe it would, but not such a devastating one; such a make-or-break one; not an all-consuming one." God! Americans could speak a load of mess when they wanted to, I thought. What a waste of words!

"So is it love that is missing?"

You've already asked that you goddamn self-reflecting Yank.

And then it all went quiet. So I left.

Chapter 9—Dana

Beruriah's fifth baby, a girl, was born just two months after Rachel joined us. She was woken in the middle of the night by wet sheets and he drove her in Amelia's— well the Family's—car to the hospital.

We woke up to a house minus Beruriah and him.

~~

We crowded around the kitchen table, our focal point in times of change or celebration.

"They must have gone to the hospital," I said, settling down to feed a hungry Isaac. "Amelia, will you start breakfast?"

Amelia, her eyes full of sleep, sighed and slowly began setting the table with bowls and spoons.

"Let me help!" cried Rachel, eager to prove her commitment to her new family.

"The cereal's in that cupboard," I pointed, "And milk in the fridge. Oh, and there are bananas there in the bowl!"

The children crowded around the table, taking their usual seats and fighting over their usual bowls.

"Where's Ima?" asked Sara. Her sleepy eyes matched Amelia's, if not in colour, then in tiredness.

"We think they've gone to the hospital," I replied, holding Isaac across my shoulder and rubbing his back. He emitted a loud burp and the children laughed.

"Is she OK?" asked Sara with an air of constant worry that seemed to follow her around as the eldest child.

"Of course," I reassured her, "I'm sure Abba will call soon."

Sara nodded and returned to her cereal.

The phone rang, disturbing our breakfast. Amelia dashed out to get it. She returned minutes later.

"They're OK," she said. "No need to visit, they'll be home tomorrow." And she returned calmly to her cereal.

"And?"

"And what?"

Well, how is Beruriah? and the baby?"

"Oh, they're fine. A girl."

"How much did she weigh?"

"I don't know."

"You see," I said turning to Sara, "Ima is OK, and so is your new sister. How about we make a big card for Ima and your new sister, and they can have it when they get home."

"Can we use the glitter?" Tamar asked.

I turned to my daughter with a smile, "Of course."

And a general murmur of approval went around the children.

"And we can write our names inside," said Sara.

"I don't know how to write my name," said Tamar, almost tearfully.

"That's OK," I reassured her. "I will help anyone who isn't yet sure how to spell their name."

"Must I help?" asked Amelia stacking the dirty bowls up by the sink.

"Of course."

"Really?"

"Really! What else are you going to do?"

And she shrugged her shoulders.

"I'd like to help," offered Rachel a little too eagerly. She was still so keen to please, still so aware of being the newest, the non-Israeli.

"Great," I replied.

"Great," said Amelia. "Dishes need washing first," and she pointed Rachel towards the stack of bowls.

I shot Amelia a look, which she ignored. Placing Isaac in his playpen I went to root out card and glitter and glue and scissors, leaving Rachel to the dishes.

~~

With the card finished I suggested we return to our normal weekday lessons.

Sara sidled up to me, "Do we have to, Auntie Dana? I mean today is kind of a special day. It's not every day we get a new sister."

I smiled, "No, it's not. But I think Ima would like it if we had school, as normal."

Sara was gracious in defeat, "So what are we going to do today, Auntie Dana?"

"Well I think Auntie Amelia and Auntie Rachel can take the little ones out to collect some leaves and pebbles and maybe some flowers for some painting, and we are going to see if we can use some of those same objects to write some poems."

I looked to Amelia and Rachel for approval. Rachel practically beamed back at me, but I'm sure she would have done the same regardless of what I had suggested—even if that had been walking over hot coals and glass; and Amelia looked moody.

"Coats on!" I cried. "It's cold outside." And a stampede rattled the stairs as a mass of children went looking for coats and outdoor shoes.

We roamed the hill at the back of the house, combing it for leaves, and flowers and pebbles; and with coat pockets and little hands full of such treasures, we trooped home again, ready to document them.

The little ones painted, and the older ones wrote, and then it was time for lunch.

I pulled Isaac to me again as he squawked to be fed. I felt him tug on my breast and his relief as the milk filled his mouth, and then his tummy.

Rachel ladled out soup from the night before into the now clean bowls and the children drank it hurriedly and hungrily. Bread was passed around and vanished as soon as it made contact with mouths. Beruriah made the bread, her mother's recipe. I burped Isaac again and hurriedly drank my own soup, now lukewarm.

In the afternoon the younger ones slept and the older ones practised their reading—their voices droned over the words my finger pointed to. Amelia was in charge of making dinner; she had no patience for the readers.

As the younger ones began to stir upstairs I sent Rachel upstairs to bring them back to the land of the awake. She brought down a troop of sleepy-eyed, yawning children.

We played backgammon, and chess, and snakes and ladders on the carpet of the sitting room. We each took a game and a group of children to play with. I casually let my group win for the fourth time, while Amelia screamed with delight as she secured her victory yet again over her little team.

The games had been mine and Anton's and it made me happy to think that they once again made children happy, as they were supposed to.

I brought in plates of cookies and they vanished in seconds. Someone cried, someone had taken their cookie. I offered them mine and peace was restored in our little kingdom, where the stealing of a cookie was a grave crime.

The time before dark the children spent in the garden—building forts and castles with the old furniture and playing hide and seek amongst the weeds.

I watched them from the kitchen window and smiled. Amelia added more salt to the chicken and vegetables and tasted it reluctantly. She pulled a face and added more salt.

The children were fed, the food vanished. More dirty plates stacked by the sink.

Amelia and Rachel bathed them. I put them into their pajamas and their bed, kissed them goodnight and went wearily down the stairs.

Rachel placed a cup of hot tea in front of me and I nodded my thanks. I added mint, and sugar and stirred it with my spoon. I took Isaac from his playpen, all warm from his bath and held him to me. His eyes lowered and then he was asleep. I held him for a little longer, not wanting to let the warm bundle go. I kissed his tiny fingers, his tiny cheeks, everything of this little person in miniature. In a flash he would be sitting, crawling, walking, and talking. I wanted to enjoy this quiet, this tiny little being now while I could, before these days when he was so small became nothing but a distant memory.

His chubby baby fingers chased my pen across the page. It was a new game—similar to the one involving hitting Ima with an empty plastic water bottle, or poking Ima in the eye with a chubby finger to test her reaction.

~~

In the evening we chatted around the old oak table. Rachel helped me plan the next day's lesson. Her Mom was a teacher, she explained, she taught grade school and so she had plenty of ideas to offer. I asked her about her family, and she told me about her parents, her brother, and her life in America.

Amelia listened with one ear; with other, she listened to the music booming from her i-pod. How the older children envied her that i-pod, and how difficult Amelia found it to share it. Old as she was, and young as they were, she just couldn't. Beruriah had tried to take it away from her. She didn't want the children exposed to the commercialism of it, of what it represented. That and the fact we could never afford one for any of the children. She didn't want it there as a reminder of what they couldn't have. If they didn't know it existed, they couldn't miss it. She'd tried and Amelia had screamed and shouted and swore for days. She wouldn't eat, she wouldn't sit with us, and she wouldn't help with any of the chores. Beruriah, pregnant and exhausted, gave in. She would try again though, that I knew. This was Beruriah's house, Beruriah's Family and Beruriah's rules. We all knew that. Amelia could enjoy her respite from the fight now, but she'd not won the war, not by a long shot. Beruriah wasn't going anywhere; she had all the time in the world.

We went to bed at the same time, wishing each other good night and sweet dreams.

Rachel slipped into the bed beside mine and I turned off the light. I was slipping into sleep when Isaac's cries filled the room. Murmuring my apologies to Rachel I cooed my way over to Isaac in his cot and brought him back into bed with me where he slept until dawn.

Chapter 10—Rachel

In the morning on Friday Dana and I took the children to the park before lunch.

"Work off their energy before *Shabbat*," Beruriah explained as she bundled us out of the door.

The park was full of others doing the same. Crowds of *kippa*-wearing boys chased their friends, their *tallit* dangling. Long-skirted little girls slid down slides. Six, seven, eight brothers and sisters ran along the grass, touched the sky with their feet from their swings constantly chaperoned by their sober, black-clad fathers.

~~

At home, *Shabbat* wasa time my parents reluctantly remembered—as if it was a sacrifice, a trial rather than a celebration. Things were different with the Family. Here *Shabbat* was a celebration and treated with as much respect and as much anticipation as any other holiday.

Beruriah had us cleaning the house from the morning onwards—dusting, sweeping, mopping, wiping, washing, ironing, and tidying. No mean feat in a house of five adults and six children.

Dana dressed the children in their best clothes—the little boys in their white shirts, the little girls in their dresses. Hair was braided, *kippots* placed on heads.

Amelia had the older children in hysterics as she tried to place and keep a *kippot* on Dana's toddler—it kept slipping over his eyes and forcing a wail from him.

"Stop that," commanded Beruriah as she swept past, grabbing the *kippa* as she did so.

The candles were lit, always by Beruriah; the wine and *challah* were blessed and dinner began.

And everyone could sense that tonight was different from all others that tonight heralded the coming of the *Shabbat*.

"But of course," said Beruriah as I voiced my thoughts out loud. "The *Shabbat* is our gift from G-d. As he rested, so we rested. It is only natural that we welcome it with joy."

Amelia frowned, "Of course, because it is great to have a day where everything is forbidden!"

"It is not a case of being forbidden," argued Beruriah. "It is a case of forcing us to rest, and to be free from the restraints and worries that imprison us during the week. It is our own day to be free from chores and work."

"Yes; but maybe some of us would actually like to do stuff on our day off."

"But that is the point," argued Beruriah, quietly but firmly. "We are not supposed to be doing anything but resting—we have six days to go out to restaurants, to go to the park or the beach, to take a yoga class or to sell just one more diamond. Shabbat is to be different from all the other days, and in not doing anything we are reminded that the day is special. That it is the most special day. Every time we remember that we cannot do something, we remember why we are not doing it and that it turns us or brings us to G-d. For he created the *Shabba*t for us to rest in; it was a gift not a burden."

Amelia didn't look convinced, but then she wouldn't agree with Beruriah on principle, even if what she said made perfect sense.

I liked the idea that G-d had created a special day for us to rest on. A day when we could put aside the modern world and just focus on each other and G-d. One day when we could really be free...well free from everything but our thoughts. If only it were possible to put a Shabbat ban on them.

~~

Dinner was special. As if it were someone's birthday. The children had had their hair brushed, the girls' hair was braided and Dana had found a piece of colorful ribbon for each braid, and they all wore their best clothes. The

166

majority of them were hand-me-downs or second-hand, but they were clean and neat and the children were dressed as if for a special occasion.

The table was full of food and everyone ate and chatted with high spirits as if knowing this was the last chance before the quiet and calm of Shabbat started.

I couldn't think of anything better than having this holiday to look forward to every week. It was how I imagined a Christian or a little kid would feel about Christmas—excited and so special, and yet here we had it every week.

Chapter 11—Amelia

It was strange, having to celebrate every holiday. I'd never realized before how many of them there were. At home Papa had rarely been there, and we'd celebrated the holidays depending on Mama's mood. Some holidays she would be full of holiday spirit and would get out the candlesticks days before the holiday and start polishing them; she'd have our housekeeper baking holiday food, more than any of us could ever eat; and she'd invite friends and family around for the day, or night.

Other holidays she would be in a dark mood and would either forget the holiday even existed or she would cry her way throughout the holiday dinner that I had tried to finish.

~~

Rosh Hashanah was one holiday which, when Mama decided to celebrate, we celebrated in real style. New clothes for us all were always the priority; and she'd whirl us through Benetton, and Diesel, and Mango and Max Mara. Some years, she would insist that Papa take us to Paris to do our new clothes shopping and she'd whirl us through clothes shops and boutiques there.

She'd make the housekeeper take out the best china, and the table would groan under the weight of the food especially cooked for the holiday. And there'd be friends and family in their best clothes; diamonds glittering; pearls dazzling…. Soft music would play, sometimes jazz, something purely instrumental and people would gather about with champagne glasses in their hands discussing the stock market and the state of Israel's museums, and the peace process.

Papa always seemed to be home for the Rosh Hashanah—as if it was the one concession he made to family life, and to Mama. As if playing the role of husband and father on the holiday made up for all the times he wasn't there, and for all the women.

He was always the one who proposed a toast to the new year—and the champagne glasses would clink; and a toast to Mama, the prettiest lady there—and again the champagne glasses would clink and Mama would blush with pleasure, a smile reaching right across her face as she sat at the head of the table in her new gown from Paris. G-d knows how many valium she had to swallow to make it through the night, but she always did.

It used to make me think—maybe this year would be different. Maybe it meant a new start. But our happy family never stayed together long. With the holiday over, it didn't take long for Papa to need to be back in Paris for business, and for Mama to spend whole days in her dressing gown, crouched on the sofa with her valium on the table in front of her.

"Oh," said Dana, close to tears, "What a sad story!"

"I don't know," I said. "There are happy memories in there."

Rachel looked sad too and even Beruriah looked sympathetic.

"What?" I demanded, "It wasn't all bad." I threw the quartered apple pieces onto the plate in front of me and grabbed another whole apple to cut up.

We were sitting round the table, each of us with a pile of apples in front of us; each of us with a knife—and in the middle a rapidly growing pile of apple pieces filled the plate.

"It would be nice to buy all of our children new clothes," said Dana, slightly wistfully.

"Well we can't," snapped Beruriah." So there's no point in wishing."

Dana smiled bravely, "No; of course not."

"It'll take everything we've got just to feed everyone."

"Of course," replied Dana.

"Anyway there is more to the holiday than new clothes and food," insisted Beruriah. "We need to reflect on any past mistakes, and look to the future, and to G-d."

Chapter 12—Amelia

Yom Kippur was one holiday Mama always remembered. Perhaps because it was such a depressing one.—It gave her an excuse to be miserable, again.

"Depressing?" asked Rachel as we congregated in the kitchen.

The rain beat against the windows and Dana set up board games on the table for the older children, and crayons and paper for the younger ones.

"Depressing," I said, taking out the monopoly board from the box Dana had pushed at me. "Who wants to be the car?" Three hands shot up.

"Is Yom Kippur supposed to be depressing?" asked Rachel, as she counted out paper money for the children. "I don't remember the Rabbi at home ever using that word before."

"I don't think 'depressing' is the right word," said Dana handing out chocolate biscuits. I took three.

Beruriah shook her head as she distributed glasses of milk. "No; 'depressing' is not the right word."

I shrugged my shoulders, and threw the card at Shoshanna. "It always was in our house."

"So what is the right word then?" asked Rachel

"Solemn," came Beruriah.

"Reflective," added Dana, "It can't be depressing because Yom Kippur is not without hope—Yom Kippur is the last day when you can get your name taken off G-d's book of judgment, so you still have a chance."

"Assuming you have asked atonement for your sins against others," argued Beruriah. "We have to do that first, and then on Yom Kippur we can ask atonement from G-d for the sins we have committed against him." Why her eyes rested on me during this speech I will never know—interfering old bat!

"So fasting is a way of asking for atonement?" asked Rachel, looking confused. Dana pushed a cookie into her hand, as if that would appease her curious mind.

"Something like that," agreed Beruriah. "With no food we can concentrate on what is important—atoning for our sins, rather than focusing on the 'pleasures of the flesh'. If we fast we have no other temptations."

Rachel took an absent-minded bite of her cookie. And just as absent-mindedly threw back the dice that had escaped from the monopoly board and over to her arm.

"Well it's depressing to have to fast," I said through a mouthful of cookies.

"It's only one day," argued Dana. "It's not much of a sacrifice."

"No," said Beruriah, "It's not." And she gave me a look as if daring me to refuse to fast, the following day.

But I wouldn't give her the satisfaction of another argument. I shrugged my shoulders, partly because I knew it would annoy her, and partly because I didn't know what else to do. "Whatever."

"And we pray," said Beruriah. "Almost the whole day, we pray."

Chapter 13—Rachel

Five days after Yom Kippur the atmosphere of the house changed—as if someone had opened the door and let the light in.

The children begged to be able to build a *sukkah*.— There was plenty of space in the plot of land outside and they would help collect the materials to build it.

"OK, OK!" cried Beruriah. "Let's build a *sukkah*!"

"A collective cheer went up—the eldest cheered for having broken down authority so easily and the youngest cheered to join in with the noise and general feeling of celebration.

Dana took the eldest children on a hunt around the neighbourhood for old pieces of wood. "Look out for nails!" she called, "And watch out for splinters! ... Rachel, do you want to help?"

"Sure I said," grabbing the other end of a piece of wood that Dana's daughter, Tamar, was trying to drag along behind her.

It was fun. The eldest children ran ahead and whooped with joy every time they found a big enough piece of wood. Dana checked each piece for its suitability—making sure it wasn't too old, too wet, that it didn't have too many nails. And then we helped them drag the wood back to the house where Beruriah, Amelia and the younger children were trying to work out how to get the *sukkah* to stand.

"It needs two and a half walls," commanded Beruriah. "Let's use the wall of the house as one of the walls and then use the wood for the other walls. We need something for the roof," she called out. "But remember only *sekhakh* can be used for the roof."

I looked puzzled and one of the elder children whispered to me, "She means we can only use things that grow in the ground, and that we cut off from wherever

173

they are growing—you know branches and sticks and stuff." And he dragged me to a tree at the end of the plot and proceeded to collect sticks from its bottom.

Beruriah oversaw the *sukkah*'s construction while the rest of us watched it come together.

"Her father was a carpenter," Dana confided in me. Then, "It needs decorating!" she cried, rushing inside to collect paints and brushes and crayons. She began directing the children in the drawing of *etrog* and *lulav*, *aravot* and *hadassim*. She handed me a brush dripping with green paint. "You too," she said.

Not one painting or drawing would have made an Old Master—or even a good art teacher—very happy; but as the children showed off their masterpieces to their respective Ima, each managed to display enough pride to please every child.

"Leaves for the floor!" cried Dana, as she led the children on a leaf-collecting mission, like some female pied-piper.

And they returned, plastic bags overflowing with green, yellow, brown and red leaves.

"The floor, on the floor!" cried Beruriah and Dana together, as the children and Amelia pelted each other with the leaves and the roof began to tremble.

Promises to let each and every child eat their dinner in the *sukkah* got the floor finished and then the children lay in the leaves, side by side, admiring their handiwork. Just enough space in the roof let the stars be seen in the night sky, while still allowing the shade to dominate over the light within the *sukkah*.

"It's not bad!" enthused Amelia.

"It's great!" insisted Dana.

"Pretty good!" said Beruriah, "I like it."

"It's fantastic!" I added. And it was.

~~

Later that night, with the children in bed and after he had given his approval to our efforts, Dana suggested that

174

we take our turn in the *sukkah*. "We are suppose to spend as much time in it as possible," she coaxed.

And so we crowded in, each looking forward to a night under the stars, and we settled into the imprints left by the children's smaller bodies.

Dana moved from picture to picture that adorned the walls, lingering just a little longer on the ones her own children had painted. Having admired their work yet again, she sank into the leaves. "We never had a *sukkah* in Russia," she said. And then by way of explanation, "It wasn't a good idea to advertise that we were Jewish and, well, a *sukkah* would have been a bit of a give-away." She grinned, which was unusual when she talked about Russia. But she smiled again. "Papa use to make one inside, under the dining table with old sheets hanging down. It used to drive Mama crazy but we loved it. He even let us eat in there," and she smiled again at the memory. "He called it our Jewish haven."

"Papa used to bring ours from France," said Amelia deciding to join in on the storytelling, "It was ready-made, you just had to assemble it.—He used to get the gardener to put it together, while we watched." She tore a leaf into tiny pieces as she spoke.

Beruriah took my hand and smiled, it was an evening of smiles. "Yes. It used to take us all day to drag enough wood home for a *sukkah* big enough for all of us," and her smile turned into a laugh.

Dana turned to me, keen to keep the story-telling ball rolling, "How about you Rachel, what's your *sukkah* story?"

I shrugged my shoulders, "I don't have one." It was my turn to shred a leaf to pieces.

"Come on!" demanded Amelia. "It doesn't have to be a happy memory. My Mama used to refuse to eat or even sit in our *sukkah*—'too many insects' she said, so Lucille and I use to play and eat in it for hours. We used to steal wine from the cabinet for the blessings and say them ourselves, or what we could remember." She laughed, "That must have been the first place I got drunk."

Even Beruriah smiled; it was that kind of an evening.

"And Papa would scream at her that he'd brought the damn thing all the way from France, and that he hadn't lugged it all the way just for her to refuse to sit in it. We kept it up for months, though, as a playhouse."

"But I have no memories, good or bad. We never had a *sukkah*. My parents would never remember when the Sukkot holiday was supposed to be, and probably never would have celebrated it even if they had known."

"Oh," cried Dana, "How sad! We thought we had it tough having to make do with a *sukkah* inside, but even that is better than no *sukkah* at all!"

"But you have a memory now, Rachel," said Beruriah. "This *sukkot* can be your first *sukkah* story."

They all smiled at me, and I had to admit, "That would be perfect. Thanks." And it was.

Dana took my hand in hers. Amelia slapped me on the back and Beruiah smiled over us all like some kind of mother-hen.

~~

This is it, I thought, this is my Jewish family. I have finally found them. This is where the real memories start.

~~

"It's a memory for you," interjected Beruriah, as if she could read my thoughts, "And it's also a memory for every child in the Family."

Dana nodded, and Amelia turned away.

"You see if you have one child—well that's a memory for one child—but with so many children we have so many memories to set them on their way. Rather than just one getting a happy memory, now eight do and the happiness is shared."

"And if one gets a crappy memory, they all get one too," was Amelia's contribution.

"Life is full of ups and downs," replied Beruriah. "Everyone has to learn that."

"Sure, if you're going to fuck up the life of one child, why not fuck up the lives of as many as possible!"

Dana frowned at Amelia's choice of language.

"Oh relax Dana, there are no kids here," Amelia scowled back.

"But we have no intention of ruining any child's life," insisted Dana. "In fact, quite the opposite."

"The more children," said Beruriah, "The more opportunities we have to make the lives of those children great and happy."

"Or bloody awful," insisted Amelia, "The more lives you have to ruin."

"But it's so much better to take the risk," argued Dana, "And to try to do good, isn't it?"

Beruriah nodded and I wanted to join in. "A bad childhood doesn't have to define you forever," argued Beruriah.

Dana nodded slightly as if she wanted to believe that, but not sure if she fully could yet.

"Yeah?" scoffed Amelia.

"But what defines a bad childhood?" I asked. "I mean, is it not having enough to eat? Or abusive parents, or another abusive family member? Or just parents who think they are doing the best for you, but who somehow manage to get it completely and utterly wrong?"

"Children are a blessing," declared Beruriah, as if to cut the argument short. "They are a blessing bestowed by G-d. They are a present from G-d, a favour from G-d."

Dana nodded and Amelia sighed, "Do we have to sit through another bible lesson?"

"It's sad though," Dana said. "In the Torah, I mean, there are so many women who can't have children."

"But they have them in the end, when G-d allows them."

"Yes, but that's a little sad. I mean you have all these women who adore their husbands and their husbands adore them and yet they can't have children. They tell their husband to go sleep with someone else to have children and within days that mistress or concubine is pregnant. It's sad."

"It's insane," cried Amelia. "What kind of a person won't give someone a child when they want one, but will let their man sleep around to get one. It's bullshit."

"Amelia!" cried Beruriah.

But Amelia was defiant. "Well it is! It's bullshit!"

Beruriah frowned.

"It's not very nice," said Dana more tactfully.

"Sad," I agreed.

"It is G-d's way."

"Oh for crying out loud!"

"Enough!" cried Beruriah.

And that was it.

Chapter 14—Dana

They say that *Chanukah* is the holiday for the Jews of the disapora. That the Jews of the disapora have taken *Chanukah* and made it a much more important holiday than it was ever supposed to be because it falls in the same month as Christmas. That *Chanukah* is the weapon for the Jews of the Diaspora, in their attempts to prevent Christmas from invading their homes, and their children.

~~

Maybe that is why Mama and Papa always made such a big deal of it. On each of the eight days we lit the candle, one night I did it, the next night Anton, so that we each got to light four candles each.

"Careful, careful!" cried Papa as I held the flickering *shammus* in front of me. As steadily as I could, I brought the flame to the candle and watched the wick blaze alight.

Anton clapped his hands in glee, and even Mama smiled as Papa took her hand.

There were *latkes* to munch and *dreidels* to spin.

"The story, Papa!" I cried to him as we sat down to dinner, "Tell us the story!"

Papa smiled, "What, now?"

"Oh yes please, Papa! Now!"

Papa smiled again, "OK, well here goes....A very, very long time ago there was a very, very bad King called Antiochus."

"How bad was he, Papa?" I asked.

"Oh very bad," he assured me, "He treated our Jewish ancestors very, very badly."

"Worse than they treat us now, Papa?" I asked

Papa smiled, "As bad as that and may be worse."

Mama grimaced. She was never comfortable when Papa criticized society in front of us. We would be better off being taught to fit in with society rather than shun it.

"So what did the Jewish people do then, Papa?"

179

"Well, some very brave men known as Matthias, Maccabee and members of the *Chasidim* revolted."

"What's that?" asked Anton

"It means they decided to fight the very bad King and all of his supporters."

"Oh," cried Anton, the thought of fighting very appealing to him—as appealing as the idea that Papa's story was sanctioning fighting, something Anton was regularly getting told off for doing.

"And did they win, Papa?" I asked, knowing that they did, but never quite believing it until Papa confirmed it.

"They did, Dana. They did. Even though they were so much weaker and so very much fewer in numbers. They were brave enough to beat Antiochus and his men and all their weapons."

Anton squealed with delight and threw himself into the cushions on the sofa, "Hooray," he cried, "Hooray, hooray!"

And Papa smiled.

"And then what Papa?" I asked.

"Well, they went to the Temple to light the candles, but they only had enough oil to last a day."

"And?"

"And do you know what—that little bit of oil lasted for eight days. It was a…"

"Miracle!"—Anton and I finished his sentence for him.

"A miracle." he said. "Just like you two." And he hugged us to him. Our Papa. Our *Chanukah*.

Chapter 15—Amelia

Purim—now that was my kind of holiday!

"It's great!" I cried. "You get to drink as much alcohol as you want. You are practically ordered to drink as much alcohol as you want and that's how you celebrate *Purim*."

Rachel looked confused, Beruriah frowned and Dana—ever the peace-maker—smiled,

"You are supposed to get so drunk that it's impossible to tell the difference between Haman and Moredechai, but it's not mandatory."

"I always treated it as mandatory."

"Yes, we have no doubt that you did," sniped Beruriah as she wiped glitter from the table.

"Drinking? Really?" said Rachel, "That seems a little crazy."

"And G-d forbid that we should ever do anything crazy," I cried back.

"No, I mean, crazy for a religion to allow. I mean a lot of religions see alcohol as bad."

"As they should," replied Beruriah. "It's just for *Purim*, and it isn't mandatory. It certainly won't be in this house this *Purim*."

~~

"Now this is a holiday," I cried as I entered into the kitchen and saw the children gathered around the table, making their masks for *Purim*.

"Mmm, nice," I tried to say enthusiastically, as a brat shoved what apparently was suppose to be a mask in my face; one of the eyes was lopsided and the rest of the face was covered in so much glitter I had no idea what it was suppose to be.

"Do you want to make one?" asked Dana as she passed more glitter to the brat who had just covered me in it.

"No thanks," I said' heading for the fridge.

Rachel patiently helped the little ones glue eyes into place and suggest possible colour co-ordinations and extra decorations.

"It's fun," she said.

I brought my chocolate milk to the table, "No thanks, I'll just watch."

Glitter flew everywhere.

"Beruriah is going to kill you all," I commented, as yet more glitter and scraps of paper landed on the floor.

"We'll clean it up," replied Dana.

"You'd better. Anyway where is she?"

"Gone to her mother's for Haman's ears."

The glittery mask was once again shoved in my face for inspection, by glitter-covered hands, "Mmmm, nice—don't you think it needs more glitter?" To which the "artist" agreed and proceeded to throw more glitter everywhere.

"Wouldn't it just be easier to buy them?"

"Amelia! Where is the fun in buying the masks? Anyway this is a great creative activity for the children, and while we work I'm going to tell them the story of Esther, Mordechai and Haman."

"My cue to leave!" And I stood up as if to go.

"Don't be silly! Stay! It's a nice story."

I sank back down in my chair. It wasn't as if I had anywhere to go. And no stereo, television or computer in my room to lose myself in.

Rachel handed me a round piece of pink-coloured card,

"Here, make a mask!"

"The story!" cried one of the brats, "Tell us the story!"

Dana took a deep breath, "Once, a long, long time ago..."

"How long ago?" piped up another brat.

"Oh, thousands of years ago."

"Before I was born?"

"Of course."

"Before I was born?"

"Of course."

I sighed and reached for the glitter—this was going to take awhile.

"Once upon a time, before anyone of us was born— before Sara was born, before Shoshanna was born, before Yonathan was born, before Rivka was born, before Yeshua was born, before Tamar was born, before Yuval was born, before Isaac was born—there lived a very pretty girl called Esther. She lived with her uncle Mordechai. One day Esther won a competition, and the King of the land chose her as the most beautiful lady he had ever seen. The King liked Esther very much."

"Boohoo," shouted the almost teenaged Yonatan, not yet made awkward by spots and angst. He pretended to kiss the back of his hand until I yanked the back of his hair and he stopped.

"Ow!" he cried looking at me with hurt eyes.

I put my finger to my lips, "Sssh, listen to the story!"

"Unfortunately there was a very bad man who lived in the land. His name was Haman."

And here the older children filled the room with "boo"s and screams.

Yuval burst into tears at the noise and burrowed her way into Dana's lap where she kept her head down for the rest of the story.

"He was jealous that Esther and Mordechai were the King's friends and so he made the King make a law that would put to death all Jewish men."

The room was silent as the children's eyes widened at the thought of such a law.

"This would mean that Mordechai would be put to death too. So Esther went to the King and told him that it was Mordechai who had once saved his life...."

"I have them!" cried Beruriah as she entered the room her arms taken up by a giant box. She placed it carefully on the table as the children begged to be able to eat just one *Haman's ear* tonight.

"Just one!" Beruriah cried, giving into the pleas of the children. And a smile crossed her face as they gathered around to take a pastry. She looked almost human.

I took two from the box and went to make off with them.

"One!" Beruriah cried, her face twisted and distorted again—definitely not human anymore. I threw one back into the box and Beruriah sighed.

Dana, ever the peacemaker, picked up the pastry I had thrown back and took a bite.

"These are fantastic," she exclaimed.

Beruriah managed to smile again, "Yes, mother had just finished them when I got there."

"Great!" cried Rachel, eager to please.

"Mmm," I said. They were good, but why give smug Beruriah the satisfaction? It wasn't even as if she had made them. Her slave of a mother had.

"Ima, Dana told us the story of Esther," Sara told Beruriah as she sat down.

"Well that's wonderful! Did you all enjoy it?"

They chorused, "Yes!" and started their whinging for another Haman's ear.

"No, I said one; and one you have had. Come on, it's bath time!" and she began herding the brats out of the kitchen and up the stairs.

We trooped up after her, it took all of us to get eight brats washed and into bed.

Beruriah and Dana were on bath duty, Rachel and I on pajama and tucking into bed duty.

The little ones came first—clean for the first time that day, their hair still damp, the smell of soap and bubbles still clung to them. I pulled arms and legs through the holes in their pajamas and let Rachel help them up into bed and tuck the duvet around them. She planted a kiss on each forehead and whispered good night to eyes already closing shut.

The bigger ones came with protests and wails, "But it's so early, why do we have to go to bed so early?"

"Bed!" Commanded Beruriah, and her word was law.

It did seem bloody ridiculous for them all to be in bed so early. I mean who went to bed at seven thirty? But it was Beruriah's rule and we all had to follow her rules. "Heil Hitler!" I would have said behind her back if it had been funny. But being all Jewish, I guess it wasn't very funny. A bit like holocaust jokes. My high school playground had been awash with them. You would have thought a bunch of Jewish kids who lost grandparents to the event would have had more sense than to find holocaust jokes amusing. I still don't know if anyone ever actually made them funny; or if they were seen as some kind of really cool, ironic thing to do—Jewish people making fun of the holocaust. And yet in some countries to deny, or belittle, or support the holocaust was illegal—a sign of what a tremendous happening it was. And yet across Israel thousands of high school kids were making jokes about it. I guess that was one way of dealing with what happened back then.

We went on a trip when I was in high school to Auschwitz. Ever since then I hadn't been able to hear a joke about it. Because when you get there, you realize how it never was, nor ever could be, something to laugh about. There isn't much left of the camp. Just a few ruins. But there is an air about the place that just isn't right. As soon as you get within a few kilometres of the place you can feel it—a stillness, a darkness, a heaviness that is just different from how the air feels everywhere else. As if the air holds all of what happened there, so no-one can forget. When I think back on that visit now, all I see is grey and us trying to walk through that heaviness, but feeling it pushing back at us with every step we took. We wrapped ourselves in Israeli flags and cried, in part because it was the thing to do. Photographers from some European newspaper took our photo. It was weird to think that, so many years later, here we were—Jewish children—wrapped in the flag of a Jewish state, standing on the ground where other Jews once stood and died on. I bet they never would have believed that we would be there. That's the kind of stuff that made me feel. Not the crap Mama was always shoving down my throat about our famous ancestors. But the feeling you get when you walk amongst the ruins of a camp where thousands of men, women and children were gassed to death; starved to death; shot to death; starved to death. That's creepy—I can't quite believe I am standing here—stuff. That I am standing here where someone died, or even just where someone in history stood—be they a Nazi or a Jew. I couldn't get my head around it, and yet it was so obvious standing there, that this had been a place where something horrible had happened. You could just feel it.

"What are you thinking about?" asked the intuitive Sara as she climbed into bed.

"Nothing," I replied.—Beruriah and Dana would kill me if I gave the children nightmares.

"You looked sad," the nosey little beast said.

"Go to sleep," I told her and got up to leave the room.

A series of "good night"s chorused around the room and I left turning off the light and shutting the door behind me.

~~

I had to admit *Purim* was fun. So the children might not have won any best fancy dress costume prizes, but they looked OK, and they didn't seem to mind that everything was second-hand, or home-made.

~~

His reading of the *megillah* went on a bit. He stood in the living room, under the portrait of some dreary Yemenite landscape, with the story in front of him, and read it all.

186

Missing none out. His voice deadly serious, as he worked his way through the story of Esther, her uncle and Haman.

The children—an array of tigers, princesses, Buzz Light-years, and other beasts and characters—screamed and shook their noisemakers every time his voice said out loud Haman's name.

The atmosphere was obviously infectious and Rachel shook her noisemaker as hard as any of the children, and even joined in their yelps and shouts. She sat on the floor with the rest of us, Princess Tamar in her lap.

Dana flashed me a huge smile as she waved Isaac's arm as his podgy hand clasped his noisemaker. I managed some kind of a smile back.

Dana of course was in costume, Rachel had a mask, and even Beruriah had some brightly-coloured party hat on that some child had made for her.

~~

"This is so much fun," cried Rachel. "So much better than any other *Purim* I've had!" and she seemed genuinely happy.

I sat watching a rapidly disappearing plate of Haman's ears as the children crammed them into their mouths, spraying crumbs everywhere. I grabbed one from under the fingers of someone's snotty brat, ignoring their wails of protest.

"Really?" I said, not very interested in another of Rachel's sob stories about her lack of Jewish-holiday memories,

"We celebrated *Purim* in Asia once, with *Chabad*, but it wasn't the same. Mom and I went to Hong Kong once with Dad on a business trip and I wanted to celebrate *Purim* so we found *Chabad* and we went there."

I could barely hear her amongst the noise of the children with their noisemakers and some music Dana had put on.

"There were a lot of Israelis there, a lot of children; but it was different somehow."

"How?" asked Dana, always keen to draw Rachel out.

"I don't know. People didn't seem to be there to celebrate the holiday, but more so that they would be able to *say* that they'd celebrated the holiday—and that they'd made sure their children had celebrated it too. The *megillah* was read, everyone ate and then left. It was bit empty I guess."

"So," started Beruriah, "The question Rachel is asking is: is it enough to turn up and go through the motions of celebrating the holiday, or does more need to be done to feel and understand it?"

Dana looked up. She was stapling string to the back of a tiger's mask, that had come off in the excitement of the party, "No you must feel it!"

~~

It was a little weird. I looked around at the party that filled the living room and realized how strange it was that it was just the Family. I don't know, the children screaming and running around high on sugar didn't seem to notice the absence of anything—nor the absence of other playmates. Did I miss that? Did it matter? Was family, was this family enough? My own family had never been enough. But was this one? And if they were, was that OK? Family was kind of unfashionable in the modern world. I mean, tune into any popular TV show anywhere in the world and where were the families? Nowhere to be seen! Groups of friends relied on each other. And yet here I was in the middle of the opposite. Here family was the only thing.

Two extremes. Some shrink the school had once sent me to had said that I was only happy when I was living an extreme. Well this family was one hell of an extreme. 'Way to go, Amelia!' I thought. God, the shrinks would be pleased with themselves!

Chapter 16—Beruriah

It was the night before the eve of *Pesach*. We gathered around the kitchen table as I directed the rest in preparing the *Seder* plate for tomorrow's dinner. The *Seder* plate had been my great grandmother's, one of the few things she'd managed to smuggle out of Yemen. It was silver and well polished and it had been on every *Pesach* table I had ever known.

Dana was in charge of the *beitzah* and I could see the eggs roasting nicely in the oven. The lamb bone from dinner lay all ready to be used.

Amelia and Rachel were washing the parsley and *marror* together, at least Rachel was, Amelia stood next to the sink pretending to be busy, but she fooled no-one and didn't seem to care whether she did or not.

The *charoset* was my specialty and all I had left to do was combine the apple, nuts, cinnamon and dash of wine to bind the marror together.

With the eggs roasted, Dana turned to the *Seder* plate and *Kiddush* cup and offered to polish both. I gave her the *Seder* plate and Amelia the cup to polish. Dana began with a nod and a smile; Amelia scowled and scuffed her feet as she found a chair.

~~

"Let's tell how we made it to Israel!" cried Dana enthusiastically polishing away at the plate with all her might.

Amelia made a face into the *Kiddush* cup, "Storytelling? Again?" she groaned.

Dana looked hurt, "We don't have to."

"No, "I interrupted. "I think we should share it, especially tonight. It will help us connect with the Exodus story tomorrow."

Amelia rolled her eyes, and only I seemed to catch the evil twinkle in them, "Shall I tell you mine?"

I nodded. Heaven only knows what she would come up with.

"Well Papa took his trousers off, and Mama took her dress off and I'm guessing her knickers too and...."

I closed my eyes, "Amelia, enough! Must you ruin everything with your inability to behave like an adult?"

Amelia just smiled a rather infuriating secret smile to herself and began her tale with a laugh. "My Papa's parents came here from Switzerland after the war. They were from France until they decided that Hitler and his goons were getting a little too close to France for comfort. My great-grandfather had a lot of business contacts in Switzerland and they helped him move there. When Israel was founded he saw it as a business opportunity—a new country, plenty of new money to be made. But my grandmother always hated it here and when he retired they went back to France."

"And your mother's parents?" asked Rachel, accepting the hot tea Dana brought around on a tray.

Amelia reached for her cup of hot tea, stretching her arm out for a biscuit too, "Do I have to tell?"

"Why not?" asked Beruriah.

Amelia sighed and took a bite of her biscuit as if to fortify her for the story ahead, "My mother's grandparents were Zionists, they moved to Israel from Poland when it was still Palestine. Sometime in the 1920s. They helped fight against the British. My great-grandfather was a farmer, they helped to start a Kibbutz, and my great-grandmama was a teacher.

"Wow," said Rachel, "They helped found Israel."

"I guess," Amelia replied, cramming the rest of her biscuit in her mouth and reaching for another one.

"You're not proud of that?" asked Dana reaching for a biscuit too.

"Proud of what? It's not as if I founded a nation. They did. What has it got to do with me?" and she dunked the biscuit in her tea.

"I would think," I added, "That you would be proud to have such brave, principled people as your ancestors. As Jewish people we pride ourselves on the direct link between each of us to our courageous and morally strong ancestors—the matriarchs, for example. Your great-grandparents helped to carry on that tradition."

"It's too much to live up to," replied Amelia by way of explanation.

"But of course," I cried, "We all, as Jews, have a lot to live up to. We are the direct descendents of Sara, Rebecca, Rachel, and Leah. We are the chosen people, and so that's a responsibility we bear and enjoy everyday whether we have famous great-grandparents or not."

Amelia shrugged her shoulders, "It's not a burden I like to have."

"No, we don't always like it," I agreed more gently.— She was just a kid after all.—"But whether we like it or not, it's ours to carry."

"It's difficult though," agreed Rachel. "I guess I'm trying to work out just what the burden is and how best to carry it. My parents tossed it away pretty easily, but I'm pretty sure I want to keep and remember it. I can't seem to be able to toss it away. Not that I want to," she added hurriedly.

"So how did you get here?" Amelia asked Rachel, although more from a desire to turn the spotlight from herself, than any interest in Rachel's story.

"By airplane from New York," said Rachel matter-of-factly. "It's not very dramatic or exciting—no fleeing from any Pharaoh, no fleeing from any Nazis."

"So your parents," encouraged Dana, "How did they make it to America? If America is their promised land, then their journey to America was their exodus."

All of our eyes turned to Rachel who blushed at the sudden attention, "It's not very exciting either," she stammered.

"Oh just tell us!" cried Amelia.

I shot her a look and she shrugged her shoulders.

"Go on!" I prompted.

Rachel took a deep breath, "Both sets of my great-grandparents came from Poland. They left for America sometime in the nineteenth century...at the end of it, I think. They all lived in New York first and then later Florida and then they moved to where we are now. They were all pretty desperate to assimilate and so never really lived anywhere with a big Jewish population. My parents met at college in New York. It was just an accident that they were both Jewish; something they discovered later. They lived in New York for a few years and then when they wanted to start a family they moved to our town." She looked apologetic, as if the story wasn't worthy of a place in our midst.

"But their journey to America would have been dramatic," insisted Dana. "I mean in those days a journey like that would have been tremendous. And there must have been something that made them all leave Poland, maybe the pogroms?"

Rachel's face brightened a little, "I guess I never thought of it like that. I always figured, because they left Europe so early, they escaped the real persecution, you know."

"So are we saying," I began, "That to be Jewish we, or our families, have to have suffered in their need to survive? Are we saying that a lack of suffering makes us less Jewish? We all know how our people have been made to suffer, but are we now making that a prerequisite for being really Jewish?

My words brought silence.

"I'm just thinking aloud." I explained. "What does everyone think?"

"I guess," started Rachel, "I've always thought that my family couldn't be really Jewish because they haven't really suffered. I mean they fled to America before Europe got really dangerous and they have had nothing to do with the fight to build and keep Israel. I supposed that, without that suffering, I never really had a right to be properly Jewish."

"But you're here, aren't you?" said Dana, "Living in Israel as a Jew?"

"Yesssss.....but sometimes I feel like an imposter, as if I don't really belong and everyone can see that I'm just pretending."

"But that's awful!" cried Dana. "If you are born Jewish and if you practise and live as a Jew, well, then you are Jewish! Why must we always link Judaism and suffering? Why can't we be Jews without having to suffer all the time? Isn't that why we have Israel; why we have our own homeland, so that the suffering can finally end? I'm tired of suffering. My children will be Jewish. They will be Israeli. And they will not be sufferers." And her eyes blazed as she spoke, as if directing her passionate speech at an imagined form of suffering.

"Yeah! Until they get blown up by some crazy Palestinian or shot by one!" cried Amelia.

Dana winced, we all knew about Anton. I shot Amelia another stern look for her insensitivity and she scowled back at me. "What, I can't say what I think?" she demanded to know.

"Not if it hurts a sister, no."

"I'm only saying what's true. Just because we live in our own country we don't suffer? Hello? Human bombs in coffee shops and weddings. Um—hello, how about kidnapped soldiers, settlers shot at, rockets aimed at kindergartens?"

"She has a point," agreed Rachel.

"Thanks for the support!—Is that why you came here, finally to be able to suffer?" Amelia's words were cold and taunting.

"Amelia, that's enough!"

"Why am I the only one not allowed to have an opinion?" she wailed.

"You can have an opinion," I insisted. "Just stop using your opinions purposefully to hurt others."

Amelia sniffed and Rachel to her right looked hurt,

"I didn't come here to suffer. I just wanted to understand more about being Jewish. It's not something you as Israelis have to think about. Living here, your lives, your week, your schools, your supermarkets, your holidays are all naturally Jewish. It's not something you have to think about or actively do. It's just an obvious, unchangeable fact, regardless of how observant you are." Rachel looked pained, "I just want a little of that certainty, that confidence. That's all!" And then she looked apologetic.

I smiled, "Then welcome!" And I held out my hand for her to clasp, which she did gladly. Dana smiled and reached her hand forward to join ours. Amelia continued to sulk in her corner.

"How about Dana's story?" she demanded. "And yours?"

"I'll go first," offered Dana.

I nodded at her and she started. "My grandparents were Russian and also did their best to assimilate...." And, with that, she smiled at Rachel as if that bonded them. Rachel smiled back gratefully.

"They did everything except actually be baptized. But, as a teenager, my father discovered Judaism and the fact that he was Jewish, and soon became a devout Zionist, if not a devout Jew. My two sets of grandparents were great friends and my parents grew up together. They married, and just before we were born, my father made the decision to go public with his Judaism. It ruined his career and my mother's life. Things got even worse when he applied for visas for us to come here. The authorities refused to let us leave, and eventually my father gave up and killed himself." She said it calmly as if referring to a stranger, rather than a man I know she adored. "Not long after that they let us leave; so mother, Anton and I came. That was our exodus."

The room was silent, even Amelia was quiet.

~~

A break was needed I thought.

"Tea with *nana*?" I offered around.

Three heads nodded back.

"And some *bamba*!" Amelia cried.

~~

I placed the cups and *bamba* on the table, Amelia reached across for the orange packet and turned to me. "Your turn!" she insisted, as she crunched on her *bamba*.

I told them my mother's story. Of how she left Yemen. Of how she never meant to leave, but ended up here anyway. I told them about her Exodus. And we all went to bed with it fresh in our minds.

~~

Peasch or Passover.—It starts with the cleaning of the house. Amelia complaining and moaning with a mop in her hand; Dana encouraging the children to help with the sweeping and the dusting; Rachel scurrying about eager to help everywhere she could.

I stayed in the kitchen, clearing the cupboards and fridge of anything leaven. Stray pieces of pasta that lurked in the backs of cupboards, crusts of bread that had been dropped by little fingers down the side of the oven; half eaten cake from the fridge.

And then, later, we gathered again in the kitchen, the little ones swarming around. Dana checked on the lamb as she did so, roasting in its own juices, ready to provide the *z'roa* for our *Seder* plate, and to provide dinner for hungry tummies.

Rachel helped to combine the apple, nuts, cinnamon and wine for the *charoset* and, as we did so together, I explained to her and the children, how it represented the mortar used by our ancestors in Egypt as they toiled for the Pharaohs, but how we made it sweet, to represent the hope our ancestors had had, that one day they would be free.

"And the parsley?" she asked, as she brought it from the sink where Dana had been washing it.

"The green," I explained, "It symbolises hope." Then, speaking to one of Dana's children, "Yuval," I said, "Get me the salt!"

"And the salt?" she asked, as innocent and as ignorant as the very youngest Jewish child.

"We make salt water," I explained, "To represent the tears the Israelites cried while they were slaves.—The parsley is bitter," I added to my earlier explanation, "To remind us of how they suffered.—And also, I suppose," I added, "To remind us how lucky we are to be free."

"It is a good Pesach question to ask," I continued, noticing as I did so Amelia rolling her eyes as she plaited a little one's hair. It was a remarkably kind thing for her to do and I wondered if the holiday spirit had managed to get to her too.

"Are we really free?"

"Of course," sighed Amelia, reluctant to be drawn into what she called another 'Jewish' debate. "We're not slaves, are we?"

"No, perhaps not," I agreed. "But imprisonment doesn't always take on physical forms. Do we have to be bound by chains to be imprisoned? To not be free?"

Rachel looked thoughtful, and looked to Dana for support.

Dana shut the door of the oven and sat at the table. She looked across at me, "I know what you mean. We are all imprisoned by something.—For some people it is the pressures of work, a demanding boss, and a mortgage to pay. For others it is their family—a demanding family, or a family with a lot of problems, or with no money. For others it is their past—a bad experience, a traumatic childhood. Very few of us are able to do exactly what we want, when we want."

Rachel stared at Dana as if taking in words and ideas from an oracle.

Amelia looked unimpressed. "So?" she asked, pushing away the child whose hair she had plaited, with an impatient push. The little girl looked hurt at the sudden reversal of her fortunes and ran away to join the others in the garden. "How is celebrating Pesach going to help us with any of that?"

"By giving us time to think," I said. "By reminding us that we are physically freer than the Israelites were, but that at the same time we are all working towards our own freedom—be it physical or mental."

Ideas churned in Rachel's head, and the questions tried to form on her tongue, but she was scared of asking something stupid, of getting something wrong.

"Rachel?" I asked

"I'm just trying to understand what could imprison someone. I mean, if a woman, for example, is stuck in an abusive relationship...well, she wouldn't really be free, would she?"

"No," I agreed. "She would be a prisoner of her husband's brutality and her own inability to free herself. Pesach is a time to allow us to remember how brave the Israelites were in their bid for freedom, and perhaps can impress on us some of that bravery too."

Yonatan came in from outside. "Ima, I'm starving!" he cried at me. As my eldest male son, he had been fasting from the day before, to remind him of how he and his Jewish brothers had been saved, while his Egyptian counterparts perished in the tenth and final plague.

"Dinner will be soon," I reassured him and got up to start the preparations.

~~

The candles on the table glowed, shining their light over the food that decorated the table.

Was I free? My mother had never been free, nor her mother before her. Tradition and family had imprisoned them in their own version of slavery. But I was free, as they had never been. Free to love, to have my children, to lead this family.

And I was free to live. Something so many people I knew had lost. Like, Lilach—my sweet, innocent cousin Lilach.

She had wanted her baby born at home. No hospital. No sterile lights. No labyrinths of corridors. No gruff Doctors in their white coats.

"No hospital!" she continued to beg as the contractions came closer and closer together. She tried to smile, "No hospital!"

She paced the floor, hands on her lower back, teeth clenched. Sweat gathered on her forehead at what seemed to be an alarming rate and amount, and still she paced with the pain until it finally defeated her and she doubled up onto the floor.

"Let me call an ambulance!" I cried, my turn to beg, as she bent over the palms of her hands pushing onto the floor.

"No," she cried. "No hospital!"

A midwife was supposed to come, but she was stuck in traffic leaving Tel Aviv.

It was the Family's first baby. Or his first baby. He always counted Sara as his own, but it took me a while to count her as his.

Back when the Family was still very, very new. I'd been the first here but Lilach had joined me soon after, back when Sara had still squirmed and kicked inside me.

Lilach doubled over again and crouched on the floor breathing deeply.

I saw the blood first, but that was normal, wasn't it?

It soaked through her skirt, a dark stain spreading itself wider and wider.

"You're bleeding," I cried and then as the blood spread from her skirt to the floor, to the rugs, "Lilach, you're bleeding a lot."

Lilach was white—sweat continued to course down her face. She grabbed my hand and I winced at the shock of her grip. I helped her up, got her to the sofa, where blood dripped, trailing behind us. She lay against the arm of the sofa, her legs wide.

"Can you see anything?" she panted.

But there was just blood, a lot of blood.

"No," I whispered, "Let me call an ambulance, Lilach, please!"

She shook her head and bit her lip, "No, the midwife will be here soon. Everything will be fine, she just needs to get here."

By the time the midwife arrived, blood soaked everything surrounding Lilach—the sofa, the cushions, the floor, me.

Lilach didn't have the energy to talk. I held her white hand in mind and stroked her hair, as she learnt her head against my shoulder.

The midwife's face was serious as she calmly called for an ambulance. I asked her if everything was going to be OK, and she smiled at me softly and told me not to let go of Lilach's hand, to be there for her.

They placed Lilach in the back of an ambulance, and she didn't have the strength to protest. Ghostly pale, she could barely open her eyes. Now it was my turn to grip her hand.

I willed her better. I sent all the strong, healthy life vibes I could muster from my hand to hers; from my body to hers. I prayed and prayed, over and over, for her and the baby.

G-d doesn't make deals, I knew that, but I pleaded with him anyway. To be merciful, to be compassionate. I cried inwardly, and I prayed and prayed and prayed.

~~

Lilach died at the hospital. On a bed of blood-stained sheets. She'd lost too much blood, the young obstetrician told me. Her placenta had been too low and as the baby had tried to push her way out, the placenta had erupted and Lilach had bled to death. He was sorry, very sorry.

I couldn't bear to look at either of them—at Lilach or her little girl born dead.

I had the freedom of life that Lilach had lost, and that her little girl had never had.

Chapter 17—Beruriah

On *Rosh Chodesh* we came together much as we did every night when the children had been bathed and put to bed—something that required the skill and precision of a military operation.

It was the one night he was not allowed to call any of us. That was the agreement.

As the first day of the month, *Rosh Chodesh* was our day. The day for women. Something that was given to us because we did not join the men in the building and worshipping of the golden calf. Well, of course we didn't. The men got carried away and impatient waiting for Moses to return.—We didn't, as we were too busy nursing our babies, changing nappies and keeping our toddlers entertained, as well as preparing three meals a day, keeping the clothes clean, and our men happy. When did we have time for such frivolities as golden calves?

Anyway, we were rewarded for it with *Rosh Chodesh*. So it seemed only right that we took advantage of the gift and made it truly our own. Hence he was not allowed to call any of us that night.

Where we gathered was dictated by the weather. On warm evenings, we sat outside, each on a rickety plastic chair surrounded by weeds and toys. Sipping limonana from a big glass jug.

On cold evenings we sat around the kitchen table and drank hot cocoa and munched biscuits.

Each week I tried to get going a meaningful conversation—about Judaism, about G-d and women within our religion.

~~

"But men enjoy it, no matter who they screw," advised the ever knowledgeable Amelia, with the weight of more than twenty-four years of life-experience on her shoulders.

201

"...Although some women are like that too," she added and smiled to herself as if she were one of them.

"But a lot don't," insisted Dana. "For most of us, it takes some attachment, some feeling."

Rachel's head swiveled from Dana to Amelia, as if desperate to absorb all that they said.

"But that attachment is dangerous," said Amelia, "Because they screw you and then run off."

"And leave you holding the baby," finished Dana.

Amelia looked at Dana with surprise.

Dana looked back. "I was young and single in Tel Aviv once, as well."

"All of which makes a good argument for abstaining until you find your soul mate," I advised.

Amelia scoffed, "As if finding your soul mate makes a man less of a bastard."

"It's more difficult," said Dana quietly," To trust your judgment of them, then it is to trust them."

"So we are better off out of that silly game," I told them all, but looking at Rachel, as I spoke.

She gave me a small smile, "I guess so."

Dana nodded her head in agreement and Amelia characteristically shrugged her shoulders.

"I use to think," said Dana more to herself than to us, "that you had to go through the pain, to get to the happiness."

"You mean," interrupted Amelia, "You had to kiss a lot of frogs to find your prince."

"Something like that. But then I thought, what if there is no prince? Where is that guarantee?"

"In G-d," I added. "Everybody has a mate for life. It's preordained—one mate for each women, although a man may obviously have more than one soul-mate."

Amelia sighed, "You see even G-d approves of letting the bastards sleep around!"

I gave her a stern look and she slumped into the sofa.

Rachel looked confused, as if G-d sanctioned adultery.

"There is no approval for adultery," I explained. "But he approves of a man taking the wives preordained for him and of being faithful to each."

"Whatever!" was Amelia's intelligent reply.

Dana was quiet. "There's something to be said for arranged marriages," she finally said. And then as if by way of an explanation, "It saves the pain of kissing the frogs...saves the pain of being used and then spat out."

"Wow!" exclaimed Amelia, "Some asshole got you bad." And then, "They're not worth it," she insisted. "What do we need them for anyway?"

"For love, for comfort, for friendship, for a shared life and a family," said Dana, as if she had spent a lot of time and thought on that exact question.

Amelia wasn't convinced and disgust and doubt lingered on her face.

"For everything we have," I said smiling at them all, as if to include them all in my smile, in my Family—even the scowling Amelia.

~~

But Amelia had to have the last word.

"This is an honest conversation right?" she asked, taking us all in with her blue eyes. "We can say what we want, ask what we want?"

Dana looked unsure as if she expected Amelia to drop a firecracker in her lap. Rachel looked to me, unsure as ever.

I smiled thinly, "Of course, we are free to talk as sisters do."

"So," asserted Amelia, "that means no secrets, right?"

Dana shifted uncomfortably in her seat, as if Amelia had pulled a fire-cracker from somewhere and was just about to put the flame to it.

"Of course," I insisted, unsure of where Amelia was heading with her thoughts.

"Good, so tell us about the people who lived here before us. Tell us about your cousin!"

Judging from Dana's face and posture, Amelia had just put a flame to the fire-cracker and sent it spinning around the room. Rachel looked even more confused than usual, as if not understanding why a harmless question about someone's cousin would cause such tension in the room. She coughed as if to disperse the tension but it was too thick. It radiated out from me, from Amelia and now from Dana too.

"Amelia!" cried Dana, diverting herself from the squeals and shrieks and flashing lights of the fire-cracker. And then as if able to distract Amelia that quickly, "Anyone fancy something to eat, to drink? A game of cards maybe?"

But Amelia wasn't giving up that easily. She shrugged off Dana's words and faced me, much as a predator might face its prey in the Serengeti or other such environment. "No secrets?" she asked. But it was more a reminder to me of what I had just said about sisterhood and honesty, than a real question.

"She died," I replied flatly. I was trapped, and felt much as prey must feel when it realizes it has nowhere to run to, and even if it did, it couldn't run fast enough to escape anyway.

"Obviously," retorted Amelia. "But how? But why? And why is it such a big secret?"

"No secret," I replied. "You never knew her; I didn't think it was of any interest to you. She died giving birth, here in this house. The baby died too."

Dana's eyes welled with tears and Rachel looked uncomfortable. Only Amelia remained brazen, "So why the secrecy?"

"There is no secrecy," I insisted. "It was a long time ago. It didn't concern any of you. And it's over. She's gone."

"Oh Beruriah, I'm so sorry," Dana offered softly and I smiled in return. Rachel offered a smile of sympathy too; she hadn't the words to express herself, something of this magnitude being outside her range of experiences.

"In which room?" Amelia demanded to know.

"Amelia!" came Dana's shocked reply.

"What?" came Amelia's equally fierce reply. "I have a right to know, I could be sleeping in the same bed where someone died!"

"Amelia!"

"It's OK," I said. "She died in hospital."

"Enough!" claimed Dana. "This is ridiculous; this is Beruriah's private story. Amelia, shut up for once!"

The spirit of Dana's words took even Amelia aback.

And that was the end of it. It wasn't the end of Amelia and her challenges though.

~~

I spoke to him about Amelia.

I told him she wasn't with us because she believed in us—as a Jewish family; that her aim seemed to be solely to annoy her mother. He said, whatever her reasons were, they were for G-d alone and by choosing a relationship with him she had chosen G-d and that was his only concern. Why we chose G-d was not his concern; that we chose him was enough.

~~

"He loves her more because she's better at it."

"What? Better at what?"

"It."

"Dana!"

"Well, it's true."

"It's not true. Don't be ridiculous. Love is based on respect and friendship, not just that."

"So, he doesn't love her more. He just wants her more. She must be really good at it."

"Dana !"

"What? He's a man—aren't they all the same?"

205

"No! How could you compare him to other men? He is gentle and kind and loves us all equally."

"If you say so."

"I do!"

~~

We were a family, which meant we were all loved equally. So the younger ones could keep him amused for a little longer at night. But that wasn't the basis for everything. Maybe I resented them a little. I was once as young as them, as eager to please as them. But children and motherhood had weighed me down, shifted my priorities.

Chapter 18—Rachel

Another evening saw us gathered in the kitchen filling the time before bed with sewing, and baking, and cleaning— filling the space most people fill with television, with chores and tasks and talk.

~~

"I just want the best for my children," Dana said fiercely, as she struggled to sew back together another one of Yuval's dresses that had ripped itself on one of the stones that made up the older children's den at the back of the garden. Amelia had told her to forget it, to let her wear it ripped or throw it away. Only there wasn't money for a new one. And letting her daughter wear a ripped dress wasn't an option for Dana. There was no prospect of money for the best toys, or books or even the best clothes and so she did what she could to make what they had as best as it could be.

"Of course," laughed Amelia, "You Russians start training your babies to be Olympic gymnasts from like six months."

"I'm not Russian, I'm Israeli."

"I know that…I just meant…"

"What did you mean? You called me Russian."

"Well, technically you are."

"My passport says I am Israeli. I speak Hebrew.— Does that make me Russian?"

"Does it matter? You were originally from Russia. I just said it as a joke."

"It isn't a very funny joke."

"Well, sorry for talking!"

"I'm sorry, it's just that I've been called Russian so many times, as an insult, that I assume that if anyone calls me Russian, they must be insulting me."

"But that's awful!" I cried.

"What?"

"Well, to insult someone because of their origin, no?"

"Yes it is, but it's a fact of life. I hope my children never grow up with the stigma of the Russian label. I hope they will be Israelis through and through and that their Israeli-ness will never be questioned." And then she said, "You will always be an American here, you know."

"Yeah...I was starting to think that too; that I will never be Israeli."

"Mmm, but your children could possibly be considered Israeli, if they are raised here."

"I never knew," I said, "how people were still labeled here. I just assumed—you know—a Jewish state, all Jews and Israelis together. Only it isn't like that."

"Maybe it is also just a fight for survival...only the fittest survive. Whether in the queue at Burger Ranch, or at a Palestinian territory check-point."

"It's getting there," said Beruriah. "It's better than it used to be. But people still tend to stick to communities where they feel they belong, be that a Russian, Yemenite or American community."

"I think," said Dana, "That as people inter-marry more and more, so the labels gradually fall off and the children just all become Israeli. In a couple of years there will be no more labels. We'll all be just Israelis."

Beruriah smiled, "Let's hope so."

I almost whispered, "I hope so, too." My desire to belong somewhere was almost pathetic, I knew that; only it was the fate of so many in this country and the world, one could hardly blame me for it, could they?

Dana smiled at me. She too had known what it was not to belong. "It will happen, I promise."

And Amelia, who had always fitted, in merely cried, "Well, I'm Israeli and have always been. I have no idea what you are all talking about."

"Of course not," Dana replied, "Because you have always belonged. You have parents from Europe, parents with money, ancestors who helped found the state of Israel."

At that last part Amelia winced as if the idea was painful to her.

"You went to school, served in the army as you were expected to do. You were born here, grew up here—you know only Israel. An Israel of money and acceptance."

"So? Am I to be blamed because I didn't have a shitty life?"

"No," said Dana carefully, "but you should know that there is another side to life here. A life where people don't have money, and don't have acceptance and don't fit in."

"Like me as a child," added Beruriah. "Sometimes I use to wonder why we even lived in Israel at all. My parents spoke Arabic to each other and at home and never spoke Hebrew well. My father in particular refused to speak it, unless he had to. All the food we ate was Yemenite. The way we dressed and acted and spoke was just the same as how our family had dressed and acted and spoken in Yemen for hundreds of years. When my father finally allowed us to go to school, we were always different and everyone knew it. That's the other side of life here that Dana is talking about."

"Sure," said Amelia, "I get that. But things are changing. I mean your kids don't have that, do they?"

"No," agreed Beruriah. "They will know about their ancestors and where they came from. But, I agree with Dana, they will be Israelis. That's how it should be. Otherwise, what is the point of this country? Of course we can allow our Yemenite food and our Yemenite customs to become a contributory part of Israeli life!—And what a rich society and culture Israel will have! With food and customs and culture from Poland and Yemen and Russia and Morocco and Germany and Iran and Spain and Iraq. And yes, even from the USA. But it's time we integrated our communities and our customs rather than keeping them to ourselves."

"So you think," I ventured, "Even I could become Israeli eventually?"

Dana laughed, Beruriah smiled and even Amelia managed a grin of sorts and somehow they all managed to chorus together, "Of course!"

And there and then, in that moment, we had achieved what so many hope for—acceptance and unity. As Israelis.

I suppose, in the general scheme of things, the unity we found then wouldn't mean much. I mean there were still another almost seven million people to unite, a number that included Israeli Jews and Israeli Arabs. But it was a start.

May be though, it would be a good thing to unite us all as Israelis before we could even begin to tackle the much bigger issue of the Palestinians.

Who knew what impact our united front would have on that? But any unity between Israelis, regardless of the number, had to be a good thing. And at the very least, it made me feel as if I was a part of something, for the first time ever at that, and that my actions and behaviour could determine the future and outlook of an entire nation and even of an entire region. You didn't get that feeling in a small catholic town somewhere in America.

~~

We filled every evening with our talk. At home the evenings had always been spent with the television blaring out, Dad slumped in front of it after another day at work, his tie slightly loosened, while Mom hovered around trying to put the world and me to rights.

But here the nights weren't filled with the theme tunes from soap operas, and sirens blaring from police dramas, or the sounds of sobbing actresses from the latest movies. Here the sounds of the evening were our own voices as we shared and talked, and the occasional coo or whimper or piercing cry from the baby monitor that stood watch over the babies as they slept upstairs.

~~

"I sometimes think that maybe Yuval and Tamar and Isaac might have changed mama's life, as they have mine. Maybe they would have given her back some happiness,

"Maybe," replied Beruriah. "But that's asking a lot from the children. Children are miracles, but we can't rely on them to be miracle-makers."

"My mama has grandchildren and she's still as miserable as hell," said Amelia dourly.

"I sometimes think," said Dana looking at Amelia, "that our mamas are similar in many ways."

"How?" Amelia demanded to know, "Was your mother a manic depressive, Valium-addicted crazy person?"

Beruriah shook her head at Amelia's description of her mother.

"No," admitted Dana carefully, "But she also gave up on life. I mean she functioned—she would talk, and cook, and live; but she wasn't really there, you know?"

"There in body, but not in mind?" I suggested.

"Exactly," smiled Dana.

"Mmmm, sounds familiar," agreed Amelia.

"I can't imagine it," I admitted. "I mean, Mom drives me crazy at times. But I couldn't imagine life, or me, without her." And just like that, it hit me, like a lightening strike—a pang of longing for Mom. A yearning for the safeness she could convey with just one hug.

My mind sailed away across the sea to the States and wondered what she was doing right that second. Was she doing okay without me? Was I really okay without her? I wasn't so sure anymore. I'd spent my teenage years putting her at a distance, refusing to see eye to eye with her on anything, and yet as I got older I began to see that maybe there was something in having your family close. That it wasn't a weakness or a failing to want to be close to ones family.

"So why aren't you with her now?" asked Amelia, her blue eyes fixing on mine and refusing to move.

"I...I don't know....I guess I was upset with how engrossed everyone seemed in their own lives, that no-one seemed to be paying any attention to me and mine. That no-one seemed to be able to make family time a priority." But saying the words out loud made me think I sounded like a spoilt brat who couldn't handle growing up and on.

"What family makes time together a priority?" argued Amelia.

"This one," said Beruriah; and Dana smiled.

"And your mother?" Amelia demanded of Beruriah, as if to pay her back. And as only Amelia would dare.

Beruriah looked pained, and then sad. Her usual tough countenance changed and she seemed much weaker and younger, all at once. "She was my mother and deserves nothing but respect for raising me." But then she saw Amelia's look of protest and seemed to rethink her words. "She was my mother, so I loved her, deep down, but when I was younger I had a difficult time respecting her."

"Why?" probed Amelia, as if enjoying her mental attack on Beruriah.

"Because I had different ideas about what a woman—what a mother—should be. And because she lived, in so many ways, as if we were still trapped in Yemen. She was born here and yet she lived her life like her mother had—as one of a line of downtrodden and abused women. I hated her for being a part of that tradition....Yes, hated them," she added. "I was young once too, and I had a hard time understanding her."

"And now?" asked Dana.

"Now? Now she's elderly and fragile with Alzheimer's eroding her brain and her memory, and I pity her and miss her."

"I don't get it!" declared Amelia. "You hated her for living as if she was still in Yemen, and yet you do the same?"

Beruriah smiled. "I chose this life. My mother never did. Nobody hits me or my children, and if they did I would leave. This way of life is my choice."

"It's the choice of all of us," said Dana.

Amelia looked confused, as if trying to comprehend that she too had chosen this. Sometimes I felt the same way.

A squawk from the baby monitor sent Beruriah up the stairs to console her baby.

"She's as screwed up as the rest of us," announced Amelia, as she attacked the piece of cake in front of her.

"So?" challenged Dana, "What does it matter?"

Amelia chewed through the cake in her mouth. "It means she can get off her high preaching horse and leave me alone. That's what it means."

"You shouldn't be so hard on her," said Dana reproachfully.

"Why?" Amanda demanded to know. "She's hard on me."

Sometimes it would have been nice to give Amelia a sharp, short slap; she could be so aggravatingly childish.

Dana frowned. "She has her reasons. She has a lot on her plate."

"Really?" asked Amelia, suddenly interested. "Like what?"

Dana was flustered. "Just leave her alone, just for once."

"You aren't going to tell us what she has on her plate?" and Amelia slumped grumpily into her chair in protest.

"No."

"Why?"

"Because she told me, I don't want to abuse her confidence."

"I thought we were family. Family are supposed to tell each other everything."

"Oh really?" replied Dana sarcastically; which was not like her. "Because you tell us everything? Go on then, tell us what you spent the food money on!"

Amelia should have looked uncomfortable, but she didn't. She returned Dana's question with a signature brazen look, "I told you—food, cigarettes. Now spill the beans on Beruriah."

"It's not my story to tell." Dana was so soft on the outside and yet, when challenged, so hard on the inside. Amelia was just stone throughout. She might as well have been made of marble. She also never knew when to give up. "Oh, go on!" she coaxed, her voice and demeanor softening ever so slightly. Dana ignored her and instantly Amelia was marble again. She fumed and slammed her glass down and altogether struggled to control her anger. "Like I give a damn anyway! Why would I care about anything concerning that old hag?!" Amelia's anger controlled her words, and anger spilled out of her. She had gone too far and knew it. As a consequence, she descended into herself, and an air of gloom settled over her.

Beruriah, being Beruriah, noticed it as soon as she walked back into the room. "What have you done to Amelia?" she asked us.

Amelia sighed and fumed.

"It's nothing," promised Dana, with a smile; eager to clear the air.

Amelia cried, "Yeah, right!" under her breath.

And without really thinking, I snapped back, "Oh shut up Amelia!"

Beruriah looked from me to Amelia, and then from Dana to Amelia. "What is going on?"

"Dana seems to think families have the right to keep secrets from each other," Amelia accused, before any of us could say anything.

"I…"

But Beruriah wouldn't let Dana defend herself. "Dana," she admonished, "Families shouldn't keep secrets from each other," taking Amelia's side in an argument for the first time ever, unaware of the trap Amelia had laid for her. Amelia smiled suddenly, secure and happy in the knowledge that she had Beruriah well and truly where she wanted her.

Dana grimaced and put her hands up as if admitting defeat. I shot her a look of sympathy. Beruriah was now well and truly on her own, and as if to show it, Dana came around the table and sat by me, leaving Amelia and Beruriah together on the other side.

"I agree," said Amelia sweetly. "Dana was just saying that you had a lot on your plate and skeletons in your closet. But she wouldn't tell me what they were. I told her we don't have secrets here, but she refused to share."

Beruriah's eyes widened and Dana shrugged her shoulders as if to say, "I tried to warn you."

"Anyone up for a game of backgammon?" I asked.

Amelia shot me a look of—well—pure hatred. Dana looked grateful. "Sure! Beruriah? Amelia?"

Beruriah ignored her. Amelia looked up at Beruria, her blue eyes refusing to let Beruriah's brown ones go.

"What do you want to know?"

"What skeletons are you hiding?"

"This is ridiculous," I cried. "You can't force someone to share their secrets. It isn't fair."

Amelia glared at me again and Beruriah shook her head, "No, Amelia is right!" And Amelia practically gleamed at her words. "No secrets!"

Beruriah took a deep breath and refused to sit down. She held onto the back of an empty chair, perhaps for support. "Ten years ago my cousin raped me."

"Oh," escaped from me.

Dana looked sad and even Amelia had the decency to look slightly sorry.

But Beruriah was determined to finish her story. "I got pregnant."

Amelia shifted in her seat and seemed suddenly to regret what she had started. I tried to catch Beruriah's eyes, in an attempt to convey the sympathy I felt for her. Although what good my sympathy would have done her, I don't know.

"My father threw me out of the house. My great-aunt took me in and she helped me." There was not a flicker of emotion apparent on Beruriah's face. "And then He came along," and she nodded her head upwards. "He was happy to marry me and to help me raise my daughter, if I would help him build a family."

"Sara?" I asked.

"Yes, Sara was my daughter. That's it," finished Beruriah, "That's my secret."

"Oh, Beruriah!" started Dana.

But Beruriah wouldn't let her go any further. She stood up tall. "No, enough! I don't want or need anyone's pity. It's gone, done. It will not define nor destroy me," and Beruriah's steely gazed dared anyone to pity her.

But we did anyway. Even Amelia, who looked slightly horrified, "Shit!" she cried, unable to keep it inside any longer. "I hope that asshole is rotting in gaol. Raping his cousin, shit! That's disgusting."

"Enough!" cried Beruriah, revealing a little of her pain, while refusing to let it all out.

I had no idea about pain like that. The longer I was here, the more I began to realize just how sheltered my life had been. But I guessed—which is all that I could do—that pain like that is too intense to release all at once, if at all. That some things, for some people, are better kept locked inside—deep inside—where no-one, not even that person, can access and view them.

"Backgammon? I asked, again anxious to save Beruriah. There was so much more to her than any of us could imagine, and I couldn't help but feel that she needed to be left alone. If only for this one minute.

"Yes," agreed Dana, and went to get the game.

~~

Later, as we brushed our teeth together in the bathroom, Dana told me that Beruriah had tried to have her cousin charged by the police, but that her father wouldn't allow it. You don't help put family in jail, he had argued—never once thinking about the pain he caused his own daughter. Ultimately, family honour was more important to him than his own daughter.

"But her mother?" I asked in disbelief. "What did she do?"

"Whatever Beruriah's father said. So, nothing."

"Poor Beruriah," I whispered.

And Dana nodded sadly, "Mama wasn't the nicest person at the end of her life, but she would never have let someone get away with doing that."

"It's wrong. Isn't it—I mean the betrayal by her own parents—worse than the actual rape?" That's at least how it seemed to me.

And Dana agreed, "Yes, worse."

I put my toothbrush back into the cup on the edge of the sink and realized again how much I missed Mom and Dad.

Dana copied me and turned to wipe her face on a towel. Then she turned back. "And when you have your own children it becomes even more difficult to understand. I mean I look at my children and my heart rips apart at the thought of someone hurting them. And I'd want to kill anyone that did. I can't understand why a parent wouldn't feel like that."

"I suppose some people allow ideas and so-called principles to get in the way and prevent them from protecting their own children," I said, as I struggled to understand how some people's minds work.

217

"Yes, perhaps," agreed Dana thoughtfully, "Like a settler who lets their children be shot at by Palestinian militants just because they think that they have a biblical right to a piece of land."

"That's insane! Why would anyone put a piece of land before their own child's safety?" I responded.

And Dana shrugged her shoulders.

"Does Sara know?" I whispered, worried that little ears might be listening at the door. Or bigger ones too, come to think of it.

"No!" cried Dana, horrified at the thought of Sara finding out. "And she mustn't know! Can you imagine what that would do to a child? No, sometimes the truth is best hidden."

And we shuddered again at the thought of what had happened to one of us.

"Mama wasn't always—well wasn't always—not with it," said Dana confidingly, as she climbed into the single bed next to mine. She pulled the blanket up to her stomach and looked across at me. On my side, snuggled in the blankets, I propped myself up on one elbow. "Once she and Papa loved each other very much. They were very happy. After Mama died, when I cleaned out the apartment, I found boxes and boxes of old photos—from when they first met, from when they were married, from when Anton and I were born. Mama is smiling in every one. But not a damp, fake smile you know—a real smile, that fills her face, her eyes. Photos of Mama and Papa kissing, laughing, holding each other." Dana was quiet, a sad look on her face, "It would be nice to be able to remember them like that. Papa tried, I know he did, to make Mama happy again, like they had been. But it didn't work. She closed herself up and no-one could enter."

I looked across in sympathy and Dana smiled bravely back.

"Sleep," she said decisively and slowly slid herself down until the blankets all but covered her.

Sleep.

When there was nothing left to say. When no words of sympathy could change a past, or even a future, what better escape, if it will come, than sleep!

~~

"Shit, no, no, no!" rang out from the bathroom—a sort of chorus of profanity!

I knocked on the door.

"Is everything OK?"

"Go away, now!"

I turned to go.

"No, wait, come in here!"

It was Amelia. Who else? She was clearly angry, but on the verge of tears at the same time. I'd never seen her so vulnerable, although she was desperately trying to hide it.

She was pacing up and down the worn carpet.

"Um, is everything OK?"

"No, it's not!" And she stopped pacing long enough to throw something at me.

I only just caught it and turning my eyes to it realized it was a pregnancy test. I was confused.

"Read the result!" she demanded, handing me a page of instructions.

"A cross for positive," I read and there in the window of the test was the cross.

"Oh!" I said.

"Oh?!" Amelia screamed. "Oh?!" she grabbed the stick from me and threw it at the wall.

"What am I going to do?" she wailed, while sinking to the floor with her head in her hands. "No, no, no, no!"

I was lost for words. What do you say to someone in this situation? It was if she was involved in some big tragedy.

~~

"What is going on in here?" Beruriah's head came round the door.

Before Amelia or I had time to think, let alone act, she had seen the stick on the floor and had pounced on it. Reading it, her eyes widened and seemed to light up. A small smile definitely appeared at the corner of her lips.

"I take it this is yours, Amelia?"

"Congratulations! I shall have to let him know straight away." She openly smiled, as she tossed the stick in the bin and waddled out.

"No, no, no," moaned Amelia, her face still hidden in her hands.

I patted her awkwardly on the shoulder, feeling even more awkward for not knowing what to do.

Chapter 19—Amelia

What a bunch of idiots, all of them! Just by existing and having all those goddam children they were destroying the children's lives. How many stable, well-adjusted adults come from a family where the 'father' had four wives? And how many homeless adults with needles stuck in their veins come from the same family? It wouldn't take a genius to work out those figures.

~~

The way I saw it, I still had plenty of options, including the old classic standby—if in doubt, run! If they thought this thing inside me would stop me, they were wrong.

~~

The positive pregnancy test still lay on the floor when I heard the faint knock at the door.

"Go away!" I cried.

"Please, Amelia!"

"Go away!" I buried my head in the pillow, as the door creaked open. I got ready to fling my pillow at the intruder and their audacity, but stopped as I saw Dana raise her arms as if in surrender.

"Please, Amelia! I just want to help."

"Help!" I scoffed, "What can you do to help?—Are you a Doctor?"

Dana stood in the doorway, not daring to come any closer. My hands still grasped the pillow, ready to spring to action if needed.

"Don't talk like that," Dana replied. You don't know what you're saying."

"Oh, and you do, do you?"

"Please, Amelia! I've been where you are now and I did what I know you are thinking of doing. Don't do it! Please! It's not as easy as you might think. Really it isn't. Promise me you will really think it over before you do anything."

I relaxed my grip on the pillow. "Please leave me alone," I said.

~~

Maybe it was better to be loved a lot by a few people than to be loved just a little by a lot of people. And maybe it was just a case of those few people learning how to show the love they felt, and how to translate it from just feelings to something concrete, something others could really see.

Hiding from the world behind others, behind long skirts and an ancient way of life—that didn't save me from the pain life had to inflict. Life still found me. I thought that I would be protected, that the Family would form a barrier that would keep the pain out. But the Family didn't keep the pain out. The Family just stopped help getting in, when I needed it most.

Chapter 20—Rachel

At dinner, Amelia's eyes were red. But she held her head high and shoveled food into her mouth as if daring anyone to question her tear-stained, blotchy red face.

"Let's raise our glasses," he called, "to a new member of our family!" He raised his glass and smiled across at Amelia, who raised her glass along with us all. The eldest children beat their hands on the tables as their own celebratory tune.

"About time too," remarked Beruriah, looking across at Amelia. "It shouldn't take so long for someone so young."

"Beruriah, please!" He was always the peacemaker, always diffusing the tension and the conflict. "Tonight we celebrate. Come, let's eat!"

And we did. Although it didn't feel like much of a celebration. Amelia was definitely not in a mood to be congratulated, not now and not ever. She didn't touch the food on her plate, just sat with her arms folded, staring straight ahead.

He and Beruriah tried to jolly the meal along, but it didn't work very well. Dana put on a brave face and spent the meal smiling across at Amelia, who didn't respond once. Which left me to return Dana's smiles, which seemed to make her a little bit happier, but she was still full of concern.

The children ate and talked and argued with each other as usual. But the warmth between us was missing that night, and we could all feel it. The children didn't, and he didn't. But we did and it hurt.

I wasn't quite sure where our sisterhood had gone and if we would ever get it back. So much for our unity and the shining example we were setting for Israel as a state. Beruriah was bitter. I'd never seen her like that before.

And Amelia was depressed. And Dana distraught. And I, I didn't really know what to feel, let alone what to do.

~~

"Rachel?"

"Yes."

"Will you come in?"

She had never asked for my company before. And after dinner she usually disappeared with him.

She pointed to the bed and I sat.

The room was bare like all the rooms. Paint peeled off the walls. Brown furniture did its job and lent nothing to the room but an air of usefulness.

"What am I going to do?" Amelia turned to face me.

She had been crying again. She took a seat beside me and picked at the hem of her skirt. "Do you think I should leave?"

"Leave? But to go where?"

"I don't know, to my sister's maybe. I can't have this baby!" She was desperate. "There are too many bloody babies in this house—the stink, the crying." And, as if on cue, the wails of a baby could be heard from somewhere in the house, "I can't take it."

"Maybe it's different when it's your own baby," I offered. But who was I to know?

"I'll have to get it taken care of."

"Taken care of?"

She ignored me. "But then I will have to leave the Family and"—she turned to the window—"go back out there…. How can I do that?" she demanded of me.

"I…I don't know."

~~

Dana was at the door. No locks in this house.

"Amelia, he wants you."

"Now?" Amelia wiped her eyes with the back of her hand.

"Yep, now!"

~~

"Is she OK?" Dana asked as we began the journey down the stairs.

"I'm not sure," I said.

Dana looked worried. "I hope she's OK?" Then, with more confidence, "She will be OK once she gets over the shock."

"I hope so."

"Do you want some cocoa? I promised the children I'd make them some."

"I'd love some cocoa."

~~

Watching Dana with the children was a real delight. She was so patient with them as she let them stir their own cocoa—never once telling them off for spilt drops or even in the case of clumsy Isaac an entire cupful on the floor. She just kissed his forehead, handed him a wet towel and set about making him a new cup.

She magically produced a bag of marshmallows from somewhere, which set the children off into squeals of delight. I'd never seen children so excited by a bag of marshmallows before. It was sweet and innocent. Wasn't that what childhood was supposed to be? The American children I knew could only get that excited over a new cell phone, or an ipod or something.

After Dana had made sure each child had their favourite colour of marshmallow, she passed the bag to me.

"Thanks," I said plunking a white one into my coca, much to the delight of the children who were soon chasing marshmallows round their cups.

Dana's children stayed close to her the whole time. They clung to her skirt like little monkeys. Only they didn't have the energy or the cheekiness of little monkeys. They were like three little shadows—silent, almost not there.

Dana so obviously adored them. She gave all the children her attention—ruffled their hair, handed them another marshmallow, poured yet more cocoa, listened to them carefully and with obvious interest in what they had to say. But with her own three she was especially attentive. It almost made me rethink my decision not to have them.

~~

"Is that all you're eating?" asked Dana, her eyes on the packet of potato chips in front of Amelia.

"Yeah!... So!" The challenge came back across the table.

"But it's not enough for the baby. The baby needs more than that, and something healthier."

"Do I care?" retorted Amelia.

"But you should!" protested Dana. "It's not about you now. It's about your baby."

"Do I care?" repeated Amelia.

"Oh grow up, Amelia!" Beruriah snapped. "Dana is just trying to help. Can't you at least try to do something right for your baby?"

"For the last time," screamed Amelia, "You are not my mother! Leave me alone!" And she slammed the kitchen door behind her.

The room was silent, but tension hung in the air like a dead weight. "That poor baby!" said Beruriah.

"But we're here," offered Dana. "We'll be able to look after it—won't we?"

"Yes," sighed Beruriah. "What's another baby?" but she was worried, and only Dana seemed relieved by her reply.

Another evening, another discussion. It was a continuous, constant thing. Tonight however, the tension of the past week still hung in the air. Beruriah and Amelia had reached an unspoken truce. You had to when living in the same house as someone. But the friction between them wasn't going to go away.

"It's funny," I said to no-one in particular, keen just to get people talking to each other again.

"What is?" asked Dana, as she handed Amelia another piece of cake.

"How we all became our mom's worst nightmare."

"Oh I was born that," replied Amelia through another mouthful of cake.

"Really?" asked Dana, "I can't believe that.... That someone would look at a new baby and think that they were a nightmare."

"No," I agreed. "We weren't born their nightmare. But see what we are now? Haven't we become their nightmare?"

Dana looked thoughtful and sat down beside me.

"Maybe," she said, "I mean, here I am an Israeli—speaking Hebrew and never any Russian, following Judaism as an orthodox believer would, and raising my children to be Israeli Jews.—Yes, that would have been her worst nightmare. She'd grieve for the lack of Russia in my children, and in me. She hated Israel when she died. And here I am, having embraced it." She looked sad. "But she was wrong, hating Israel...."

"I was always my mother's nightmare," cried Amelia. "Never quiet enough, never graceful enough, never clever enough, never brave enough...never my sister."

"That's sad," I said. "I mean, my parents worship my brother because he's smart and sensible, but I never once thought that they didn't worship me the same. They just worshipped me for different reasons."

"I don't care," replied Amelia. But it was obvious that she did. Wasn't that why she did the things she did?... Negative attention was better than no attention at all.

Beruriah came back in and looked around at us. "You all look serious, even Amelia."

"We're discussing whether we've become our mother's worst nightmare," explained Dana. "I have. And Amelia has."

"And me," I added. "I mean, not going to college, living so religiously, cutting my family off.... I'm pretty sure Mom never wanted that." And I knew that she never had, and that I hadn't just made her biggest nightmare a reality. I had probably broken her heart too. It seemed to hurt more, breaking her heart, than any breaking of my own heart had ever hurt. I hadn't even given her the chance to accept me in my new life. Just cut her off, just like that. Maybe she didn't really care about the going to college and all that, maybe right now she just wanted to talk to me, to hug me, to see and know that I was OK.

"How about Beruriah?" Amelia interrupted my thoughts. "Are you your mother's worst nightmare?" She held Beruriah's eyes in her own.

Beruriah smiled, "Perhaps.—She didn't know how to be happy, so maybe my happiness would have been unimaginable to her."

"But that doesn't make it a nightmare," I said.

"Perhaps she would have been shocked by my confidence—the control I have over my own destiny."

And no-one said anything, but I wondered if the others were thinking the same as me. That Beruriah had perhaps become her mom's worst nightmare by being in a loveless marriage just like she had been, in a family with no money, where everything had to be shared and eked out from day to day. And maybe Beruriah's Mom's biggest nightmare would have been that Beruriah was blind to just how similar her life was to her mother's, no matter how hard she tried to pretend that it wasn't.

"This is a rather depressing topic for *Rosh Chodesh*."

"Yes, Beruriah, you are right," agreed Dana. "Let's talk about something else."

And the conversation turned to the meals for tomorrow, the mending of clothes, and the shoes that needed to be bought.

~~

Amelia yawned and excused herself to the back yard. I followed her.

We sat in the yard, the dark closing around us and shivered somewhat in the winter evening.

"God," cried Amelia, "I would kill for a cigarette!"

I looked meaningfully at her ever-growing stomach.

"OK, OK, relax! I'm not actually going to smoke one!—Where the hell would I get a cigarette from around here? And how the hell would I pay for it?... You know," she continued, "Out of all of us you are the one I don't get."

"What do you mean?"

"Well look at us all—messed up beyond belief, hiding here from the world and our problems, and yet you... what have you got to hide from?"

I didn't know what to say.

"Shit! You have parents who love you, who want to spend time with you, who show an interest in your life, regardless of what you want to do or who you want to be. So why the hell are you here?"

I didn't know what to say.

All the reasons I had first had for being here seemed to weaken by the day. I'd wanted to find my Jewish self and in the process find myself. But was that what I was doing here? Looking after other people's children, cleaning and cooking and sharing all day long. Not leaving the house for days and weeks at a time.

And it made me think, did one have to live an orthodox life, or as close to an orthodox life as one might choose to get, to be Jewish? What about the Israelis who drove their cars on *Shabbat*, went to synagogue only at *Yom Kippur*, if then? Were they any less Jewish, any less happy? Weren't they Israelis too? Weren't they in fact the majority?

But wasn't that why I was here, because it meant I was safe and secure in our own Jewish world, without having to deal with everything out there? Here I didn't have to take any risks, make any bad or wrong decisions, and decide anything for myself. Life wasn't bad, it was easy.

Was I running away from my life? From responsibility?

"Shit, to be free!" cried Amelia bringing me back to her and the yard.

And I realized, then and there, that, right now, freedom to be and do whatever I wanted—mistakes included—was the greatest thing I had. And maybe it was time to start doing something about claiming that freedom back. Before I was no longer able to.

~~

Dana opened the back door and came to join us. The night stirred with cicadas and the odd cat and not much else. Some people—and some newspapers—called us a country at war. It didn't sound like it that night.

I wondered if Dana remembered what freedom felt like? I wondered if she ever craved it. I was too chicken to ask her. She seemed to believe so wholly in this ideal of the Family. Or she was a great actress.

She sat down next to me and looked up at the sky.

"Beautiful," she whispered. And with the stars twinkling ahead, it was. More stars than you could ever count.

It brought back that rhyme from my childhood, "First star I see tonight, I wish I may, I wish I might, the first star I see tonight."

Here I was, almost grown up, and still wishing on first stars. Not that I believed any wish would come true. It was more habit—more superstition—than anything.

If I could wish for anything now, what would it be?—The answers. The answers to my life would be nice. A sign. A sign telling me which way I needed to go next, what step I needed to take.

Were we all wishing for the same thing? Even Amelia was quiet as she stared up at the sky.

Did she know her next step? And Dana, did she even want to take a step, or was she happy standing still?

We shared so much and yet so little. We slept in beds next to each other every night. Shared the same three meals everyday. Worked beside each other. Shared family stories and memories. But the present? We never shared that.

It was supposed to be unsaid. That the Family would go on, and we would go on with it.

We were all entranced, lost in the stars and our thoughts. Secret thoughts. We shared everything, but not those.

~~

"Can you feel the baby yet Amelia?" Dana asked pulling herself away from the stars and whatever thoughts crowded her mind.

"Don't know," replied Amelia, pulling up the grass beside her.

"Oh," said Dana, thwarted slightly but gallantly powering on. "It's amazing, the first time you feel them, because you're not sure, you know, if it's really what you feel and then you realize it is, and you've been taken quite by surprise." She smiled to herself. "And then you begin to worry when you don't feel something, and you spend whole days waiting to feel something," and her face dropped slightly.

Amelia shrugged her shoulders, "If you say so."

"It's amazing," said Dana almost to herself.

"I'm sure," said Amelia as a gesture for Dana. She didn't sound convinced herself.

"Amazing but worrying," continued Dana. "I mean just being pregnant used to give me this excited feeling every time I woke up, or thought about it. But then there is the worry too, you know, if everything is going OK, if the baby is going to be healthy, if you're going to make it to the nine months with a baby. It's hard but amazing."

Amelia smiled reluctantly. My smile was more enthusiastic. I liked Dana. She was real. And more than anything she wanted to help.

"Even the second time round...I mean you're more relaxed because you've done it before...you know what's coming each month...but still you worry. Sometimes I think maybe it would be nice to go without the whole nine months, you know, just have the baby delivered or maybe just be pregnant for a few months, but I suppose the baby needs the whole nine months to develop and grow."

Dana was thinking aloud. It didn't seem necessary to say anything. I had nothing to say anyway. No experiences of pregnancy. Amelia had the experience but I doubt she shared the same thoughts as Dana. But then, who knew what Amelia thought? Sometimes I wondered if she even knew herself. If she ever spoke to herself. If she ever spoke to herself just before or just after she had done something. If she ever had that little voice inside her.

Chapter 21—Amelia

"So we'll go to Shilav, go crazy buying things. It will make you feel better." Lucille was desperate for me to go home with her. She'd been trying, in vain, for the last eight months to get me to leave the Family.

"No thanks," although I wanted her to know I did appreciate the offer. "It will only end up in Beruriah's hands and every baby born between now and the next twenty years will use it."

"You could leave, come to us."

"You don't want me living with you."

"Why not? You're my sister and you're in trouble. What could be more natural than you coming to us?"

"I'd be in the way."

"You wouldn't. Please come with me. Then we can sort this out. Together."

I shook my head, but she continued,

"I should have offered you this a long time ago. With Papa always in France and Mama as she is, it was my responsibility to be there for you. And I wasn't. I'm sorry Amelia, really I am, But I am here now," and she reached across the table with a smile.

"You are welcome in our home Amelia, I want you to know that. But there are rules—no alcohol, no drugs. And you have to find something constructive to do with your life."

"And this?" I asked pointing to my stomach.

"That we will deal with, I promise."

~~

I didn't know what I wanted. Only that it was time to do something, to take some kind of action. I could go with Lucille and face life again and my future within it, or I could stay hidden away from it in the security of the Family. And let them make the decision, let them determine my future.

"Please Amelia, let me help show you how good life can be."

"Can I come now?"

"Right now?"

"Yeah."

"But what about your things? You don't want to tell them you are leaving?

"No."

"Then of course you can come now."

~~

At 6pm that night, as my nieces trooped home from ballet, I pictured the Family gathering around the table in the kitchen. Wednesday night was always Dana's night to cook and she would be making her children's favourites. Which would mean schnitzel and mashed potatoes again.

Dana would be heaping the food onto plates as the elder children called for more chicken, more potatoes. Beruriah would be hushing everyone as Rachel helped the little ones onto the benches and strapped Isaac into his high chair, where he would be beating his chubby fists on the tray in front of him and waving his piece of pita in the air.

After the prayers for the food, you would barely be able to hear yourself think as five, now four adults, four children, two toddlers and a baby started to eat. Would anyone notice I wasn't there? Beruriah with her hawk eyes surely would.

But apart from my obviously missing physical presence—would they miss me?

Chapter 22—Rachel

"Where is Amelia?" Beruriah asked, as I strapped little Isaac into his high chair. He began to squeal in protest, so I handed him a piece of pita, which he twirled above his head.

Dana turned from the stove to face us, a plate of crisp schnitzel in her hand, "Is she not here?"

Thunderclouds developed over Beruriah's head and a storm began to brew on her face, "Is she even in the house?"

Children began to traipse into the kitchen begging for food. Dana swatted the older ones away from the chicken as I shepherded the younger ones to their places around the table.

I took the chicken and then the potatoes from Dana who then handed me a spoon and I began to spoon out the food onto the waiting plates. The children eyed me with big round eyes and hungry, rumbling tummies.

"I don't know," Dana and I said at the same time, and despite the storm obviously brewing, we both couldn't help a small smile at each other.

"Amelia!" Beruriah shouted through the house and up the stairs.

"Amelia, Amelia, Amelia," chanted the children until Dana hushed them with more chicken.

"She's not here," Beruriah thundered.

"Where could she be?" I wondered outloud.

"She better have a good explanation!"

"Let me go look for her!" said Dana.

"No! The children are hungry. We'll eat and then worry about Amelia later.

"Where is Amelia?" he asked, once the plates had been emptied and the children sent out to play in the yard for an hour before their baths.

"We don't know," answered Beruriah.

"You will find her?" he asked.

"Of course," replied Berurirh, who looked exhausted at the thought. She put her hand to her stomach as if seeking energy and reassurance from the baby inside.

"It's Amelia's turn tonight," he said.

Beruriah looked as if she wanted to sigh, or maybe cry—or perhaps do both.

"Let me take her place!" I said, keen to help after he had left the room. Wasn't that what families did? Helped each other?

Beruriah shot me a look of pure gratitude. I smiled back rather nervously and she put a hand on my arm and squeezed it as if to give me reassurance in her gratitude.

~~

He always asked for one of us as soon as dinner was finished and the dishes were washed. This always coincided with when the children needed to be bathed and put to bed, which always left us one short. Tonight Dana and Beruriah would have to manage alone.

~~

"Will you manage?" I asked Beruriah as she closed the door on the cutlery.

"Of course!—Go, enjoy yourself!" and she pushed me out of the door.

~~

"Come," he said as I knocked on the door and entered the one truly masculine environment in the house.

He usually started with a passage from The Torah. But it was just words to me, and in my fear even more so. He wanted me to enjoy it. G-d meant for man and wife to enjoy it—to enjoy what brings children into the world.

~~

Amelia always said that you could enjoy it with anyone as long as you approached it with the attitude that you were in it for yourself—to get yourself off as she used to put it, much to Beruriah's disgust. She said it was just a case of mind over matter. Whatever your fantasy was, put that into your head regardless of the reality, and you'd get what you needed.

Dana had responded to that with, "That sounds like something a prostitute would do."

And Beruriah shook her head as if actual words failed her.

"I'm just trying to help Rachel out," she snapped back moodily.

"Let's not forget what it essentially is, said Beruriah, "and that is an act for the bearing of children."

Amelia pulled a face, "Must you ruin everything?"

~~

I don't know if I would ever enjoy it. Amelia obviously had a more vivid and ultimately stronger imagination than me, because I could never get my mind to work so as to make me enjoy it.

I grinned and bore it—not as Dana did, for precious babies, and not as Beruriah did, who saw it as her duty—but because I saw it as the price I paid to be a part of the Family.

~~

"Thank you," He would say and that was the cue to go, at which point we'd rejoin the rest downstairs as if we'd just popped upstairs to go to the toilet, or to check on the children.

The next day it rained and rained. Dana covered the table with glue, and glitter, and scraps of coloured paper and engaged the children in a huge craft project.

Beruriah paced up and down the kitchen floor.

Dana bounced Isaac on her knee as he attempted to grab the glitter and fill his mouth with it. Dana appeased him with a strip of coloured paper and he tried to cram that in his mouth instead.

"Beruriah, sit down!" she insisted.

"Where is she?" Beruriah demanded to know, still pacing.

"Maybe she went home," said Dana, handing Isaac a piece of felt to play with.

"This is home."

"I meant, back to her parents' home."

Beruriah sank onto the bench.

"Maybe."

"Does it matter?" I asked

"No, I suppose not." But to Beruriah it obviously did matter. It was her job to keep the Family together and regardless of how much she and Amelia fought like cats and dogs, Amelia was still a member of the Family, still someone Beruriah was responsible for.

Chapter 23—Amelia

"Just cut it out of me," I screamed as the pain coursed through my body. Discomfort followed, and I just wanted it to stop.

"Relax!" the nurse by my side said, as she offered me another dose of gas, "You need to relax."

"Don't touch me!" I cried, "I want drugs, real drugs. And I want this cut out of me now!"

She looked horrified and unsure of what to do. Lucille marched into the room.

"Amelia, shut up! Leave the nurse alone!"

The nurse looked even more horrified.

"I'll get the Doctor," she said, glad to have an excuse to escape.

"Bitch!" I hurled after her retreating back.

"Amelia! Stop it! This could take awhile. You need to calm down."

The pain again, the discomfort paralyzing my whole body, making me powerless in the face of it.

"Drugs!" I screamed, somewhat hysterically.

The Doctor entered the room.

"Everything looks good. Baby is good. We are 6cm dilated, so getting there. But you need to relax. The nurse will call me when it's time to push," and he made to leave.

"I'm not pushing," I screamed at him. "Cut it out!"

"Look," he said calmly, "I know you are in a lot of pain, but everything is going to be fine. Believe me!"

"I won't do it," I swore. "I won't push an inch!"

He looked at Lucille, puzzled.

She shook her head, "If she says she won't, believe me she won't. Maybe a caesarean is best."

"But we don't like to perform caesareans unless absolutely medically necessary," he tried to protest.

"Oh come on," argued Lucille, "This is a private hospital. You do whatever we pay you to do. She wants a caesarean, and so that's what she'll get."

The Doctor nodded, "Fair enough," and then to the nurse, "Prepare her for a caesarean," and he headed out of the room.

~~

Then I remember fear. Gripping Lucille's hand as the anesthetist prepared the needle that would shoot the epidural through my spine and down to my legs. Fear as my legs deadened and refused to lift themselves, or to respond to a pinprick. Fear that I might feel the surgeon cutting away at my engorged stomach.

And then relief when they pulled the baby free and began to stitch me back up.

"A boy," the surgeon cried and handed him to the pediatrician who cleaned him and weighed him and sucked mucus from his nose. His screams filled the room and Lucille smiled and stroked my hair.

"A boy," she gleamed and took him from the pediatrician and brought him to where I lay on the operating slab.

"Would you like to feed him now?" asked the nurse.

I shook my head.

"Maybe later," she said with a smile.

I shook my head again.

"Are you going to try breastfeeding?" she asked rather worriedly.

And I shook my head.

The smile fell from her face and she took the baby from Lucille. "We need to take him to the nursery," she explained slowly, "To measure him, and to make sure everything is as it should be."

"I'll go with her," said Lucille and she followed the nurse out.

~~

240

The next few days passed in a blur. The nurses forcing me to get up and have a shower almost as soon as the epidural had worn off; the discomfort and pain as I stood bent over in the shower. Lucille stayed the whole time—she changed his nappy, his clothes, wrapped him in a blanket, and gave him his milk.

On the fourth day she agreed to go home, to see her own children, before coming back to help me check out.

~~

Once she was gone, I knew what I had to do. I picked him up, placed him in the Moses basket. Shoved his clothes and stuff in a plastic bag. I signed myself out of the hospital, accepting their offer of a car seat, putting the deposit for it on the bill Lucille would have to settle later, and hailed a taxi. I gave him the address and sank back in the seat, my eyes closed.

The taxi-driver drew up. I paid him and lifted the baby from his car seat. I placed him in the Moses basket, put the basket outside the door, placed the car seat and plastic bag next to him and walked away. I didn't look back once. Didn't look back or wait around to see who found him and when. I just kept walking. And that was it.

He would be better off here. Here he would be wanted and loved. At Lucille's he would always be "that other one," and "Amelia's mistake," but here he would be one of them. So he might not always have the coolest trainers, or the latest i-pod—or hell, even an i-pod at all—but he would at least belong. And if he needed money, well I knew Lucille or Papa would always give that. He just had to ask, or Beruriah had to. There was plenty of money to go around in my family, if not attention.

I called Papa and asked for a ticket to Bangkok and money to travel for a few months.

"Are you out of that cult?" he barked down the phone.

"Yes," I said wearily too tired for once to argue.

"Have you seen your mother?"

241

"No," I said and stopped myself from asking, "Have you?"

"You should go to see her."

"I will," knowing full well that I wouldn't. But he couldn't hold me to that. When was the last time he had seen her?

"I'll transfer the money now."

"Thanks, see ya."

"Amelia?"

"Yes?"

"No, nothing!...Have a good time! I'm…I'm glad you are OK."

"Yeah, thanks! I am."

~~

"A ticket to Bangkok, tonight?" asked the girl at the El Al desk.

"That's what I said."

"I don't know. The Bangkok flight is always very busy."

"Can you just look?"

"OK, we have. But it's really expensive. Do you want to go away and find a travel agent to book you a seat for another day?"

"No, I want to go tonight!"

"OK, but you're crazy! This is like three times what you would pay if you went through an agent."

"Shut up!" I wanted to shout. "Are you being paid to have an opinion and then to broadcast that opinion to every bloody person in the airport? No, I don't think so. Take the damn money and give me my ticket."

The plane was full. Businessmen, travelers fresh out of the army.

This was it, I thought, as the plane taxied down the runway and the engines whirled. I finally get to be free from everyone—from Mama and her drugs, from Papa and his women, from Lucille and her perfect life and from

242

all the perfect people that came before me. Finally I could be anonymous, free to be myself and live my life.

So long, suckers!

Chapter 24—Dana

She left him on the doorstep. It was like something out of a book, or a film. There he was snuggled in the most exquisite blue baby-blanket in the most gorgeous Moses basket. On his back, his little fists curled. Newborn babies appear to sleep so soundly—only the experienced know how quickly they can go from sleeping soundly to being wide awake and screaming with hunger.

Who knows how long he had been there, resting on the step. Even Amelia couldn't have left him there for hours, could she? Maybe she was watching us from across the street, from behind a car, to make sure we took him in.

There was no note of explanation just a scrap of paper, with "from Amelia," written hurriedly on it. His birth certificate had been folded and pushed under his sleeping body.

And there he was—so tiny, so perfect and so blissfully unaware of his being abandoned.

~~

"How could she do it?" I wailed as Beruriah lifted the delicate Moses basket and carried it through to the kitchen. She rested the sleeping baby on the table and shook her head.

I wanted to understand what would make a mother abandon her child. It was one thing to make the decision to terminate the life of a baby-to-be; quite another thing to carry a child for nine months, give birth to a baby, hold that baby, feed that baby, dress and care for the baby— and then abandon him on a doorstep.

My babies were my life, and even a few hours separation was too much for me. Losing them was my greatest fear. And yet here Amelia had purposefully lost her baby.

"She wasn't ready," remarked Beruriah, as she lifted the sleeping baby from his basket. She cradled him and kissed a little cheek. It was the only time I saw the tender side of Beruriah—when she held a baby. She passed him to me and I stroked his cheek, ever so softly, as his little eyes blinked in wonderment.

Could he tell his Ima was gone? Would he know and feel it, even now? My heart ached at the thought of such a tiny thing, aching with pain for his Ima.

"We could have helped her..." I said sadly, "...helped her with everything."

"Yes," agreed Beruriah. "But having a baby is much more than changing nappies and feeding them every two hours...." And Beruriah's voice was surprisingly soft. "...Only when your baby is born do you realise that suddenly you are responsible for who and what this baby becomes. You will be the one that instills the values in this baby. You will be the one to teach it almost everything it will know. You will determine its life. That's a huge responsibility and it's no wonder it scares a lot of people."

"It never scared me," I replied.

"No, because you know what you wanted to instill in your children, and what it is important for them to learn. Amelia had no idea what her own values were—let alone what she should teach her baby. Amelia still struggles over what to have for breakfast, let alone what she would want for her baby. He's much better off here with us." And she took him from my arms and began to rock him back to sleep, his eyelids slowly lowering with each rock.

"A baby is always better off with its Ima."

Beruriah shook her head, "No, not always. Physically we were all meant to be mothers, but emotionally some of us are just not ready for it. You will see. He will be happy here with us."

"It's just so sad. So many people in the world desperate for a baby and yet unable to have one. And Amelia, who had this little one so easily, doesn't want him. Sometimes I can't help but think that G-d works in mysterious ways."

"Well we want him, and so he is meant to be with us. There is nothing mysterious nor sad about that."

And as always, Beruriah with her practical stoicism was right.

Although I still couldn't help thinking that maybe, just maybe, this little boy could have gone to a childless couple after all. It wasn't as if our home was lacking in children.

~~

He was my especial care. With my little Isaac weaned, I had begun to miss the closeness that comes from a new baby and its complete and utter reliance on you. I took it upon myself to make sure that Amelia's baby would never feel the absence of his real mother.

~~

Several weeks later as I rocked Amelia's baby to sleep in my arms and attempted to spoon Beruriah's youngest's cereal into her mouth, at the same time appeasing Isaac with a packet of *bamba*, the doorbell rang.

"Can someone get that please!" I cried as Isaac emptied the packet of *bamba* onto the floor and proceeded to stamp through it in his barefeet.

"No!" I cried as the *bamba* began to mash under his feet.

Someone came bounding down the straits. The door opened, then voices.

"Who is it?" I called, appeasing Beruriah's youngest with a spoonful of cereal.

"Dunno, some lady."

I placed Amelia's baby in the Moses basket and, handing Beruriah's youngest a spoon to play with in his high chair, lifted Isaac onto my hip and began to head for the door.

A clear—not cold…but yet not quite friendly—voice from the hallway called, "Please don't get up! I've let myself in."

I sat back down and left Isaac to the crumbs of bamba decorating the floor.

"I'm Lucille," she explained coming into the kitchen, "Amelia's sister."

The resemblance was there—the same honey-coloured hair, the same slimness and height. But while Amelia slouched, her sister stood tall. I took her in—her shiny hair, her manicured nails, her linen skirt without a crease, her designer handbag.

"Is this…?" and she pointed to Amelia's baby in his Moses basket. Lucille smiled as she leant over the basket, "He's gorgeous," and I nodded. "I've come for him," she said. My heart sank into my stomach.

"What?" I managed to stutter.

"I've come for him, to take him home." And she moved her elegant being closer to the basket.

"But he lives here," I managed to get out. "Amelia left him here."

"Amelia didn't know what she was doing. She didn't want to burden me, but she was wrong. He's family. He's ours," and she let him grasp her finger, no doubt entranced by the diamonds sparkling on it.

"Amelia left him here," was all I could repeat.

"No need to pack his things," the intruder said. "We have plenty for him." And she made to pick up the basket.

The door slammed. Beruriah came in with Hannah on her hip and a parade of children around her, laden with grocery bags.

"Dana, who is this?" she asked, motioning to the children to put the bags next to the fridge and then amuse themselves in the garden. She handed Hannah to Sara, and the children trooped out.

"Lucille, Lucille Bernstein." And she calmly held out her hand.

Beruriah shook the offered hand warily. "Amelia isn't here."

"Oh no, I know that." And Lucille smiled, "She's in India, finding herself. Whatever that means. No, I've come for her baby," and she turned back towards him.

"No," replied Beruriah calmly, unperturbed and unchallenged by the elegance of the lady in front of her, "You haven't!" And she put herself between Amelia's baby and its aunt.

"He is Amelia's baby, and he belongs with our family." Her eyes were ablaze, her voice calm, but her eyes spoke volumes. She had the composure on the outside that Amelia had always lacked, but inside she was as fiery as her sister.

"Amelia left him here," came Beruriah's equally calm reply, but she refused to move an inch. "She gave up any rights to him the day she abandoned him here."

"You won't get away with this," cried Lucille, losing some of her well-bred reserve. "I'll hire the best lawyers!" She clearly wasn't accustomed to being thwarted in any way.

"His mother isn't in the country…. The baby was left with his father…. What do you need a lawyer for?" Beruriah crossed her arms over her chest.

"I'll call social services, have you and this dump investigated."

"So go ahead!" replied Beruriah. "We have nothing to hide."

"I can give him a better life," Lucille had resorted to pleading, "Everything money can buy. The best of everything."

"And we can give him everything money can't buy— love, happiness, security."

Lucille's blue eyes flashed, and she was furious in defeat, "I will fight you on this," she cried, and without a glance at the baby, she turned on her heels and left, slamming the door behind.

Beruriah said nothing and turned to the shopping.

"What are we going to do?" I asked, feeling physically sick with worry.

"Nothing," and Beruriah opened the fridge to put away the milk.

"Nothing?"

"He stays here. End of story." And then with a small sigh, "Only Amelia could continue to cause so much trouble from so far away."

She never mentioned it again. For days I lay in wait for the heavy thud of a lawyer's letter on the doorstep, forcing us to give up Amelia's baby. Or I anxiously feared the heavy knock of a social worker at the door, ready to take the children away.

But my fears were unfounded. All in my head. Beruriah snapped when I tried to ease the fear by sharing it. Beruriah refused to take it on board.

There was no fight for Amelia's baby.

He was ours.

Chapter 25—Dana

"Dana, what can I do for you?"

I looked at my children clinging close to me, their hands gripping my skirt. "I need more money."

"More money? Well of course! Can I ask for what?"

"For the Family!"

"The Family?" And I saw him take in my children—their sickly hacking coughs, their eyes rimmed with dark shadows, their quietness, their nervousness and I saw his concern.—His eyes on the children, he said, "I'm sorry Dana, but I can't."

"There is no more money?"

"There is. But I think one day you will need it much more than the Family will."

"But I have only the Family. There will never be anything else."

"But there may be. And I would rather your father's money was there for you and his grandchildren. I understand if you are angry. But I won't change my mind."

I wasn't angry; more, concerned. What would I tell the Family? "What will I tell them?"

"Tell them I said 'no'; that there is no more money. Tell them that your father's books aren't selling at the moment."

"And they will believe that? They won't believe that!"

Tamar and Yuval looked up at me. Concern filled their little faces. I squeezed their hands in reassurance that everything was OK. Ima was OK.

"Tell them as if it is the truth, and they will. Either way, you will have no money to give them. But for your children, there is always money. Is there anything they need?"

"No, they have no priority within the Family. No-one child or person does."

He had that concerned look on his face again. "Dana, is everything OK?"

"It's fine." I gathered my children to me and headed for the door.

"If there is anything you need, you know where I am. Anything at all."

His words were at once cold, business-like; and I decided that everything I had imagined, fantasized about was just a silly dream I had had. It had been all one-sided and he had never felt anything similar for me. What a fool I was, forever thinking that he would feel anything for me.

~~

"Dana?" I stopped on the way to the door and turned around, worried that he had known all along how I felt and yet had been laughing at me and my feelings.

He got up from his chair and came around the table. He went to take my hand but I didn't have a free one, Tamar and Yuval had one each and didn't look likely to give one up. He looked uncomfortable and drew his hand back. "Dana, there's something I have to say."

My heart leapt.

"I think, I think I want to spend more time with you. I think I want to get to know you better. I think we were meant to be together."

~~

So this was my prince. How Amelia would shout at me for such a corny expression.

Nothing else mattered anymore. And suddenly I found happiness in the most simple of things—a telephone call from him; a card from him.

A lifetime with him wouldn't be enough, and I began to see why and how Mama fell to pieces after Papa died. How she couldn't live without him.

But with that happiness came the fear—the fear of losing them; not wanting to spend a second apart, of always wanting to keep them near and safe.

To suddenly be comfortable and at ease; to be able to say, do, reveal anything without any hint of shyness or reluctance. To be oneself and to be naked—comfortably and with confidence—whether physically, mentally, or emotionally.

To have found equality in a relationship, to know that we both felt the same way and to both equally contribute to our relationship. With honesty as its corner-stone, with no games, no riddles—just honesty and a craving for physical contact of the simplest kind—a kiss, a hug, a hand to clasp, an arm to hang on.

~~

Was it luck or fate? Were we preordained to be together, or had it just happened? That was a question I couldn't answer and a question I didn't need to answer. We were. And that was all that mattered.

And the question I never dared to answer, or begin to answer—I tried hard enough to not even ask the question in the first place but would I be here with him today if Papa hadn't died, if Anton hadn't died? Did they have to die for me to get here?

~~

He made his secretary take Tamar and Yuval out for ice-cream so that we could talk.

He wanted more than I could ever have believed possible. He wanted me to leave the Family and live with him.

~~

"I can't, you don't really want me."

"Oh Dana, but I do, I really do."

"But I come with so much baggage," and I thought of Papa hanging from the rope above the bed he shared with Mama, and I thought of Anton standing in the queue to the nightclub, and then his body blown into a million

252

pieces, and then I thought of Mama pale and thin in her hospital bed, crying out in pain for her lost boys; and then my three children, Isaac not even out of nappies.

"I don't care, we all have baggage. Isn't that what makes us human? And anyway we are Israelis—aren't we born with baggage?" his weak attempt at a joke didn't help.

"But why would you want to take on so much of someone else's baggage?"

"Because I love you."

"Enough?"

He looked offended at the question.

"Because," I explained, "You'd have to love someone an awful lot to take on that much baggage."

"And I do. I can't promise you a perfect ending," he said, not letting go off my hand. His eyes held mine, and he wouldn't let them go, no matter how much I shifted from foot to foot, uncomfortable under his gaze.

"I can promise to be faithful, to love you forever, and to do everything I can to make you happy." My eyes tried to waiver, but his drew me back. "But you have to trust me, and to trust that I love you. I can't control everything or anything that might be thrown in our path. But you have to trust that whatever comes our way, we can get through it together." He let my eyes fall, as if letting me know, that he had said his piece, he had made his promises.

Now it was my turn. But this was it. This is what I'd been hiding from. Once upon a time, hadn't Papa promised Mama the very same thing? And even though he'd never gone back on his promise, what he was capable of wasn't enough for Mama.

"It will be OK," he said, as if reading my thoughts, my hesitation. "Happiness is something we can find, cultivate and keep a hold of. We're not your parents, Dana! We aren't going to share their fate. We are not them."

Could I do it? Could I take a step without knowing what might come next? Could I give up the security I had, for something that would bring me happiness I could never remember having? I knew I wanted to. I knew that this was what I needed to do. But did I dare?

"It's OK to be scared," he said softly, and then more firmly, "I think the fear tells us that we are about to make a huge decision. But you have to decide if the fear is valuable and reasonable, or if it's holding you back."

But it wasn't just the fear holding me back. Tight ropes seem to tie me to an invisible post. Papa, Mama, Anton. Tamar, Yuval and Isaac.

"Let them go," he said pulling at the ropes as he did so. They began to shake and slacken a little. "Or bring them with you."

And for the first time I considered that possibility. Could I take them with me? Not forgetting them, but not letting them take over. I could pack them away somewhere safe, where they wouldn't interfere with my daily life, and then go over them, through them occasionally, when I wanted to remember the good.

~~

"Why are you so scared?" he asked.

He asked me so directly, so openly, I couldn't help but speak my mind. "Because you might walk into a coffee-shop one day, just in front of a suicide bomber, and never come out. And I would be alone, forever. Unable to touch you, unable to hear you, unable to talk to you. I would be alone...alone...!" My words gave out.

Ilan looked sad, "I used to think I could promise that wouldn't happen. Call it the arrogance of youth, or the arrogance of a man...the idea that I was invincible. But now I know—call it the wisdom of age—that I'm not invincible. I'm not going to take any risks. That, I can promise! But that is all. No-one—but no-one—Dana, can promise you invincibility."

I knew that—Papa, Mama, Anton, none of them had. Maybe I was the bad luck. Maybe I zapped the invincibility from those around me.

~~

I was tired. Tired of worrying. Tired of seeing and fearing death everywhere.

~~

Was it so hard to believe that there was a man, who really did love me enough to take on all my baggage (or all my crap, as Amelia would say)? Was it so hard to believe that men were also looking for the one, as much and as naturally as women? Are there men out there, ready and willing to make a commitment to someone else? Why and when had it become so difficult to believe in a man like that?

~~

It reminded me of a conversation Amelia had started, one *Rosh Chodesh*.

"Men are assholes because we let them be assholes. If we got rid of them as soon as they cheat, or as soon as they even think about cheating on us, then they might think twice about doing it again, or to someone else. If every women in the world refused to go out with, or marry a cheating bastard, well…then men might not do it! But we don't, we close our eyes, cover up the bruises and let them get away with it, and let them be assholes. So of course they keep on doing it."

Amelia's father's behaviour had shattered her mother's heart, but hardened Amelia's beyond belief.

But did I want that?

~~

I wanted to believe that he loved me. Would love me. But even if I got past that and could somehow believe that he wanted me—how could I live day-to-day, fearing for his life every time he left the house? Fearing that he might have a heart attack, or get run over by a bus, or be blown up or…or…or…and then how would I live without him?

Because isn't that what love did? It lured you into a false sense of security and then the world and all the horrors it contained took them away?

My children, I could keep safe. That was my power and responsibility as their mother. But him? How could I keep him safe?

~~

But was it better to have months or years of real, true love only to lose it, than to live decades, centuries, with someone you didn't love?

~~

And then one day it hit me. I couldn't live without him. Not even for a second. I had to be with him, my heart ached when I wasn't with him. My whole body physically hurt when I wasn't with him. It didn't matter how long we would have together. And the sooner we were together the more time we would have. I thought I could live without love for a man, but I was wrong. And suddenly I needed it more than ever.

~~

But the Family?—Beruriah, Amelia, Rachel.—How could I leave them? They had taken me in, when no-one else would or had even noticed me. I didn't know if I had the right to abandon them. I didn't want to lose them. But I couldn't live without Ilan. It took me almost me a month to realize it, but there it was.

"Take a chance on me!" Ilan had said.

We'd laughed.

"That sounds like a corny ABBA song," I'd said.

He'd beamed back at me. "Sorry!" and then, "So will you?"

How to explain that it wasn't just taking a chance on him, but on life and everything it had to throw back at us. And that it wasn't just my life I had to chance, but three others too.

His smile was infectious.

"Throw a dice?" I asked, smiling back.

"Something like that," he said, slipping his arm around my waist.

I looked up at him, "But doesn't the house always win?"

"Not always," he laughed, "Some people get lucky." And he bent to kiss me.

And then I felt as if I might just be ready to throw a dice again, even if I had my eyes shut with fear as it left my hand.

"No dice-throwing!" said Ilan, suddenly serious. "This is you and me. Not luck, not chance; but love, patience, hope, and hard work."

So I didn't shake and roll the dice, with fear and reluctance. Instead I tossed them high into the air, eyes open wide, and I didn't even stop to look where or how they had landed. Trust.

~~

I packed our things. It didn't take long. Most of Isaac's things I left behind. They were never his, just borrowed from the last baby and worn until the next one came along.

He was waiting outside in the car and I hustled the children down the stairs and into it. I passed him our bags and went back into the house.

~~

I wanted to tell them the truth, to let them know why. But I was too scared and too much of a coward to face their anger and also their disappointment.

~~

"I'm just going to the publisher's office, to collect the cheque for this month."

I could hear the children in the yard, their yells and screams carried through the house by the autumn wind.

Beruriah stood in the kitchen doorway. "Of course," she replied. We will see you for dinner," and she was gone. She assumed, I supposed, that my children were with hers.

I knew that no-one would question my going into Tel Aviv to collect the cheque. With Amelia gone, the cheque and the meagre social welfare payments the government gave us were all we had to live off. Oh, and what he managed to collect in donations. It all depended on how many people he had managed to convince that they would be better Jews by feeding our Jewish Family.

The government had just cut the social welfare payments again and my cheque was needed more than ever. What would they do when the cheque was gone for good? But then, there would be four fewer people to feed and clothe.

Rachel came up behind me, "Hi, where are you off to?"

"Just into town, to collect the cheque."

She smiled back. "Sure, see you later!" and she was gone also.

I thought they might have been a little suspicious. After all Amelia had vanished while going to collect her money. But nobody had questioned me. They had no idea. Did I want them to beg me to stay? To go down on their knees, grab at my skirt and insist I stay? May be, just a little. I would have settled for a hug and a goodbye.

~~

Then it was my turn. I closed the door behind me and couldn't resist one look back. This is where my children had been born. This is where I had lived when I fell in love with Ilan.

I got into the car and turned to Ilan.

He smiled. "Ready to go?"

"Yes." And I turned to my children in the back and smiled, "Are we ready to go?"

They looked confused but saw my smile and returned it. "Yes!" they shouted.

It was sad, driving away. I wasn't consumed by grief or wracked with guilt but I did feel sad. Sad that a part of my life was over. That that part of my life would never be again. I closed another door on my memories.

Sadness mingled with excitement, who would have thought two contrary emotions could have occupied the same space and mind at the same time; excitement that this was the beginning of something new.

Chapter 26—Rachel

I stirred the rice on the stove. It was almost done and just in time as hungry children began to crowd around the table.

"Go wash your hands!" Beruriah called over the din, counting heads as she did so. She counted once, and then again. "Where are Dana's children?" she asked me, a puzzled look on her face.

"They were in the yard," I replied turning off the heat and bringing the rice to the table.

"They're not here," insisted Dana, "I just counted them all and they're not here."

And there they were—one, two, three, four. Then Beruriah's youngest in the highchair and Amelia's baby upstairs asleep.

"They're not here," I repeated. "Maybe she took them with her?"

"But why?" Beruriah demanded to know. "She hasn't taken them all with her since Isaac was born."

"She'll be back soon. We can ask her then." And I began to spoon rice onto plates.

Beruriah left the room and I heard her feet on the stairs.

I wondered if she had reason to worry. Why would Dana take her children with her? Was it really that odd? She hated to be separated from them.

~~

"She left this," and Beruriah thrust a piece of paper in my face. I took it from her and opened it.

Dear Beruriah and Family,
I know I am being a coward for writing this to you rather than telling you straight but I was just too scared. The children and I have gone to live with Ilan, my father's

lawyer. I love him and he loves me and we want to be a family.

Sometimes I can't believe that I am leaving you all. I will miss you all deeply.

Please take the cheque and use it for the children. Maybe one day you will be able to forgive me.

Love, Dana

I handed the cheque to Beruriah who fingered it absentmindedly. The room was quiet.

"Eat!" Beruriah commanded. And the children picked up their forks.

"She's gone?' I asked, not quite believing it.... Dana gone?

That left me and Beruriah, and the children. And him.

It was a silent meal. The children piled the dishes into the sink and went to amuse themselves in their room with the promise of ice cream if they were quiet.

Beruriah stacked dishes as if everything was normal. Ideas that had been forming in my head for several months suddenly became crystal clear and a reality. It was time to go to.

I suppose it would seem as if I had taken all I needed from Beruriah and her Family of sisters; that I had learnt all I needed to know...and hence was moving on. But it wasn't like that.

~~

"Everything OK?" I asked as she handed me the dishes and I placed them by the sink.

"Of course," and she scrubbed away at the table for all she was worth.

I took the dirty dishes one by one and slipped them into the hot soapy water. It burnt my hands but I didn't care.

Was it, then, ...was this the sign I needed to make my own escape? With Amelia gone, and now Dana, what was there here for me anymore?

Beruriah looked up from her scrubbing, "You want to leave."

I jumped and the plate slipped from my wet hands back into the water. "I...."

"It's OK. I'm not as blind to what you all are thinking, or at least not as blind as Amelia thought I was. What is there here for you without the others?"

And she was right.

For the first time ever, Beruriah looked defeated. And tired. And worn out. "Go!" she said, "Just go!"

I didn't have time to shake the soap off my hands before I was dashing up the stairs, two at a time. I threw clothes and shoes into my bag as quickly as I could, worried that at any minute Beruriah would change her mind and come up the stairs to lock me in my room and stop my getting away.

But she didn't. And with my bag safely packed I went back to the kitchen. She was still scrubbing away at the old oak table.

"Good-bye Beruriah. I wanted to thank...."

"No need," she said ,without looking up.

"But I've learnt so much and...."

"No need."

"So, good-bye."

"Good-bye."

And just like that, I was out of the door and walking down the street...and free.

I took the bus into Tel Aviv, called Mom collect and she promised to wire me money straight away. I got a hotel room, and then a ticket home and then decided it was time to say good-bye to another good friend.

~~

I went to see Leah before my flight home.

"Hi!" she said, as she opened the door.

"Hi!" I said, as I walked in.

"How are you?"

"I'm good. I'm going home."

And she smiled, "I'm so glad. Maybe we'll see you. Jonathan has agreed to go to the States, to visit Mom and Dad....Their treat."

"That's great news," I replied, and smiled back.

Leah looked happier, more at ease—almost like the Leah I had once known in Ugg boots and denim miniskirts.

"You look good," I said

"Yeah, well; I finally lost the baby weight from the last one and I'm trying to keep myself baby-free for a little while."

"Sounds like a good idea."

"And you know, with Mom and Dad in the picture again, it's nice to know I have my own family there."

"It sure is," and I smiled again. "So I'll see you soon."

Leah smiled back and hugged me close, "You bet."

~~

Mom had wanted to meet me here, in Israel. They would fly over, she said. We could have a family holiday. But I said no. I wanted to go home. Israel was special to me now, and I wanted to keep it for my own. It was selfish perhaps, but it was what I wanted: to keep my memories of my time here intact.

It had all happened so fast. For months, doubt had been growing in my mind. I had agonized over whether I really wanted to leave, or not, and if so, how I would do it. That it had been so easy was a little disorientating and a little surreal. When I woke up that day, I had no idea that by evening I would be in a hotel, on my own, with a ticket home the next day.

For the first time in a year I took off my skirt and put on jeans. They were tight, having not been worn or washed for so long. I laid my blouse beside the skirt and pulled on a T-shirt. My arms felt eerily naked and rather exposed all of a sudden. A bit like how I felt.

Even just going to a coffee shop and ordering a coffee and salad was an ordeal. I hadn't interacted with

263

normal people for so long, that I worried I might have forgotten how to do it. My palms sweated as I relayed my order to the waitress. It was weird to have time to myself, with no-one else around. No Beruriah, no Amelia, no Dana. No kids.

~~

I never thought I'd ever get excited about putting on a pair of jeans. And yet here I was, as excited as a kid in a candy-store. Who would have thought that clothes could symbolize so much? And yet as I took off one set of clothes and put on another, I was saying 'farewell' to one life and 'hello' to another. Only now did I recognize the symbolism and the meaning.

I would keep my skirt and blouse as a reminder, They would take the place of the photos I didn't have.... Although that wasn't entirely true. There were some photos.... I turned on my camera and flicked through the few photos I had.... Dana with the children gathered around her, *Purim* face-masks on their faces or on top of their heads.... Beruriah stirring rice on the stove, her face protesting the presence of my camera.... And here was Amelia sunbathing in the yard, her pink designer bikini in contrast to the weeds and mouldy garden furniture.... And here we all were, the day we all went to the park in Tel Aviv.... There we were, with our matching dark skirts and blouses:—baby Isaac grinned in his Ima's arms and Rivka's legs could just be seen, kicking above the front bar of her stroller. Cheeky Shoshanna grinned for the camera from her big sister's knee. Serious Sara held her little sister tight and smiled shyly into the camera. Yuval lay with her head on her mother's lap and Dana stroked her hair almost absentmindedly as she hung on to Isaac with the other. Tamar sat by her mother's side and leant against her for comfort. Beruriah's boys stood at the back, their hands on each of their Ima's shoulders.... Then Amelia, just before her baby was born; and she looked big and bloated.... And then me, grinning with all my heart into the camera.

~~

That had been a great day. On *Yom Atzmaut* the Russian billionaire had hosted a free party in Yehousha park in Tel Aviv, with live shows, food and games for children.

As it was a rare free activity Beruriah decided we could go, with the words, "We are Israelis; it is our duty to celebrate."

Amelia cheered at the opportunity to be out amongst the public, although she soon descended into a state of gloom when she realized that she was still eight months pregnant and there wasn't a lot she cared to do, bar going to the toilet every five minutes and eating large quantities of cake. And even her enthusiasm for cake seemed to wane, the closer she got to her due date.

Dana was excited for the children's sake and they talked about little else, the whole week before the party.

This was my first *Yom Ha'Atzmut* and I couldn't wait to be a part of it as an Israeli.

Dana, Beruriah and he would take the older ones by bus. Amelia and I would take the babies in the car.... The car trunk was piled with rugs, a travel cot/playpen, a stroller to share among us, bottles of cola and Nestea, a big bag of sandwiches.

Amelia parked the car and we waited by it for the others. She was feeling particularly pleased with herself. She had found a parking space in Tel Aviv, relatively close to our destination; an achievement any day, let alone on *Yom Ha'atzmaut*, when parking spaces were rarer than gold dust. It seemed almost to make her forget that she was eight months pregnant.

~~

It made me remember once, many months ago, when I was new to the Family and Beurriah needed milk or something, so Amelia and I had gone out in the car to get it. We'd just driven to the nearest kiosk.

~~

"I'll park here," said Amelia making ready to do so.

"But this is a pedestrian crossing," I protested.

"So? It's close to where I need to go and there is nowhere else to park. We'll only be a little while," and she pushed her hazard lights on, as if that made it OK. "With these on, people will know we will be back in seconds."

~~

But back to *Yom Ha'atzmaut*.

The others soon arrived and, loaded down with paraphernalia, we crossed across the grass, past the lake and over to the party-site. The sun shone on us all as we waved for security to check our bags and let us through.

Music blared from one stage where one act had already begun, and a bouncy castle was already groaning under the weight of many bouncing children.

"Please Ima, can we go?" cried the children pulling Beruriah and Dana in all directions.

"Wait!" cried Beruriah. "Let's find a place to sit down, then you can all go off."

Israeli flags flew from strollers, picnic boxes, bicycles and dog collars.

I was so proud to be here. Proud to belong here. To be a part of something so fantastic and meaningful and special as a Jewish state. Pride in my Jewishness filled me. Proud that after more than two thousand years of being pushed and thrown from country to country, of being ostracized, beaten, isolated and persecuted, not to mention murdered in our diplomatic mission buildings, we were finally home.

And here we were—a modern, functioning country with a democratic government. What other fifty-eight year old country could boast of that? Today we celebrated the reality of our own homeland, finally returned to us. I tried to imagine what it would have meant to my Jewish ancestors, and I could see how it would have meant everything. And here I was; a part of history.

But even at the tender age of fifty-eight, there was no doubt that she was taken for granted. My mom was not much older and I'd taken her for granted for years.

But today I promised there would be no taking for granted our Jewish home. Today was the day to appreciate her and all she meant to us.

So the day passed. The children sang and danced along with the performers; among them.

They jumped and splashed in a fountain of foam and bubbles that someone had created on the grass. They bounced in the castle and ate candy-floss until their teeth hurt and Dana had to start pulling it out of their hair.

~~

We sat on blankets on a little grass hill overlooking the whole party-ground. Nothing could ruin our day, not even the despairing looks of people who walked past, confused and unsure of our family situation.

"Snobs in Israel, that's a strange idea," I thought outloud.

"Why?" asked Dana, lying on her side next to me, her head propped up by her hand. Isaac lay on the grass beside her and she tickled his tummy.

"Well, because Israel is so, so equal? No?"

Dana laughed, "There are snobs in Israel. Apart from the fact that every Israeli, regardless of wealth or background, thinks himself or herself better than the next man!"

And I laughed too. Israeli arrogance could put American arrogance to shame.

"But snobbery exists, as in any society. The wealthy, the educated, even the middle classes look down on the poor, the orthodox, the immigrants."

She paused to tickle Isaac's toes and to meet his smile with one of her own. "We live in a land made up entirely of immigrants. Every Israeli was once an immigrant, however many years or generations back. And yet we

have a snobbery based on how early you or your relatives
came here, and where they came here from."

"Ashkenazi versus Sephardim," I said.

Dana nodded, "The Ashkenazi-Sephardim divide is
eroding. It's taken sixty years to do it, but it's finally
going. Now it's Israeli versus the Russians, versus the
Ethiopians. Almost as if there always has to be a
downtrodden lesser class of people to look down on, until
everyone is assimilated. But assimilation takes time. And
placing Ethiopian immigrants in half-empty, deserted,
kibbutz in the middle of the desert, with no transport links
to jobs and Israeli society will only slow the assimilation
down."

Dana was flushed, carried away with her words; and
then in an instant, was almost apologetic. "I know I get
carried away with it all sometimes. But I feel as if I have
to. Everyone complains about the Russians who
emigrated. Because the government gave us apartments,
money for cars, that kind of thing. As if we weren't
grateful for it, which of course we were. When really all
we wanted was to belong.

"Oh, I know a lot of Russian immigrants were
economic refugees, looking for high salaries here, and
nothing more. But a lot of us wanted to be here, so we
could be home. We might have got a better deal from the
government, but the Ethiopians get a better deal from
society. Everyone thinks we are gun-wielding mafia dons,
while the Ethiopians—well, no-one thinks badly of
them!" Dana was flushed again. She sat up and held Isaac
on her knee; from where he waved at the people and
sights below. Dana stroked the dark fuzz on his head. "I
just want my children to be so assimilated that any
Russian in them has gone forever. I don't even want them
to be aware of it. Russia never really wanted me, and I
certainly don't want it. We are Jewish, we are Israelis. We
don't need any more labels than that. There is nothing we
need to remember or hold on to. We have our Jewish

culture, customs, traditions and history. We don't need anything from Russia. We were unwelcome guests there, and so we left. I just wish sometimes we didn't feel so unwelcome here."

Even Amelia was quiet. She too lay on her back, allowing the sun to radiate over her. She used her hands to shield her eyes from the sun. But it was Amelia who eventually broke the silence. "Whew! Talk about patriotic!"

Beruriah shot her a look, daring her to ruin the day, "We should all be proud to be Israeli," she shot back.

Amelia glared back at her. "Some of us are patriotic," she replied. "Some of us served in the army!"

Beruriah held her gaze on Amelia. "Patriotism is not all about holding a gun in your hands."

"No, nor is it about hiding at home behind the Torah, when others are being shot at and blown up defending this place," retorted Amelia. Her reply was surprisingly quick and surprisingly intelligent. And then she turned on me. "I'm surprised you didn't go knocking on the door of the IDF. That's what most lost American Jews do."

I didn't dare admit that it had been an option, and one I had perhaps been about to pursue, had I not found the Family when I did, or if they had not found me.

"I never held a gun," said Dana calmly. "Apart from during basic training, which only lasted three weeks. The rest of my two years I was in an office."

Amelia shot her a look. "That's not the point," she almost snarled. She also was now sitting upright, as if lying down gave her some disadvantage in the argument.

"You served, that's the point!"

It was strange to see Amelia so passionate about something so politically important and relevant. The only thing I'd seen her this worked up about before, was when Sara had finished her last diet coke from the fridge.

It also wasn't characteristic of Beruriah to reveal much of herself. But now, perhaps to protect her patriotism from Amelia's spirited attack, she did. "Joining the army was never an option for me, no matter how much I love Israel," she stated clearly.

You had to give it to Beruriah, she knew how to stay calm when under attack. "Even my brothers weren't allowed to go. They were expected to study to be closer to G-d, not to take up arms. I was a girl; my place was at home with the other women, with the babies and the washing and the cooking."

Amelia didn't look convinced, but then she so rarely was convinced by anything, especially not by anything Beruriah said.

Beruriah was still patient. "I don't expect you to understand, Amelia. We live in the same country, but we might as well have grown up in different ones. Our childhoods, our upbringings, our families were so different. Joining the army, any branch of it—be it in the battlefield or in an office—was never an option for me."

"And your children?" Amelia demanded to know, refusing to let Beruriah off that easily, or without a fight.

"They are Israel's," was Beruriah's calm reply. "They must choose for themselves if G-d is asking them to fight or to study his teachings. I hope that they love their country very much and that they are able to decide the best way to serve her—either by defending her, or by building her up with religion and following the best way to live."

"Whatever!" snorted Amelia, who was never gracious in defeat. "They'll be like the rest of the Orthodox…hiding behind their black hats and Torahs."

Beruriah was still calm. "It is easy to be angry at what seems unfair, but G-d works in his own way and wishes us all to serve him and Israel differently."

"What a cop-out!" cried Amelia. "Just because they are too scared to get out there and give their lives for this country they use G-d as an excuse. When they don't want to go out and work, they use G-d as an excuse. When they can't stop getting their wives pregnant and producing yet more screaming brats that they expect the government to clothe and feed, they use G-d as an excuse."

"G-d has different paths for everyone," insisted Beruriah.

"Bullshit!" cried a very angry Amelia, as Dana rushed to cover Isaac's ears from Amelia profanities.

"He's just an excuse for laziness and cowardice and everything else!"

~~

"Ladies, ladies are we enjoying ourselves?" And then he was there and all conversation stopped. Amelia still seethed with anger, but she did so quietly and turned away.

"Of course, of course," cried Beruriah. Whether her enthusiasm and happiness was genuine was always too difficult to say. Amelia insisted it was forced. Dana insisted that it was real. I just didn't know.

He stroked Isaac's head. I wondered if he even remembered his name. "It's a wonderful day!" he cried.

And we all nodded. As one Family, we agreed with him. "Lunch!" he cried again. "Come, let's eat lunch!"

And with that command, we set about laying out food. Beruriah called the children in. And we sat and devoured the picnic.

~~

The babies slept at the back of the car. At home I helped Dana put them to bed without their baths. We took off their socks and slipped them under the covers.

In the yard he had the barbecue alight. The boys fanned the flames as the girls helped Beruriah and Amelia chop vegetables for salads and season the meat.

I went straight to the bread and started cutting it into thick slices, while Dana mixed Tahini to go with... well... with everything. Beruriah made fresh limona, which she poured from the jug into our waiting cups, and we drank cupful after cupful of the sweet and sour drink.

We ate the meat with our fingers or sandwiched between the bread. Tahini and meat juices dripped onto my fingers and I licked them up with delight. Even Amelia got down and dirty with the rest of us and ate her way through what she claimed was almost a whole cow!

We took ourselves out of the yard and sat on the hill. And we watched the fireworks over Rosh Ha'ayin. They weren't the most spectacular fireworks I'd ever seen, not even close. But they suited us and Rosh Ha'ayin just fine. I don't know if we—or Rosh Ha'ayin—could have handled anything more spectacular anyway. When the fireworks were gone, and all that remained was their smoke that clouded the sky, we stayed and waited for the stars to re-appear.

I wondered, who had walked on this land before me? … Jew, Arab, Jew, Arab… And now the bottom of a Jew sat upon it!

Lights twinkled in the distance…. Artificial stars…. From here it was hard to tell what was Palestinian territory and what was Israel…. But from here it didn't matter…. From here it was all just light and stars. This had officially become my most favourite holiday ever.

"So how did you like your first *Yom Ha'atzmaut*?" asked Dana, resting her head on my shoulder. And there and then, I had felt truly accepted.

"It was fantastic! Words can't describe it."

"That was your proper welcome to Israel. Sorry it was almost a year too late."

I laughed, and Dana laughed with me.

"What's so funny?" Amelia demanded to know. She lay flat on her back, her tummy a large mound up above her. God knows how she was going to get back up again.

"Today. Life."

"It's beautiful," whispered Beruriah, as one by one the stars reemerged from the smoke left behind by the fireworks.

And it was. All of it.

~~

And yet I decided that I had more to give than this. I loved the Family. I had come to love them. But this wasn't for me anymore. There was a world out there, a world that I wanted to be a part of. A world that I wanted to learn about. A world that I wanted to make a difference in. I wanted all the things the Family could offer—the company, the sisterhood, the children—but I wanted more than that too. I wanted to make a difference, to really help and I wasn't able to do any of that here.

Sometimes we need to go to extremes to find ourselves. And, yes, it sure would be easier if we could do it from the comfort of our own homes. But sometimes that just isn't possible, and we have to go on crazy journeys to find out who we are and what we believe and what we need.

I miss them all... the stern—but motherly—Beruriah.... The gentleness and eagerness of Dana.... The prickliness and yet fun that was Amelia.... They were my sisters and my Family. And they taught me so much about Judaism and my place in Judaism. About life and my place in life. They taught me things I could never have learnt by myself. I owed them a lot. I missed them a lot.

It would have been nice to have thought that we could have all met again one day and that in doing so we'd be able to recreate the family we had—if only for an afternoon. But as close as we had been—it had been the Family that had kept us close and without that we had nothing in common anymore. No shared memories or interests to talk about. No common understanding.

I spoke to Dana on facebook—from sisters, to facebook friends. It doesn't seem like a fair trade somehow, but we know how much we love and miss each other.

Amelia dropped off the radar and Beruriah would always be there, in the home. But could I ever go back? ... We had abandoned her, deserted her.... Who could face the awkwardness of that?... I was a coward and couldn't.

Dana was braver than I and had tried. She'd wanted to see Beruriah, and Amelia's son. But Beruriah wouldn't let her. She wouldn't let her further than the front step. It was a punishment she had decided upon us for leaving, and it was a punishment we all accepted with a great deal of guilt.

"Please Beruriah! Just let me see the children. Just to say hello. I brought presents!" Dana's tone was pleading, verging on the brink of begging.

But Beruriah held her head high and refused to crack. Her stone eyes met Dana's soft ones and refused to melt.

"No, it will only upset them. I won't have them upset again."

Dana tried to smile, anything in an attempt to soften Beruriah. "Come on, Beruriah, we're family. I just want to say 'hello'."

"*Were* family," said Beruriah, with the emphasis very much on the 'were'. "You have your own family now." and she nodded to the car parked on the road, where Dana's children and he sat.

Dana turned around to look at the car too and something inside her seemed to snap. Her whole body sank and she turned to Beruriah with—if not acceptance—then defeat. "So this is my punishment!"

"Not punishment. Just what is best for the children."

Dana turned to go, the Toys'RUs bag, full of presents, still swung from her hand. She didn't dare leave it.

Beruriah was hurt, anyone could see that. She was hurt too badly to forgive Dana, or any one of us. She forgave Amelia only for her son's sake. You can't raise a child and hate its mother, its real mother. You can never love a child that way.

~~

Amelia never went back to claim her son. That much Dana learnt from Lucille. She ended up in Thailand with an Englishman and together they ran a guest-house. So she had found her calling.

Of all people, Dana kept in touch with Lucille. Theirs was an unlikely friendship, forged from Beruriah's refusal to let either into her Family. I always hoped Amelia's son knew how many people loved him. His mother never did, or could never bring herself to; she didn't even try. But there were so many other people desperate for just a glimpse of him.

Maybe it wasn't right for Beruriah to use him to punish those who had hurt her. But she did it anyway. Who was to stop her?

~~

Amelia's mother died the same year that her grandson was born and abandoned. The newspapers quoted a suspected suicide and something about an overdose of valium pills. According to Lucille, Amelia never saw her mother before she died. And her mother never saw her grandson.

Her surname headed each newspaper, its bold print staring out at me from the kiosk. Even in death, that name—the name of those who had come before her—was bigger than her, much bigger than she could ever be, To Amelia that name had been a curse. Even when attached to her father's name, it towered over every thing. But Amelia never realized that it had been just as great—if not a greater burden—on her mother, as it had been on her. On her mother it had been heavier, with no other name to balance it or distract from it. And even in death, it overpowered her.

~~

That was the biggest tragedy... that no-one mourned Amelia's mother in death, in much the same way that they had ignored her when she was alive. The more hysterical she became, the more pills she took, the closer to self-destruction she got, the more people turned away. The louder she screamed for attention, the less people listened. And in death it was no different. She had a big, elaborate funeral. Lucille made sure of that. Hundreds of mourners filled the cemetery, but how many really grieved for her? Lucille tried, but it had been years since her mother had been anyone she could recognize; and she was not sure who or what she was grieving for. She grieved, not for her mother as the person she was, but for an idealized picture of what she had always wanted her mother to be. Amelia's father was there, suitably contrite. Lucille held his arm, the two of them matching in black Armani. Amelia was missing. Who knows how she felt about her mother's death, or even if she felt anything at all? Guilt? Sorrow? Regret? Relief? Sorrow? Joy? Whatever she felt, it wasn't strong enough to compel her to attend the funeral.

Chapter 27—Beruriah

My life fell part. I, who had never let myself get too close to any of them, had lost my sisters. They were quickly replaced, and I welcomed my new co-wives as I had the others, but things were never the same.

Lonely Dana, confused Rachel, rebellious Amelia—they had been my sisters. Something I realized only after I had lost them. The only reminder I had of any of them was Amelia's son.—His blonde curls stood him out from our brown-haired, dark eyed sons and daughters.—He would know he was different; and one day I would have to tell him about the Mothers and Family he once had.

I would have to put into words for him how a group of women, with nothing in common but one man, the house they lived in and a shared religion, came to be a Family. How they came together to be a Family, without meaning to; and in some cases with some resistance.

But if I know anything, it is that families change. That there is no permanence in the idea of a Family. And that families must be rebuilt again and again. Which is what I'm doing—rebuilding this Family again.

There isn't time for me or my thoughts, when there are children to put to bed, to feed, and new babies to be clothed and a house to run.

This is my life. This is my role. I am not running from that. Not for me the luxury of running off to Thailand, or of returning to a family in the USA, or of starting a new life with a lawyer from Tel Aviv. When I was younger, I used to think I had those choices. But I know now that I don't, that I have never had those choices. This is my life. This is my role. I am not running from that. I am a Jewish woman living in our ancestral homeland, and I have a Jewish family to raise. The luxury of thinking about myself does not exist. It did not exist for Sara, for Rebecca, for Leah, or Rachel. And it does not exist for me; no more than it existed for my mother or her mother, or the countless women who came before them and whose blood I share.

If it was their life then; it only follows that it is mine too. It is not a burden; it is simply my life. I will be here, I will live, and I will die. My children will live, and die. Our lives are nothing but a tiny drop in the ocean, compared to the lives that came before us and will come after us. Why then should ours be any different, any better, any worse? Why should mine be any different, any better, any worse?

I never mourned the opportunities I didn't get to explore, because I never had them. This is the life I was born into; this was the only life I was going to get; this was the life that was intended for me.

For Dana, Rachel and Amelia, this life had been just a chapter in their lives, a temporary thing. But for me it was real life. The only life I had. The only life I was going to have. But that didn't depress nor sadden me. It was the life my ancestors had lived, and it was the life the matriarchs of the Torah had lived. What was good enough for them was good enough for me.

Dana, Rachel and Amelia were looking for something more than what they had. They weren't happy with the cards, or the family, that life had dealt them and they were seeking to change that.

At home, in the Family, I knew how it worked. There were set, known, rules and we followed them. I had a large amount of control over the things we did, and saw, and said and ate. It was my Family.

Out there, beyond the walls of our home, well, that was something different. A large, hostile world, where you were nobody, vulnerable to attack and abuse and hurt and pain.

No, better the devil I knew between these four walls and the pages of the Torah, than to even begin to face what was out there.

A modern woman would scorn me—like Amelia did. Or pity me, like Rachel did. Or feel torn between her desire to be content with what she had, yet craving love and society's acceptance, like Dana did.

She was the only one who understood why she lived as she did. It was a life she had committed herself to. Only it wasn't her destiny, wasn't in her blood, the way it was in mine. But she was the only one who had come close to understanding it—her, the professor's daughter from Moscow.

So while their leaving was sad, and sadder than I at first realized, and while I missed them as sisters, life went on. It had done so after Lilach had died, and it did after they left. Children would continue to be born, to grow older and to start the cycle all over again. Who was I to want for anything more than that? Who was I to interfere with that?

I didn't need more than that.

I will never forget them, though, my sisters.

Did Dana find her happy ending? I don't know. But she got to be happy in the meantime, which I think she realized was a much better deal.

Did Rachel find herself? Maybe, but ultimately she learnt something more important—that it takes a lifetime to find oneself and that it's in living that we find whoever we are. It's not a destination but a journey.

Did Amelia achieve the ultimate? Running as far away as possible from her biological family; hurting her mother beyond belief?—She was in Thailand when her mother committed suicide, so on some level, she did.—I don't know if she ever wanted more than that, but if she did, I hope she found it…. Poor, lost Amelia!

And me? I wait to welcome my sixth child into the world, as our new sister and mother waits to welcome her first. I light the candles on Friday night to welcome in the *Shabbat*, the children around the table watching and listening as the candles flicker and my voice fills the room. We sit down and we eat.

I don't need more than that.

WRITE TO US!

We are interested to read your comments on
Rebecca Tomasis, *Mishpacha – Family*.
Write to our email address,
info@proversepublishing.com,
giving us a few sentences
which you are willing for us to publish,
describing your response to this book.
If your comments are chosen to be included
in our E-Newsletter or website,
we will select another title published by Proverse
and send you a complimentary copy.
When you write to us, please include your name, email
address and correspondence address.
Unless you state otherwise, we will assume that we may
cut or edit your comments for publication.
We will use your initials to attribute your comments.

Mishpacha – Family by Rebecca Tomasis
A Universal Issue of Love, Pain, Struggle, and Healing

I was engrossed when I first read this most outstanding piece, and could not put it down until after 2am.

Like other Chinese, I grew up in Hong Kong without attachment to religion. I am neither familiar with the Jewish life nor do I possess a strong curiosity to explore it. But my eyes were captured by the struggles of the families presented in *Mishpacha*. The families come from different corners of the world, practice extremely different cultures carried over from their host countries, yet bind into a single block – Judaism – their desire to lead a real Jewish life. As a result these families encounter traumatic transnational experiences in their "homeland". On top of these rough situations, these families are torn by inter-generational conflicts. This raises an interesting debatable question: whether the passive immigrants – the children brought to Israel by their parents' idealisms and motivations – should have the right to be nurtured by their own culture? In fact the novel's main characters constantly rethink the myth of creating a Jewish state and critically question: What has my life got to do with the state that is called my ancestral country?

In this sense the novel deals with a universal issue – the dynamic relationships between family and state, between cultures, between the varied world-views and motivations possessed by young and old generations.

My father was an Indonesian-born Chinese. He went to Maoist China in the 1950s to fulfill his idealism – building a new China for his ancestral nation. Although he lived in his "home country" for nearly twenty years, my father never felt at home there; he even refused to use chopsticks as a protest against China's assimilation policy. In the 1970s he wanted very strongly to go back to Indonesia, and claimed that he finally realized that his real "homeland" was nowhere else but Indonesia, although his daughter (me) felt Hong Kong to be her home. My father's obsession with constantly seeking a symbolic home nation is extremely beneficial as a means for me to understand the beliefs, behaviours, desires, and strategies of the families portrayed in *Mishpacha*. Although I am a complete outsider from the Jewish communities and do not even have any close Jewish friends, *Mishpacha* touches me deeply.

In the process of creating the Jewish state, the concept of Judaism can be manipulated by religious leaders and power-hungry politicians. Families residing in "host societies" also actively exploit the concept of Jewish blood to maximize opportunities by tackling rules and resources available in the "homeland". This is similar to my father's idealism that had so much included my grandparents' desire to find social mobility for their offspring, where the new-born China promised numerous privileges to "repatriates". Unfortunately, they could not foresee the traumatic Cultural Revolution, although they were good at risk calculation. In the late 1990s the world media reported that Indonesian Chinese had been brutally assaulted by indigenous Indonesians, who alleged that ethnic Chinese controlled the national economy. During that financial crisis a comparison was current among Indonesian Chinese – they claimed that their fate was similar to the history of the Jews.

As for the repatriated families, the aspirations of some have been hindered in Israel and some families have done well. Behind the moral of returning to the Jewish ancestral homeland, the motivations of these "returnees" are not so much different from those of migrants who seek social mobility or personal advancement through international migration. The difference is whether the Jews adopt unique strategies to make the best deals for themselves so as to advance a new life in their ancestral country, deals which are better than other migrants do.

However, *Mishpacha* seems to give a hint that the Jewish strategies are similar to others, and actually they often make the same old deals.

Dealing with this kind of grand topic, it is easy to present a tedious textbook somewhat like political science. However, the author sensually delivers a vividly colourful story about how young women negotiate for favourable lifestyles, love, and power while dealing with family difficulties and the external forces in Israel. From this "bottom up" angle, we learn more social and cultural implications of a peculiar transnational environment rooted in the history of Judaism.

The transformation of people's private lives is one of the very characteristics of modernity. In the past neighbours or fellow villagers could be ascribed as one's life friends, whilst making friends nowadays is up to personal choice and mutual interests that require individuals to present a best self to others. Family, traditionally an economic unit, is now injected with new ideas: marriage is increasingly based upon emotional communication; having a child is more related to psychological and emotional needs; parental authority is replaced by equal interaction with offspring.

Leading a city life in Hong Kong, we get used to measure an ideal family life with liberal and modern values. Interestingly, *Mishpacha* sketches some young women who grew up in the modern world who want nothing, but desire to lead a rigid religious lifestyle and form a feudalistic family. Even though the desire for fundamentalist tradition requires them to sacrifice the comfort, education, and parental love they had at home in the US. Perhaps this is the only part of the novel that I could not relate to. However, I believe in differences and I accept differences. There are some women who can find a sense of security and thus happiness in strict religious rules, and they do not need modern women to liberate them from tradition.

In this sense, the novel presents more than a dynamically exotic culture to non-Jews. Its charm lies in its clever way of delving into the myth of religious institutional systems. People who want to make their lives meaningful tend to use cultural and religious logics to restructure their lifestyles. The more extreme tradition they practice, the they may feel themselves to be heroic.

From the narrations of several Jewish women, the novel reveals that the Jews from a variety of countries who practice the Jewish culture and religion are extremely diverse – from ultra orthodox to modern liberal. Yet these dissimilar people are urged by a peculiar obsession – going "back" to their ancestral land. Through the young women's painful experiences, *Mishpacha* creates an ambitious thinking place in itself – throughout the book it desperately tries to find out: What on earth has my life got to do with this abstract and symbolic homeland?

The novel has a rhythm composed by its black humour and sometimes by light humour. It has its own characteristic literary style. Its structural plot runs smoothly with the recurring serious discussions about Judaism and the creation of Israel. It is delightful to see that Hong Kong – an international city upholding freedom of creativity – has eventually become the birthplace of *Mishpacha*.

Yeeshan Yang
author of *Whispers and Moans* and *Palma's Tears*

Glossary

Abba: father/Daddy.

Abu Ghosh: an Arab village near Jerusalem, famous for its hummus, and popular with Jewish Israelis looking for good food.

Aravah (sing) / Aravot (plural): willow(s).

Arava: a plant or bush with no taste and no smell. One of the symbolic plants used during Sukkot.

Ashkenazi: Jews who originated from Eastern and Western Europe.

Azrielli: an office and shopping complex in the centre of Tel Aviv.

Bamba: a popular Israeli peanut-flavoured snack, popular with babies, children and adults.

Bar Mitzvah: marks the Jewish girl's acceptance into maturity.

Bat Mitzvah: marks the Jewish boy's acceptance into maturity.

Bedouin: desert-dwelling Arabic ethnic group.

Beitzah- Hebrew for egg.

Bisli: a popular, savory, fried-wheat snack, eaten by Israeli adults and children alike.

Blag (verb): to convince someone to give you something by words.

Bnei Berak: a city of mainly Orthodox religious families, located just to the East of Tel Aviv.

Breslev Hasidim- an Orthodox Jewish group that promote spirituality, mysticism and the joy of worship. Named after the town, Breslev, where they originate.

Burger Ranch: local Israeli kosher fast food chain.

Burqa: head-to-toe covering worn by devout Muslim women.

Café Aroma: a chain of popular Israeli coffee shops.

Café Netto: a chain of popular Israeli coffee shops.

Chabad: founded in the late 18th century, Chabad is a powerful force within Judaism. It has institutions in 75 countries, providing outreach and educational activities for

Jews through Jewish community centers, synagogues, schools and camps.

Challah: a Jewish egg bread that is eaten on the Sabbath and often plaited.

Chanukah: Jewish festival of light. It lasts for eight days.

Charoset: a sweet paste made of apple, nuts, wine, sugar and cinnamon. It is eaten on Passover to symbolize the mortar used by the Israelites on the bricks they used during their forced labour in Egypt.

Dizengoff Street: one of Tel Aviv's most popular boulevards, full of shops and restaurants. Named after the first mayor of Tel Aviv, Meir Dizengoff.

Dreidel: spinning top, usually wooden. Played with by children on Hannuakh.

Etrog: yellow citron.

Fox: a popular and reasonably priced clothing chain.

Galgalatz: a popular Israeli radio station broadcast by the army and liked for its English and Hebrew popular music.

Gefilte fish: a sweet stuffed fish patty, favoured by European and American Jews.

Ha'aretz: how Israelis refer to Israel, when they are abroad.

Hadassim: bough of a myrtle tree.

Haman: vizier of King Ahasuerus in the 6th century BCE. (See also "Purim" below and Notes to Chapter 14 below.)

Haman's ears: a three-cornered sweet pastry filled with poppy-seed eaten at *Purim*.

Herzeliya: a costal district of Tel Aviv, known for its wealthy residential areas and its marina.

Herzeliya Pituach- a very wealthy residential area within the district of Herzeliya.

Hummus: a popular Middle Eastern dip made of chickpeas.

IDF: Israeli Defense Forces.

Ima: mother/Mummy.

Irgun: a Zionist militant group during the British Mandate over what was then called Palestine. Their aim was the creation of a Jewish state.

Jaffa: an ancient port, and part of the Tel Aviv municipality. Now famous for its Arabic food and artists' colony.

Kadima: the middle school age affiliate of United Synagogue Youth and The United Synagogue of Conservative Judaism. Kadima is Hebrew for "forward."

Khat: natural stimulant drug, deriving from the *Catha edulis* shrub.

Kibbutz: co-operative agricultural community.

Kiddush: Jewish prayer for the dead.

Kinneret or Lake Kinneret (also "Kineret"): the Sea of Galilee, Israel's largest freshwater lake.

Kippa (singular) /kippot (plural): Jewish skull-cap worn by males over the age of three years old. Worn to show reverence for God.

Kuba: fried Iraqi dish containing minced meat.

Latkes: fried potato cakes, popular amongst Ashkenazi Jews. Eaten mainly at Hannukah.

Limonana: a popular Israeli cold drink of lemonade and mint.

Lulav: closed frond of the date palm.

Ma'abarot: refugee camps in Israel in the 1950s.

Magen David: the star of David, used as a symbol of Judaism.

Makot: a popular game played with two bats and a ball; played primarily by Israelis on the beach.

Magic Carpet Operation: this took place between June 1949 and September 1950, when many Yemenite Jews were airlifted from Yemen to Israel in transport airplanes.

Manga: Hebrew for barbecue.

Marror: refers to the bitter herbs eaten at the Passover Seder in keeping with the Torah commandment, "With bitter herbs they shall eat it." (Exodus 12:8). The word derives from the Hebrew word *mar* (מר — "bitter"). (*Wikipedia.*)

Mazel-Tov: Hebrew for Congratulations.

Megillah: means 'scroll.' The Megillah Esther is the scroll containing the Book of Esther which tells the story of Purim.

Meir Panim: a soup kitchen mainly for children from poor families.

Mishpacha: Hebrew for family.

Mitzvah: See "Bar Mitzvah" and "Bat Mitzvah", above.

Mordechai prevented the annihilation of the Jewish people.

Moshav: an agricultural settlement. Very few are now co-operatives.

Nana: Hebrew for mint. Tea with fresh mint is a very popular Israeli and Arabic drink.

Parve: neutral foods that are neither dairy products nor meat. In Jewish dietary practice, parve foods can be eaten with dairy products or meat.

Passover: Jewish festival celebrating the Jewish people's Exodus from Egypt.

Pesach: Passover.

Purim: a celebration of how in the 6th century BCE, Queen Esther foiled the plan of Haman, vizier of King Ahasuerus, to kill all Jews. (See also Notes to Chapter 14 below.)

Ramat Ha'sharon: a wealthy suburb of Tel Aviv, famous for its strawberries and Tennis Centre.

Rabin Square: a public square in the middle of Tel Aviv. Rabin, the then Prime Minister was killed here by a Jewish extremist in November 1995. Rabin Square is still used for public rallies and celebrations.

Reviva and Celia: restaurant in the up-market residential area of Ramat H'Sharon.

Rosh Chodesh: —the first day of the new month; a time for women to get together.

Rosh Ha'ayin: city in the centre of Israel, founded largely by Yemenite Jews.

Rosh Hashanah: the Jewish New Year, celebrated on the seventh day of the year.

Schnitzel: a traditional Austrian dish consisting of an escalope coated in breadcrumbs and fried

Seder: the Passover Seder is the dinner held on the eve of Passover to remember and relive the Exodus from Egypt. Seder literally means 'order'.

Sekhakh: literally, "covering". As one of the children explains to Rachel, *sekhakh* must be something that grew from the ground and was cut off, such as tree branches, corn stalks, bamboo reeds or sticks.

Sephardim: originally used to describe Jews with Spanish origins, now applied to Jews from Spain, North Africa and the Middle Eastern States.

Shammus: the main candle used to light the other candles in the Chanukah (Chanukah candlestick).

Seder Plate: used to hold the symbolic foods used during the Passover meal and celebration.

Shabbat: Jewish Sabbath/day of rest. Begins on Friday evening and ends on Saturday evening.

Shekel: unit of currency used in the state of Israel.

Shenkin Street: a trendy and popular street in Tel Aviv. It is lined with local and international designer clothes shops.

Shilav: a chain of stores selling baby products, clothes and toys.

Shwarma: meat kebab wrapped in pita or Arabic bread.

Sixty Minutes: a current affairs news programme from the USA.

Sukkah: literally means "booths". These are built on Sukkot to remind Jewish people of the temporary shelters their ancestors lived in during their forty-one years of wandering, after leaving Egypt with Moses.

Sukkot: a festival to celebrate the harvest and to remember the forty-one years the Israelites spent in the desert trying to find Israel.

Tallit: Jewish prayer-shawl.

Tel Aviv: second largest city in Israel and her financial capital.

Todah: Hebrew for "thanks".

Torah: one written part of the Jewish Bible, more familiarly known to non-Jews as the Old Testament.

Ugg boots: "Ugg" is an Australian brand of high-quality sheep-skin boots made famous when worn by pop-stars and actresses in Hollywood.

Yehousha Park: a large park situated to the north of Tel Aviv.

Yeshiva: a school where the Jewish Torah (bible) is studied by males.

Yom Ha'atzmaut: Israel's Day of Independence.

Yom Kippur: the Day of Atonement, and the most solemn day in the Jewish year.

Z'roa: usually a lamb shank bone, a part of the Pesach plate, there to symbolize the Pesach sacrifice of a lamb, which was once the sacrificing of a lamb at the Temple in Jerusalem.

Chapter Notes

General

Tomasis uses both "G-d" and "God" and explains her usage as follows. "Religious Jews do not write God on any piece of paper or document that might be or could be destroyed. So when Beruriah speaks, for example, I have it written 'G-d' as this is how she would write it. However when Amelia and her sister and Ifat speak, it is written as 'God' as this is how they would write it, not being religious."

Chapter 1

On 12 August 1952, fifteen Soviet Jews were falsely charged with capital offenses. Thirteen of them were executed in the basement of Lubyanka Prison in Moscow, Russia. This event is known as the Night of the Murdered Poets (although five only were actually poets).

The arrests of these fifteen occurred in September 1948 and June 1949, as a result of Joseph Stalin's increasingly violent antisemitism. All were falsely accused of espionage and treason as well as many other crimes. After their arrests, they were tortured, beaten, and isolated for three years before being formally charged. Ironically and cruelly, the five Yiddish writers among these defendants were all part of the Jewish Anti-Fascist Committee; a World War II organ dedicated to rallying support for the Soviet Union against Nazi Germany. (Wikipedia, 21 June 2010.)

Chapter 9

"A house of five adults and six children": The five adults are: Beruriah, Dana, Rachel, Amelia and Him. There are seven children in the house when Rachel joins it; Beruriah gives birth to a daughter (Rivka), and Amelia gives birth to a baby boy, unnamed, after Rachel joins and by the end of the novel.

Chapter 14

"The difference between Haman and Mordechai".

The Purim story can be found in the Book of Esther, in what non Jews call the Old Testament. (To the Jewish people there is only the one Testament, the Torah. They do not recognize the New Testament.) Esther was Jewish and chosen by the King of the time from all of the young and beautiful women in his kingdom to replace his wife. Esther did not reveal to the King that she was Jewish. Esther's uncle, Mordechai, uncovers a plot to assassinate the King and as a result his dedication to the King is remembered. Haman is appointed by the King as his prime minister and soon issues a decree that all the Jews in the Kingdom be killed. The King agrees to this. However Mordechai is owed something in reward for saving the King's life, while Esther reveals her Jewishness and begs for her people to be saved. Haman's actions anger the King and he orders him to be hanged on the gallows originally meant for Mordechai. The original decree calling for the killing of all Jews cannot be rescinded but the King allows the Jewish people to defend themselves. Mordechai goes on to assume a high position in the King's court.

"We trooped up after her, it took all of us to get eight brats washed and into bed." — At this stage in the story, the eight are: Tamar, Yuval, Isaac, Sara, Yeshua, Shoshanna, Yonatan, Rivka.

About the Author

Rebecca Tomasis was born in the United Arab Emirates, spent her later childhood years in Turkey and has called Hong Kong home since she was eleven. She is married to Ido Tomasis. She has three young children, a daughter (Tamar Naomi Tomasis) and two sons (Yuval Ethan Tomasis and Aviv Nathan Tomasis). None of the family is described in any way in the book, which is a work of fiction.

Although she has been writing all her life, "Mishpacha – Family" is her first completed novel. Tomasis attributes her love of writing to two sources, her passion for reading and her interest in people and how people think and feel and interact with each other. During her history studies at University it was always the stories of the people involved in each particular time period or historical event, that gripped her most. Her travels across the world have served to fuel her interest in people and their families and she has a particular interest in the Middle East and its fascinating culture, history and people.

About Proverse Hong Kong

Proverse Hong Kong (PVHK) is based in Hong Kong with long-term and expanding regional and international connections.

Proverse has published novels, novellas, non-fiction (including autobiography, biography, history, memoirs, sport, travel narratives, fictionalized autobiography), single-author poetry and short-story collections, children's, teens / young adult and academic books. Other interests include diaries, and academic works in the humanities, social sciences, cultural studies, linguistics and education. Some Proverse books have accompanying audio texts. Some are translated into Chinese.

Proverse welcomes authors who have a story to tell, wisdom, perceptions or information to convey, a person they want to memorialize, a neglect they want to remedy, a record they want to correct, a strong interest that they want to share, skills they want to teach, and who consciously seek to make a contribution to society in an informative, interesting and well-written way. Proverse works with texts by non-native-speaker writers of English as well as by native English-speaking writers.

The name, "Proverse", combines the words "prose" and "verse" and is pronounced accordingly.

THE INTERNATIONAL PROVERSE PRIZE

The Proverse Prize, an annual international competition for an unpublished single-author book-length work of fiction, non-fiction, or poetry, was established in January 2008. It is open to all who are at least eighteen on the date they sign the entry form and without restriction of nationality, residence or citizenship.

The objectives of the prize are: to encourage excellence and / or excellence and usefulness in publishable written work in the English Language, which can, in varying degrees, "delight and instruct". Entries are invited from anywhere in the world.

The Prize
1) Publication by Proverse Hong Kong, with
2) Cash prize of HKD10,000 (HKD7.80 = approx. US$1.00)

PROVERSE PRIZE WINNERS WHOSE BOOKS HAVE ALREADY BEEN PUBLISHED BY PROVERSE HONG KONG:
Laura Solomon, Rebecca Jane Tomasis, Gillian Jones, David Diskin, Peter Gregoire, Sophronia Liu, Birgit Linder, James McCarthy.

About Proverse Hong Kong

PROVERSE PRIZE WINNERS WHOSE BOOKS WILL BE PUBLISHED BY PROVERSE HONG KONG IN NOVEMBER 2015:
Philip Chatting, Celia Claase.

Extent of the Manuscript: within the range of what is usual for the genre of the entered manuscript. However, the following indications may be useful: novella – 30,000 to 50,000 words); other fiction (e.g. novels, short-story collections) and non-fiction (e.g. autobiographies, biographies, diaries, essay collections, journals, letters, memoirs, etc.) – 75,000 to 100,000 words. Poetry and poetry collections: 5,000 to 25,000 words. Other word-counts and mixed-genre submissions are not ruled out.

KEY DATES FOR THE PROVERSE PRIZE IN ANY YEAR
*(subject to confirmation and/or change)

Receipt of Entry Fees/ Forms	14 April to 31 May
Receipt of entered manuscripts	1 May to 30 June
Semi-finalists announced	July-September of the year of entry*
Finalists announced	October-December of the year of entry*
Winner(s) announced	March to November of the year that follows the year of entry*
Winning book(s) published	Within the period, beginning in November of the year that follows the year of entry*
Cash award made	At the same time as publication of the winning work(s)*

More information, updated from time to time, is available on the Proverse Hong Kong website:
<www.proversepublishing.com>.

The free Proverse E-Newsletter includes ongoing information about the Proverse Prize.
To be put on the E-Newsletter mailing-list,
please email: info@proversepublishing.com with your request.

NOVELS, SHORT STORY COLLECTIONS AND OTHER FICTION
Published by Proverse Hong Kong

Those who enjoy **Mishpacha – Family** by **Rebecca Tomasis** may also enjoy the following (all titles in English unless otherwise stated):

A Misted Mirror, by Gillian Jones. 2011.
A Painted Moment, by Jennifer Ching. 2010.
An Imitation of Life, by Laura Solomon. 2013.
Article 109, by Peter Gregoire. 2012.
Bao Bao's Odyssey: from Mao's Shanghai to Capitalist Hong Kong, by Paul Ting. 2012.
Bright Lights and White Nights, by Andrew Carter. 2015.
cemetery miss you, by Jason S Polley. 2011.
Cop Show Heaven, by Lawrence Gray. 2015.
Death has a Thousand Doors, by Patricia Grey. 2011.
Hilary and David, by Laura Solomon. 2011.
Instant Messages, by Laura Solomon. 2010.
Man's Last Song, by James Tam. 2013.
Mila the Magician, by Zhang Jian 章簡. 2013. (English / Chinese bilingual)
Odds and Sods, by Lawrence Gray. 2013.
Paranoia (the Walk and Talk with Angela), by Caleb Kavon. 2012.
Red Bird Summer, by Jan Pearson. 2014.
Revenge from Beyond, by Dennis Wong. 2011.
The Day They Came, by Gérard Louis Breissan. 2012.
The Devil You know, by Peter Gregoire. 2014.
The Monkey in Me: Confusion, Love and Hope under a Chinese Sky, by Caleb Kavon. 2009.
The Monkey in Me, by Caleb Kavon. Translated by Chapman Chen. 2010. Ebook. 2010. (Chinese)
The Perilous Passage of Princess Petunia Peasant, by Victor Edward Apps. 2014.

The Reluctant Terrorist: in Search of the Jizo, by Caleb Kavon. 2011.

The Shingle Bar Sea Monster and Other Stories, by Laura Solomon. 2012.

The Village in the Mountains, by David Diskin. 2012.

Tiger Autumn, by Jan Pearson. 2015.

Tightrope! A Bohemian Tale, by Olga Walló. Translated from Czech by Johanna Pokorny, Veronika Revická & others. 2010.

Tightrope! A Bohemian Tale, by Olga Walló. Translated by Chapman Chen. 2011. (Chinese)

University Days, by Laura Solomon. 2014.

Vera Magpie, by Laura Solomon. 2013.

OTHER GENRES

We also publish in other genres, including autobiography, biography, children's illustrated books, educational books, Hong Kong educational and legal history, memoirs, poetry, teenage / young adult books, and travel. More genres may be added.

About Proverse Hong Kong

FIND OUT MORE ABOUT OUR AUTHORS AND BOOKS

Visit our website
www.proversepublishing.com
Visit our distributor's website: www.chineseupress.com

Follow us on Twitter
Follow news and conversation:
twitter.com/Proversebooks
OR
Copy and paste the following to your browser window
and follow the instructions:
https://twitter.com/#!/ProverseBooks

Request our free E-Newsletter
Send your request to info@proversepublishing.com.

Availability
Most books are available in Hong Kong and world-wide
from our Hong Kong based Distributor,
The Chinese University Press of Hong Kong,
The Chinese University of Hong Kong, Shatin, NT,
Hong Kong SAR China.
Email: cup-bus@cuhk.edu.hk.

All titles are available from Proverse Hong Kong
and the Proverse Hong Kong UK-based Distributor.

We have stock-holding retailers in Hong Kong,
Singapore (Select Books),
Canada (Elizabeth Campbell Books),
Principality of Andorra (Llibreria la Puça, La Llibrera).
Orders can be made from bookshops in the UK and
elsewhere.

Ebooks: Most of our titles are available also as Ebooks.

www.ingramcontent.com/pod-product-compliance
Lightning Source LLC
Chambersburg PA
CBHW051334020726
47501CB00007B/2079